UNLIKELY LOVE

Emily could see that Amanda Laelard was ideal for Lord DeVere. Not only did Amanda's stunning beauty match his good looks, but her views on marriage—based on cool calculation rather than fiery passion—matched his as well.

Meanwhile, Amanda's brother Robin offered Emily all the heated emotions and poetic sentiments that Emily's heart could desire. Surely he was the man of her romantic dreams.

Why then didn't this pair of perfect matches strike the kind of sparks that flew each time that she and DeVere met? How could love be so unlikely—and so impossible to resist?

PRAISE FOR ELIZABETH HEWITT'S

THE ICE MAIDEN

"Excellent . . . one of Ms. Hewitt's best works . . . an eminently satisfying 'must' read for Regency devotees."—*Romantic Times*

"Intriguing . . . cast in an interesting period in history and told with authenticity, including colorful, colloquial language. A complete pleasurable read."
—*Affaire de Coeur*

A LASTING ATTACHMENT

ELIZABETH HEWITT

A SIGNET BOOK

NEW AMERICAN LIBRARY

SIGNET TRADEMARK REG. U.S.PAT. OFF. AND FOREIGN COUNTRIES
REGISTERED TRADEMARK—MARCA
REGISTRADA HECHO EN DRESDEN, TN.

SIGNET, SIGNET CLASSIC, MENTOR, ONYX, PLUME,
MERIDIAN and NAL BOOKS are published by NAL PENGUIN
INC., 1633 Broadway, New York, New York 10019

First Printing, April, 1989

1 2 3 4 5 6 7 8 9

PRINTED IN THE UNITED STATES OF AMERICA

1

Philadelphia, March 1812

The best parlor of the Barnacle Inn was quite dark; only a rosy glow emanating from the hearth that took up the better part of the rear wall inadequately illuminated the room. A faint, muffled sound of voices and laughter penetrated from the taproom beyond, but the only other sound in the parlor was the soft hiss and crackle of the wood fire. Jacob Farley, entering the room from the brightness of full moonlight glinting on hard-packed snow, at first thought that the room was uninhabited. It was only as his eyes adjusted to the near darkness that he became aware of the solitary figure seated at a table in the far corner of the room.

Everything about Farley proclaimed the sailor, from his ruddy, weathered complexion to his rolling gait, the result of more than two decades of maintaining a precarious balance on the uncertain surface of a sea-washed deck. He was a large man, Herculean of stature and circumference, but there was not an ounce of softness attached to his frame. At first glance he presented an awesome sight, but his expression was habitually good-humored and his eyes intelligent, dispelling any image of crudity or oafishness. His clothing, if practical and suited to an open deck, was well made and showed that Farley possessed discernment as well as an ample purse. He crossed the room without doubt of his welcome, settling himself on the broad comfortable seat of a wooden chair drawn up to the table. Without speaking, Farley drew a folded, sealed letter from an inner pocket and laid it on the table between himself and the other man, his hand coming down on the wood surface with a sharp slap, as if delivering a challenge.

The man across from Farley glanced at the letter and then away. With a graceful economy of movement he rose and in a few moments returned with a short branch of candles which he had lit from the fire. He placed it on the table almost touching Farley's hand. Farley pushed the paper across to him so that it nearly fell into the other man's lap as he resumed his seat. The man glanced at the letter and then held Farley's dark brown eyes with his own, which were a of a clear light blue. His finely chiseled and somewhat sharp features had a stern cast which suited him. He was as fair as Farley was dark. They plainly met as equals, though the fair man was fashionably dressed in a manner befitting a gentleman and one of considerable means as well. He had an air of refinement about him that was palpable and oddly at sorts with the plain room in which they sat.

It was Jacob Farley who spoke first. "It comes from England, brought over on the *Mary Leggit*, which came into port the day before last. An old mate of mine by name of Rampet is first mate and he thought you'd have it a sight quicker if he gave it to me instead of forwarding it in the usual way." The other man did not reply and made no motion to pick up or open the missive. "You've got to look at it, Galen," Farley said in a voice clearly used to issuing commands. "Kin is kin, whether you like it or not."

"Do you think so?" A slow smile spread across Galen DeVere's face and was echoed in his eyes. "But then you aren't at all acquainted with my, ah, kin." His voice was rich, resonant, and faintly drawling, with an elegant inflection that marked him as a native of the country from which the letter originated.

Farley tapped the letter with one long, calloused finger. "Kin is kin," he repeated.

DeVere picked up the letter and started to place it in an inner pocket in his coat. Farley reached out to grasp his arm, nearly toppling the candles and spattering the table with wax. He held DeVere's arm in an iron grasp. "I know your ways, Gale," he said. "You're hoping to put it into the fire later when I'm not about."

Once again their eyes locked. Something flickered in Galen's eyes that was not a reflection of the candle flames and it was Farley who dropped his gaze first. He released the other man's arm and sat back, a mulish expression on his face indicating that while the skirmish was lost, he was not in retreat.

A small, characteristically cynical smile turned up the edges of Galen's mouth. He sighed in resignation, for he was well acquainted with his friend's tenacity. He withdrew the letter from his coat and placed it on the table again. A glance at the direction written on the outside of the letter was sufficient to give him the identity of the sender and a premonition of its contents. It was news he was expecting, but not news he wished to receive, and he acknowledged to himself that Jacob was right; he might well have put the letter into the fire unopened if left to himself. He examined the seal, broke it, and unfolded a single page covered in a delicate script. He read it over carefully and then folded it again, making no comment other than to pick up his tankard and finish the remains of his ale.

"From the lawyers again?" Farley asked.

"No. My sister."

Jacob waited for him to continue but he did not, and once again silence fell between them and Jacob was obliged to break it. "Didn't know you had a sister," he said reproachfully. Galen seldom spoke of his life before he had left England more than ten years ago to sign on as a common seaman on a merchantman sailing for the West Indies.

An excellent companion and the best of good friends to those who could name him such, Galen DeVere possessed a cool, slightly cynical detachment and a bone-dry sense of humor that could turn caustic if forbidden ground were violated. But Jacob Farley had no fear of the edge of his friend's tongue. He turned the letter over so that the direction was visible again. It was addressed to The Honorable Galen DeVere. Jacob pointed to the words and said, "Is that a title of some sort?"

Galen pushed back his chair and stretched out his long legs beneath the table. "It is mere courtesy. It is my brother who holds the title."

"The devil you say!" exclaimed Farley, astonished that Galen had never seen fit to mention before that he had brothers or sisters or sprang from the nobility. "You've been mighty close about it."

"I've never mentioned it because it is unimportant."

"Unimportant to be a lord? That's not the way of it that I've heard tell."

"I have told you I am not a lord," Galen said patiently. "At least not yet, that I am aware. According to my sister Eugenia, the final payment for my brother's misspent life is about to be exacted, and then I suppose I shall be."

He spoke so matter-of-factly that Jacob wondered at it. "You weren't close to your brother?"

"No, we were not close," Galen said shortly but then smiled again and added in his more usual manner, "Rather the opposite of it, but that doesn't mean I have a wish to step into my brother's shoes, or rather wear his coronet. He's never married—I doubt there was any woman in the whole of England foolish enough to have him—so when he dies I shall be Lord something."

"Lord what?"

"DeVere. It is merely a barony; the DeVeres have been great only in their own estimation."

Emboldened by Galen's tolerance of his curiosity and the unexpected expansiveness with which it was met, Jacob dared to probe further. "What's he dying of? Same as carried off your father a couple of years ago when you had that letter from the lawyer?"

Galen seldom spoke of his family or his life before he left England for the simple reason that it gave him no pleasure to do so. Time and distance had dulled the bitter edge of many of his memories, but he seldom indulged in thoughts of his past. He maintained a desultory correspondence with his elder sister, the only member of his family with whom he had enjoyed any closeness, and an earlier letter had already warned him that Robert DeVere was in poor health and not likely to mend his ways in a hope of recovery.

His brother's death would force him, he knew, to face the life he had abandoned nearly twelve years earlier, and responsibilities he was not sure he wished to assume. As Lord DeVere he would be head of his family, however little he wished for the elevation. But he was no longer a youth, he was a man and accountable to himself if to no other. Duty and honor were a part of his breeding and though he might chafe at these virtues, ultimately he would not shirk them.

The small, resigned sigh Galen gave before replying to his friend's question was in acknowledgment that the past had caught up with him at last. "What carried off my father was apoplexy," he said, "and, given his temperament, which it would be a kindness to describe as choleric, it was long overdue. My brother has chosen a different, but equally sure route to hell. He shall doubtless expire with a brandy glass in one hand and a pair of dice in the other. My mother died of inflammation of the lungs when I was seven, but family legend has it that she dosed herself frequently and liberally with laudanum, and an accident was inevitable. When I last saw my sister she was in a fair way to making herself notorious by openly encouraging the attentions of one of the royals—I don't recall which just now."

"Sounds a rum bunch to me. Where do you fit in with that lot?"

The prospect that he might do so caused Galen to grimace. "I don't, I hope," he said with feeling. "That's why I left, or at least part of the reason. My father decided it was up to me to repair the family fortunes and found an heiress with a squint and a cit father who was willing to overlook the fact that the

DeVeres were second only to the Barrymores in ill-repute and impecuniosity in order to ally himself through his daughter with the aristocracy. She had the manners of a scullery maid and was actually known to have eaten cabbage.'' He spread his hands in appeal. ''What else could I do but sign on to the first ship out of Portsmouth?''

The landlord, who was almost as broad and tall as Farley, entered by the door to the taproom. Galen looked up and, catching the landlord's eye, held up his empty tankard in silent request. The landlord nodded and returned to the tap, leaving the door into the larger room open.

Jacob smiled. ''I don't see what there is in all this to put you in a pucker, Galen,'' he commented. ''In fact, it looks to me like you've more to gain than lose when your brother sticks his spoon in the wall. You get the title, don't you, and whatever goes with it?''

DeVere gave a sharp bark of laughter. ''But that's the point, dear boy. There isn't a damn thing except for an empty title. The estate has been bled dry by my brother and my father before him. It is certain to cost me a great deal of money to set it right again if I choose to do so.''

''Well, you have a great deal of money,'' Jacob pointed out.

''True,'' Galen acknowledged with a brief nod, ''but you may have noticed that I am not overburdened with family feeling. While it was my brother's responsibility to see to the estate, it was welcome to molder with my perfect goodwill.''

The landlord shuffled across the room and placed a tankard brimming with ale before each man and a third in front of an empty chair into which he lowered his bulk without waiting for invitation to do so. ''Come into an inheritance, have you, Captain?'' he said, somehow managing to grasp the gist of the conversation though he had heard little of it. His accent proclaimed him a countryman of DeVere's but not his equal in education or refinement. "You said before the new year you were of a mind to go back again."

"Did I?" Galen said as if surprised. He shrugged. "Perhaps it was an idle thought."

Ketch grinned. "You were on your fourth pint of ale when you mentioned it, so I suppose it might've been bottle talk, but in the usual way it would take a sight more than that to see you jug-bitten."

"The day has never been that you've seen me jug-bitten," Galen informed him indignantly. "If I said it at all, it was a mere flight of capriciousness. But now I suppose I have no choice in the matter. I can't have seven centuries of DeVeres spinning in their graves because I spurned the fruits of their accomplishments. My return as a nabob will be a nine days' wonder, I suppose. Black sheep seldom return with a golden fleece and speculation should be rampant."

Ketch snorted to show what he thought of the opinion of the world. "Let 'em talk, Captain. At least you came by your blunt honest, not just by the luck of being born on the right blanket."

There was an upturning of the Galen's lips, but it was not precisely a smile. "Much good that sort of luck did my brother," he remarked.

Jacob picked up his tankard and said, "To the return of the prodigal as lord of the manner."

The three men drank deeply and fell silent for a bit until Jacob spoke again. "This'll be the end of your seafaring days, I suppose," he said with regret as he recalled the many adventures shared together in the years since they had first met. "You'll be trading your mistress for a wife and setting up your nursery."

"I suppose," Galen agreed. "There is the succession to consider. It will be largely a matter of bloodlines."

"That's too damned cold-blooded, if you ask me," Jacob retorted. "When I take a lass to wife, I mean to have something warmer in mind."

"The trick is to have no illusions about love," Galen

insisted, "and then there is no disillusionment. Most of what we call love is just lust wrapped up in clean linen, in any case. I'd rather let my head choose a life for me than my passions."

Jacob shook his head. "Damned if I believe you have passions, Galen. In nine years I've never seen sign of one. Even your rages are cold where other men's are hot."

"I possess the usual complement of emotions," Galen replied with an arid smile. "I simply learned at an early age the folly of exposing one's vulnerability." He drank a bit more of the ale and then stood, picking up his greatcoat which was slung over the back of the only unoccupied chair drawn up to the table. "Actually, I've no wish for a wife at all," he commented, "but I shall have to make a push to secure the succession sooner or later."

"Then you're goin' back for certain, Captain," said Ketch.

"I may, Louis," Galen said as he drew on his gloves. "And then again I may not."

Emily Hampton carefully counted the strokes as she pulled the brush through her long, thick, light brown hair. Her mother had insisted that she brush her hair a hundred strokes before braiding it each night for bed, and even though Mrs. Hampton had been dead for more than a year, her daughter still did her bidding, though it was as much out of habit as in respect for her mother's advice. It was still fairly early in the evening, only an hour or so past dinner, but Emily was already attired in a soft white cotton nightdress and a sensible quilted dressing gown. Her maid had gone downstairs to fetch her a glass of warm milk and the soda crackers she particularly liked, and she wanted only the addition of a good book to make her evening complete.

There was a soft rapping sound at her door and Emily's aunt came into the room. Lucille Armitage beheld her niece with an expression of almost comic dismay. "Emily, you are undressed!" she cried. "But you said you would come with us tonight. I was quite counting on it."

"No, Aunt Lucy," Emily said in a gentle, yet firm manner, "I said I would consider going with you to the Vickersons' party, but I have decided I would not care for it after all. You must not fuss over me so. I enjoy quiet evenings and there is nothing I would rather do than read, particularly when I have something as excellent to entertain me as this," she added, picking up her book from the dressing table and holding it up for her aunt's inspection.

Lucille Armitage took the book from her without bothering to glance at the title and placed it back on the dressing table. A small straight-backed chair stood next to the dressing table and she sat down on it.

Emily spoke before her aunt could begin. "I know you think there must be something the matter with me because I prefer a good book to a party, but—"

"I most certainly do," her aunt interrupted. "You are not yet twenty-five, a pretty, intelligent girl who was used to have a wide circle of friends. I know how upsetting it was for you to lose your dear mama and so soon after your father had died as well, but you won't get over your grief sitting by yourself, hiding away from the world."

"I am not hiding away from anyone," Emily said quietly. "You should understand better than any one, Aunt Lucy. Papa was your brother and I know you loved him and were fond of Mama."

"I very much miss both David and Regina, but I wouldn't suppose I was serving either their memories or myself by falling into a melancholy."

"I have not fallen into a melancholy," Emily responded, with a flash of spirit.

"In the seven months since you came to us," her aunt said, holding up the requisite number of fingers in illustration, "I could not count as many times that I have persuaded you to come out with us, even though the strictest period of your mourning was over by then. Except, of course, for your trips to the lending library," she added with asperity. "Now *I* do not call that natural at all."

"You exaggerate, Aunt Lucy."

"I do not," replied the older woman, and she proceeded to enumerate each occasion that her niece had accompanied her and her husband on excursions of pleasure. "If you can think of any other, I cannot," she said in conclusion. "I quite understood that at first you would not wish to attend any lively entertainment or spend the evening dancing the soles out of your shoes, but it is more than a year since your mama was carried off with influenza. *She* certainly would not want you to spend the rest of your life alone, which is what you will do if you will never go out and put yourself in the way of any nice young men."

Emily vented a short sigh and put down her brush. The direction their discussion was taking was familiar to her but no more welcome for that. "I have no wish to marry, at least for now, Aunt Lucy. Surely my circumstances are such that I may please myself on that score. I have had offers of marriage, but never on that I was more than momentarily tempted to accept. Mama herself agreed that I was right to decline any offer where I could not feel more than friendship or mild affection for the gentleman who proposed marriage to me."

"Oh, yes, I am well aware that Regina filled your head with a lot of romantic nonsense," Mrs. Armitage said, adding quickly as she saw her niece tense defensively, "Don't be cross with me, Emily. Whatever your mama might say, your papa would have agreed with me. David and Regina's history was very romantic, to be sure, eloping as they did in the teeth of so much opposition from her family, but they were very lucky that their passion for each other grew into a lasting attachment. It is not always so, you know, and more couples who abandon all for love end up badly than

happily. Passion is all very well in its place, but it
seldom wears well.''

"I am sure you are right, Aunt," Emily replied with
no hint in her tone that she felt reproved. "But if ever I
am to marry it will only be with one whom I know
beyond all doubt I can love with all of my heart and who
returns my regard in full measure.''

Mrs. Armitage got up and shook out the creases
sitting had made in the dark blue satin gown she wore.
She went over to stand behind Emily, who had begun to
braid her hair. She stood there until Emily's frank gray
eyes met hers in the glass. "You won't ever meet this
paragon if you never leave the house, will you?" she
said waspishly, and then bent to kiss her niece good
night. Lucille Armitage left feeling full of her failure to
persuade Emily against her solitary pursuits, but none-
theless determined to find the way to bring these to an
end.

Emily completed the task of braiding her hair and
secured the ends with a bit of cherry-colored ribbon. As
she glanced up from her task she caught her own eyes in
the gilt-framed mirror hung above the dressing table
and looked quickly away. Aware of the absurdity of
avoiding her own gaze, she looked up again and met her
reflection squarely. She knew that she was attractive
enough in a quiet way, but certainly not the great beauty
her mother had been.

The truth she did not admit to her aunt and barely
admitted to herself was that she wondered if she was the
sort of female to inspire a grand passion in any man the
way that her exquisite mother had inspired a great love
in David Hampton. She was not even certain that she
could conjure such a degree of regard herself for any
man; certainly she had never felt the faintest stirring of
such an alarming emotion for any man who had in the
past tried to fix his interest with her. In fact, a deep
sense of modesty made her strongly suspect that the

young men who had courted her were as often as not attracted by her purse as by her person.

Her notion of the perfect marriage was based almost entirely on what she had learned of such things from her parents' example. She had not liked her aunt's comment that her mother had filled her head with romantic ideals, but in all honesty, she supposed that there was truth in it.

Her mother was the daughter of an earl and her beauty had made her the toast of the town in her first London Season, but Lady Regina Harcourt had spurned an heir to a dukedom whom her family had arranged for her to marry and had eloped with David Hampton, an American from Philadelphia visiting in England. According to Lady Regina, who had forsaken family, titles, fortune, and even honor to be with her true love, she had never had any doubt from the moment she had met David Hampton that he was the man with whom she wanted to spend the remainder of her life, and she had not hesitated for an instant to elope with him when her family forbade the match.

For Emily's parents, passion had weathered well; they had doted on each other, as much in love on the day that her father had died as they had been on the day they had met. That was the thunderclap that Emily sought for in vain. With such an example before her, Emily feared she would not be able to settle for less.

She stared intently at the glass, not seeing herself any longer but looking at an indefinite point beyond, as if she expected her true love to materialize behind her. Her aunt felt that she was too exacting and Emily began to fear herself that it might be so. However unjust it might be, spinsters were held in polite contempt by the world and at twenty-five Emily would be considered on the shelf by many. Emily disliked the thought that she had deliberately retired from the world because she had given up hope of finding herself respectably settled.

Emily's social life had been fairly active while her parents had lived, but since she had come to live with the Armitages after the settlement of the Hamptons' property had been completed, Emily had seized on the opportunity that her mourning provided to live quietly, being very content with her books and music and the company of a few friends who cared enough to seek her out in her seclusion.

She sucked in her cheeks and deliberately puckered her brow to make herself look older. No doubt in a few years people would point her out as an oddity, an heiress without disfigurement or distemper who had never found a husband. Absurd, perhaps, but quite lowering too.

Emily forced her thoughts into different channels, but she found she could not recapture her earlier sense of satisfaction with her plans for her evening.

On the following morning, Mrs. Armitage betrayed that she, too, had dwelt on their conversation after she had left Emily to her book. "I have been thinking, my love," she said as they lingered over coffee in the breakfast room, "that while it was quite natural for you to wish for seclusion when you first came to us so soon after your dear mama's death, it has become just habit now for you to go on so quietly."

Since Emily's thoughts the previous night had run in a similar vein, she could not disagree. "Perhaps I am a little too comfortable in my ways," she conceded.

"I am persuaded that what you need is a complete change to put you back in spirits again," Mrs. Armitage pronounced with conviction.

Emily regarded her fond relative somewhat suspiciously, "If you mean to suggest again that I accept Josiah Witherspoon's offer of marriage . . ."

"No, of course not, my dear," Mrs. Armitage said hastily, aware that that plan for her niece's happiness had gone hopelessly awry. "Though I do think it would have been an excellent match. You are equals in birth and fortune and he lost his wife only a few months before you lost your mother."

"And you thought we might console each other over

the breakfast table," Emily said with a smile. "I doubt that would do much to raise my spirits."

"Well, when you were so obviously set against it, I quite gave it up, did I not?" demanded her aunt defensively. "But is not what I had in mind for you, in any case. It is something quite different." Lucille Armitage delighted in matchmaking and both her sons had barely survived her machinations to make matches that were of their own choosing. But she was learning with experience to be more circumspect. The outcome of her new-formed plan for Emily's happiness would hopefully mean marriage though she had no specific suitor in mind. It was designed merely to put Emily in the way of eligible young men again. "You had another letter from Lady Laelard last month, did you not?"

"Yes," Emily admitted. "But," she added, setting down her cup, "if you mean to try to persuade me to accept her invitation to go to live with her in England as you did last time, I'll tell you plainly, Aunt Lucy, that I haven't the least wish for a long, probably uncomfortable journey to live with a family I have never set eyes on and of whom I know nothing save that they did all that they could to prevent Mama and Papa from marrying and forced them to elope."

"That is true, my dear, in a sense. But it was not your poor mama's sisters, who were younger than she and still in the schoolroom at the time, who made things so wretched for her. It was your grandfather and grandmother who were so ambitious that they placed position over your mother's happiness. But they have been gone these several years and it is quite unfair to visit their sins on their innocent offspring. You would not wish to spurn Lady Laelard's kind invitation for such a reason."

"She does not even know me," Emily countered.

"She knew your mama and no doubt loved her dearly," Mrs. Armitage replied, though she had not the least idea of the degree of affection existing between the young Harcourts before Lady Regina's elopement. "It is even possible that she may wish, through you, to make amends in some way to her dear departed sister."

Emily had not thought of Lady Laelard's invitation in that manner before, but she supposed it was possible. She had received the first letter from her Aunt Dorothea in reply to her own letter, which had informed the viscountess of her sister's death. Though she knew that her mother had maintained an intermittent correspondence with both of her sisters, Emily had assumed that the invitation was no more than a formal courtesy despite the fact that it was couched in affectionate terms. But when the second letter arrived, less than a month ago, once again urging her to come to Whistley, the Laelard estate in Sussex, Emily acknowledged to herself that her aunt must truly wish for her to visit.

Yet Emily was no more than mildly tempted to accept. She had never in her life been on a ship and had no particular desire for the experience. Every account she had ever read of ocean voyages had made her marvel that anyone was brave enough or stupid enough to suffer illness, privation, and the potential dangers of a journey by sea for the sake of travel or adventure. She also had the very natural uneasiness that anyone might feel about leaving everyone and everything that was familiar for the unknown and the unfamiliar. "It may be so," she said, "but I don't think that sufficient reason to make the journey. I shall think you wish to be rid of me, Aunt Lucy, if you persist in persuading me to go," she added with gentle complaint.

"Of course, my dear, I quite understand that you might be too timid to set off on such an adventure," Mrs. Armitage said with apparent resignation, "and I am sure it is no fault to you. Few young women possess the courage with which your dear mama was blessed. She was such a spirited and lively creature."

The suggestion that Emily had not herself the character to live up to the example set by her mother stung, as Mrs. Armitage meant for it to do. "I do not shrink from the adventure. Aunt Lucy," Emily insisted, but without conviction. "My circumstances are quite different from those my mother and father experienced. They had each other to share their adventure and to support each other, I should be quite on my own which, I admit, I do find a bit daunting."

"That is only natural, to be sure," Mrs. Hampton readily agreed. "But perhaps that could be remedied if you made up your mind to the journey. However, if you think it too great a risk, I shan't pester you."

Emily had the suspicion that she was being manipulated, but she could not dismiss her aunt's suggestion that she lacked a courageous spirit. Coupled with her troubled thoughts of the previous evening, Emily began to fear she was dwindling into a rather poor creature.

Mrs. Armitage was content that she had given her niece something to digest and was too wise to allude to the subject again. It was Emily who finally did so several days later. "Even if I did decide to go," she concluded after admitting that she had thought further of making the journey to England, "I don't know that I would wish to live in England as my Aunt Dorothea suggests. I think it would be wise not to plan on more than an extended visit if I go at all, which I am still not at all sure that I should do."

"Of course, my dear, whatever you think would be best," Mrs. Hampton said amiably as she set tiny stitches in an altar cloth she was hemming. They sat in a sunny back parlor overlooking the garden, which was just coming into bud after an extended winter. "I mentioned our discussion to your uncle and he said that you were wise to be a bit fearful of making the journey when matters are so unsettled between us and England. A timid spirit is perhaps better than an adventuresome one at times."

"Actually," Emily responded, piqued into contradiction, "Lydia Nigel mentioned when she called the other day that quite a few Englishmen have been making arrangements to return home because they fear that if the war were to escalate, their positions here would be uncomfortable. She said that her brother, who is an oficer in the navy, you know, said that with passage on a sound ship and a little careful planning, there is really little reason to be concerned.''

Mrs. Armitage was elated that Emily had thought enough of her suggestion to discuss it with a friend, but she concealed her delight for fear of appearing too eager. "I really don't think it is so very dangerous either, my dear," Mrs. Armitage said blandly, knotting and then snipping her thread. "It is just the banker in your uncle that makes him so cautious. After all, people make ocean voyages every day of the week and I am sure most do so quite without incident."

"I suppose that is so," Emily agreed without enthusiasm. "No doubt my uncle would know where I might secure a safe passage."

"Of course he would," Mrs. Armitage said encouragingly. "In his position in the city he knows all of the owners and captains of the best merchant fleets. In fact, he introduced me to one of these gentlemen last night at the Nobles' dinner party. I wish you might have come with us, for Mr. DeVere is quite personable and amusing." She saw a flicker of opposition come into Emily's expression and retreated hastily from this digression. "You may leave everything in your uncle's capable hands if you do decide to go to England, for I know he will be very happy to arrange everything down to the smallest detail. And if you find before you leave that you do not wish to risk the journey after all, you need only say so."

In spite of the careless manner in which this was spoken, Emily had the suspicion that some preparation was already underway in the hope that she could be persuaded to the scheme. She frankly did not know her own mind, but was prepared to acknowledge that it was just possible that her aunt was right to suggest a complete change for her. In any case, it would do no harm to learn what plans might be made for such a journey. However much her aunt might scheme, Emily was certain of this: she would not permit herself to be manipulated into putting so much as one foot on the deck of a ship bound for England until and unless she had quite made up her own mind to do so.

2

For Galen DeVere the decision had already been made. A second letter, this time from the DeVere family's firm of solicitors, had arrived within two weeks of his sister's letter, informing him that Robert DeVere, ninth Baron DeVere, had indeed gone to his final reward—or perhaps his just deserts, as Galen had commented dryly to Jacob Farley. In the two months that had passed since then, he had quietly gone about liquidating his assets and transferring them to English banking houses in advance of his journey. Like most Englishmen living in the United States, he was not at all sanguine about the prospects of a quick end to the hostilities that had again broken out between England and America and he had no intention of allowing his assets to be seized by the American government should all Englishmen be declared hostile aliens.

He might chafe at the responsibility that his new dignities conferred on him, but all in all, he felt it was time for him to return to his homeland, and his inclination fell in handily with events. All of his plans were proceeding smoothly and he had every hope of being able to set sail by the end of June for England via Portugal to unload cargo.

DeVere was not a man to broadcast his affairs, but it was impossible to keep his intent from being known, particularly among his business associates. Chief among these were Mr. Stephen Girard and Mr. Walter Armitage, the principal merchant bankers of the city to whom he applied for assistance in liquidating and transferring his assets. It was not surprising therefore that

Mrs. Armitage should inquire into his plans for the voyage to England when they had met at Mrs. Noble's for dinner. Her questions had almost amounted to an interrogation, but he had refrained from delivering a deserved setdown and had borne her inquisitiveness with equanimity for the sake of her husband, toward whom Galen felt a considerable debt for assistance Mr. Armitage had given him when he had first begun to assemble his fleet.

When Galen received a note from Walter Armitage asking him to call at his home on Chestnut Street on the Saturday following Mrs. Noble's dinner party, he did not hesitate to put off his plans for that morning, assuming that the request was in some way connected with the business that the banker had in hand for him. It was not unusual for business to be conducted between gentlemen in the more genteel atmosphere of a private home rather than in an impersonal office, and Galen thought nothing of the summons. Within an hour of receiving Walter Armitage's note, he found himself sitting in that man's library, accepting a glass of excellent dry sherry.

Galen did not possess the aristocrat's inbred prejudice against trade—indeed, in the circumstances he would have been extremely hypocritical if he had—but it was with the eye of a son of a peer that he surveyed the room he sat in and he noted the elegant, understated appointments with unconscious approval. He accepted a glass of sherry from his host and murmured his thanks.

Galen sat at his ease, but privately he began to wonder why the banker had asked him to call. Armitage, generally a man who did not waste time in dithering, seemed to have some difficulty coming to the point. When their discussion eventually turned to Galen's planned journey to England, he supposed they had reached the purpose of his visit at last, but he could not help wondering why the the older man had felt a need for circumspection.

"Of course I would be foolish not to regard the skirmishes that have been taking place now and again off the coast of New Jersey," he replied to Walter Armitage's expressed concern that there might be some danger attached to the journey. "But we shall sail south of the areas where there has been trouble until we are out in the open sea. It is a tiresome detour, but I don't fancy finding myself or my crew captured by an English ship of the line and impressed into His Majesty's service."

"Many of your compatriots think it a prudent time to return home. Is that what you've decided?" asked Armitage, leaning over to the table that separated their chairs to pour out more of the sherry for them.

Galen had confided his succession to the peerage in no one save Jacob Farley and he saw no need to discuss it with the banker for it had no bearing at all on their dealings. "No," he replied without having to stretch the truth very much, "it is no more than coincidence that I have decided that it is time to return to England."

"With so many hoping to do the same and so few ships braving the blockade, no doubt you've been besieged by requests for passage on your ship."

"In the common way, I don't hold with merchant-man taking on passengers, though many do," Galen replied, suspecting no special interest behind the question put to him. "Passengers are mostly a nuisance which their fare does not offset. But I have agreed to take along two passengers this voyage who were particularly recommended to me, for I quite understand the awkwardness felt by my countrymen in remaining here while our countries are at war. I do not advertise it though, or I would be besieged, as you say, and as the *Devon* will carry a full cargo brought up from the Brazils, I don't want to overload her by taking on more weight than necessary. These are times to travel as lightly as possible."

"Would you take on another passenger as a favor to

me?'' Armitage inquired with a faint deprecating smile. "It would not mean very much more weight, I promise you."

Galen regarded him with surprise. This was the last thing he had expected. "You know someone who wishes to go to England, sir?"

"Yes. My niece, whose mother was an English-woman, wishes to visit her mother's family, and I would not be easy in my conscience if I permitted her to go without being assured that she was in good hands. The Laelards live in Sussex; I believe you mentioned that your family hails from that county as well."

Galen acknowledged that this was so, though he did not immediately recall the name of Laelard. Mr. Armitage appeared to find this remark sufficient encouragement and proceeded, with considerable economy, to inform Galen of Emily's immediate history. He made it clear that the only reason he countenanced such an expedition in these uncertain times was the belief he shared with his wife that the journey was necessary for Emily's well-being and future. "The poor girl's been regularly hipped since she lost her poor mother so soon after her father, and Mrs. Armitage is convinced that the only thing to put Emily back in spirits is a change of scene. I shall hate to see her go, myself, for she's a sweet puss," he added fondly.

Galen was too well bred not to hear Armitage out, but with each word the older man spoke Galen's dismay grew as he envisioned a thousand objections to the banker's request and cast about for a graceful way of refusing him. In spite of the obligation he felt toward Walter Armitage, he had no wish to find himself cast in the role of duenna to that man's niece in payment of it.

The image Galen formed of Emily as her uncle spoke of her was of a fragile flower, cosseted, sheltered, naive, and probably spoiled—a pampered heiress who had suffered no greater physical rigor in her young life than a cold nose on a drive in an open carriage during winter. He could not imagine the prospect of finding himself responsible for the safety and comfort of a melancholy young woman—who would very likely subject him to a daily fit of the vapors—with anything short of horror.

"I can see by your expression, or rather lack of one, that you do not like the notion overmuch," Armitage said astutely at the end of his recital, "but I hope you won't reject my request out of hand. You are thinking that Emily would be a burden to you, but I assure you, she is quite a self-sufficient young woman. If I thought she would give you the least trouble, I would not ask this of you."

Galen failed to find this reassurance comforting. He regarded it as the opinion of a fond uncle and therefore not to be trusted. He cursed himself soundly for having mentioned his intention of taking on passengers, for his best excuse of never doing so was now denied to him. He was saved from the impossibility of making an immediate reply to Armitage's request by the opening of the door followed by the entrance of Emily herself.

As both men rose, Emily's gaze was drawn to Galen at once, the expression in her gray eyes assessing. As she beheld him, the sudden, absurd thought occurred to her that she had at last found her ideal. He returned her gaze levelly until she looked away, a faint tint of color coming into her cheeks. "I beg your pardon, Uncle Walter," she said a bit diffidently. "Aunt Lucy asked me to fetch you, but I had no idea you had a visitor."

Galen's regard of her continued for a bit longer and his assessment of her was not nearly as flattering. In appearance, at least, she was not at all what he had expected. She was not a spoiled beauty, at any rate; her nose was a little too straight, her face a little to triangular for beauty, and with her plain gray eyes and unremarkable light brown hair, not even her most ardent admirer could have regarded her as striking. Yet he found her attractive enough. Her complexion had the color and texture of palest pink rose petals and thick, slightly curling lashes framed eyes that were large and well shaped. He suspected that with her hair properly coifed instead of pulled back into a braided bun at the nape of her neck, and dressed in something more becoming than the dove-gray round gown which did nothing to enhance her delicate coloring or figure, she might well hold her own with other young women of more obvious beauty.

When her uncle made them known to each other, saying in his hearty way that they had just been speaking of her, Emily felt her blush deepen and found it unaccountably difficult to meet Mr. DeVere's eyes. She looked up at him for not more than a moment and then studied the pattern in the Turkey carpet like a bashful schoolgirl while he bowed over her hand.

To the sin of being a pampered heiress Galen added the equal crime of insipidness to her dish. She reminded him of a frightened fieldmouse ready to take flight, but it aroused in him no noble desire to protect. Rather, he felt irritation at the prospect of finding himself cast as her unwilling caretaker for a long and potentially dangerous voyage.

"I am very glad you are here, Emily," her uncle said, taking her hand when she would have made her escape with another murmured apology. "Mr. DeVere—or perhaps I should say Captain DeVere—and I have been discussing your passage to England on his ship, the *Devon*, which he hopes to have under sail in another month or so."

This statement did make Emily's head come up and she looked from her uncle to Galen in surprise. Her uncle had informed her that he meant to speak to a captain of his acquaintance about her passage, but the terms in which he had described this individual had made Emily suppose that the seaman was a contemporary of her uncle, an older man who would look after her welfare in the same manner as would Mr. Armitage himself. But Galen DeVere was quite young, not much over thirty, she thought, and strikingly handsome, Saxon fair with light blue eyes and a decidedly forbidding patrician cast to his features. She could not for a moment imagine him behaving toward her in an avuncular way.

Though it was no more than a fleeting expression, Emily saw that her uncle's assumption that she would have passage on his ship surprised Mr. DeVere as well, and guessed that it was not to his liking. For a moment, as they were introduced, she had felt for the first time a genuine desire to make the journey to England, the result no doubt of her instant attraction to Mr. DeVere, but now she felt ashamed of her unwarranted admiration. How could she think for even a moment that this man, with whom she had exchanged no more than a common greeting, could fill her exacting ideal, when all she knew of him was that he had a handsome face and a well-formed figure? She was mortified by what she perceived as her own shallowness.

"I understand you wish to travel to England to visit your mother's family, Miss Hampton," Galen said in a level voice that gave Emily no encouragement to suppose she had mistaken his dislike of her uncle's scheme.

Emily found herself wanting to deny it, but conscious of her uncle beside her, she said, "Y-yes, I have thought of it. Yes." Though Emily had not been much in the world of late, she did not want for social grace, and knew her reply to be insipid. She was also acutely aware of her unprepossessing appearance and could scarcely wonder that her admiration for him was not reciprocated.

She read dismissiveness in the glance that Galen swept over her as she responded to him, and it effectively stifled her ability to make any further intelligent comment. She stood silent and tongue-tied, blushing like a plain girl in her first Season. She felt a sudden vexation toward her uncle for not warning her that she would be expected to meet Mr. DeVere today and thus precipitating this awkwardness.

Galen certainly possessed the address to breach the

uncomfortable silence that had fallen upon them, but he chose not to do so. It was not in his interest to make the interview easier, for it would only serve to encourage Armitage and his niece to suppose that he intended to give Emily passage on his ship. Armitage seemed to regard it as a settled matter with only details to be discussed, but Galen had every intention of finding a way to rebuff the banker's request without giving palpable offense. Or better, he thought, his eyes resting speculatively on Emily, if he could manage to do so, he might convince the niece that she would be wise not to make the journey at this time. She appeared a timid creature so he did not regard this as a far-fetched hope.

Mr. Armitage, apparently oblivious to his guest's distaste and his niece's discomfort, enumerated, in a cheerful manner, the steps he had already taken to see to Emily's comforts both for the crossing and when she finally arrived in England. "Couldn't persuade that silly girl of hers to make the journey—has a young man here, I suspect—so I have made arrangements to hire a girl who is looking to return to her family in Dorset to look after Emily. That is, if all goes forward as planned." He placed an avuncular arm about Emily's shoulders. "My little puss has never been on a ship before and had her doubts about the scheme, but I depend on you, DeVere, to convince her that she'll be as safe on the *Devon* as if she were in her own sitting room." He gave Emily a gentle squeeze before releasing her, then beamed on them both impartially. "I'll leave you for a bit to get acquainted while I go to Lucy. I know I don't need my wife's permission to ask you to take luncheon with us, DeVere. I hope you will, for then we may discuss this matter in greater detail."

Galen's opinion of Emily did not improve as he watched her color rise and fall in an unbecoming manner as her uncle's attempts to dispel the awkwardness only served to increase it. He was considerably heartened to learn that she was not especially eager to make the crossing. "I thank you for the invitation, Mr.

Armitage, but I fear I must decline. I am expected by friends outside the city within the hour and I must leave now if I am not to keep them waiting for me. Another time, I hope.''

"Of course," Armitage said promptly. "But you must not leave without having a word with Mrs. Armitage. I know Lucy will want to ask you to take your mutton with us one night herself.''

Galen politely bowed his acquiescence and put his hat and gloves back on the table from which he had just lifted them when he had hoped to make his escape. Emily felt ready to sink at her uncle's officiousness, but she would have felt far worse if she had known that Galen heaped silent curses on the older man's head for leaving him alone with her. Supposing that conversing with this little fieldmouse would be less wearing than having to endure her blushes and darting timid glances, he repressed a resigned sigh and asked her if she would care for a glass of the sherry he had shared with her uncle. Emily declined in as firm a voice as she could muster, but did take the chair her uncle had vacated so that Mr. DeVere could resume his seat as well.

Finally, anger with herself for her foolishness came to her rescue before she sunk herself utterly in her own estimation, if not in Mr. DeVere's, and she inquired politely and very nearly in her normal accents about the nature of his ship. But she paid little heed to his equally punctilious reply. She was too sensitive and astute not to be aware that his polite mask was merely a cover for disapprobation, and she came to the conclusion that she would sooner become a complete hermit than travel to England in the company of Mr. DeVere, who was clearly as arrogant as he was attractive.

Involved in her own thoughts, she was for a few moments unaware that he had stopped speaking. Caught out in her inattention the color which sprang too readily to her cheeks did so yet again. A glance at him showed that he awaited her in civil repose, his expression slightly sardonic.

A faint smile touched his lips at her startled expression. It was the first sincere smile she had seen from him and her foolish heart beat a bit faster as the severity of his countenance lightened, making him even more attractive in her eyes. "I have just informed you that the *Devon* is a frigate and given you a little of her history," he said conversationally. "It is your turn again now, Miss Hampton."

Their eyes met for a brief moment and an unexpected spark of understanding passed between them before Emily once again succumbed to her unaccustomed shyness and looked away. She was furious with herself for her stupid, missish behavior over which she seemed to have so little control. She forced her chin up and made herself meet those cool, ironic eyes to show that she was not completely intimidated by his barely concealed contempt for her. "You are an Englishman, Mr. DeVere," she said. "Perhaps you are acquainted with my aunts, Lady Laelard and Lady Caroline Antrop?"

"No, I am afraid not," he replied civilly. "Though I once knew a Sir Timothy Antrop, who was an acquaintance of my father. Perhaps there is some connection. Your uncle informs me that the Laelards are from Sussex, which is where my home, Landsend, is situated, but I cannot recall anyone by that name."

"Land's End? It sounds as if it must be near to the sea," Emily said, deciding even as she spoke that the remark was fatuous.

"Our property reaches to the sea," he acknowledged, adding blandly, "No doubt that is how it came to be named."

Another uncomfortable silence fell between them and Emily, to her own surprise, found herself saying, "And now it is your turn, Mr. DeVere."

He smiled again, and this time Emily thought with some satisfaction that she saw a flicker of appreciation come into his eyes. "I own myself a bit puzzled, Miss Hampton," he said, "that you would choose this time for a visit to England. You could not be unaware that war has been declared between the United States and England."

"Of course I am aware of it, Mr. DeVere," Emily replied, managing a degree of cool loftiness in her tone. "But it is my understanding that most of the danger is still confined to the north. It is even the consensus of many that the war may well be over before the summer is out. My uncle has no qualms for my safety, so why should I feel concern?"

"An ocean crossing is never a thing to take lightly, Miss Hampton," he said reprovingly, "and I would be remiss in my duties as ship's captain if I did not warn you that it is a rigorous experience in the best of circumstances. I hope to sail by the first week in June, so there will be little time for more than rudimentary preparation for so long a journey, and you may find yourself making a longer visit to your aunt than you had planned. I am not so sanguine about predicting a rapid end to the hostilities between our countries."

The words informing him that she had no wish to make the journey at all, at least not in his company, hovered on her lips but instead she said with a flash of spirit, "Not all of my sex dithers, Mr. DeVere. I think I can vouchsafe not to keep you waiting at the dock for me."

"I would not," he said bluntly.

"I have no doubt of it!" she retorted, anger flashing in her eyes and making them sparkle most becomingly.

But Galen, vexed that she was not as biddable and easily intimidated as her mouselike appearance had led him to suppose, took no notice of it. Still in the guise of a responsible ship's captain—though he had never before felt it necessary to issue caveats to his passengers—he described for her all the discomfiting, inconvenient, and dangerous aspects of an ocean crossing.

Emily heard him out and though she was not unaffected by the potential horrors he described, she understood that he was deliberately trying to discourage her and would not permit him to see her squeamishness. "I think you do not wish me to make this crossing on your ship, Mr. DeVere," she said, a little surprised at her own plainspokenness, for she still felt gauche and unsure of herself with this cold, insufferable man. She saw he also regarded her bluntness with obvious surprise, and she felt emboldened to add, "If that is so, you must inform my uncle that you do not with to give me passage on your ship, for I am not so easily persuaded to cry craven." She still had not the least intention of sailing on his ship, but her spirit of defiance awakened, she refused to permit him an easy victory.

The color that stained Emily's cheeks this time was very different from the self-conscious blushes that had afflicted her at their introduction and this time Galen did notice how well her sudden flash of spirit became her. But it awakened in him no amorous response; to the fault of insipidity he added yet another: a rebellious nature.

He vouchsafed no response to Emily's declaration of hostility, but as Mr. Armitage, with his wife in tow, returned to the library he was not obliged to do so. Flicking Emily a disdainful glance which was calculated to depress her pretensions, he turned to Mrs. Armitage with a warm smile which Emily, knowing it to be false, wished she might slap off his impudent face.

Deprived of the ability to vent her rage on the source of it, she said nothing at all to him for the brief remainder of his stay, only acknowledging him, as he bowed over her hand again in leavetaking, with a furious glare which he—abominable man!—returned with a bland smile and sardonic amusement lighting his icy blue gaze.

3

Perfectly cognizant of Galen's rejection of her and painfully aware that her dowdy appearance and want of wit and grace were in good part responsible for his unfavorable impression of her, Emily was mortified by her attraction to him, but she could not deny it to herself. There was no reason why she should care a pin for his opinion of her, but it did matter to her.

Though Galen accepted Lucille Armitage's invitation to dinner, he animadverted bitterly to Jacob Farley that evening on the subject of bankers calling in favors in general and mousy young women who wanted conduct in particular. He received no joy from his friend, though, for Farley, listening patiently to these objurgations, at the end of them merely said that he saw no harm in taking on another passenger to please a benefactor. The *Devon* had sufficient staterooms to accommodate Emily and her maid in addition to those who had already been assured passage. Galen acknowledged the truth of this, but was no less determined to find an excuse to free him from his obligation to the banker.

Emily for her part had no outlet at all for her invective against Galen, for she saw plainly that her aunt and uncle held him in mistaken regard. She expressed this only in her refusal to take a proper interest in her aunt's plans for the dinner party and her defiance of Mrs. Armitage's wish that they take one of her silk evening dresses to Mrs. Rielly, the fashionable modiste on Arch Street, to have her apply her clever skills to bring it up to the current fashion.

Emily declared so mulishly that the dress in question was suitable just as it was that Mrs. Armitage gave it up at once, seeing that argument would be pointless. She was a little puzzled by her nieces behavior, but no amount of subtle probing to discover what might have passed between Emily and Mr. DeVere during his visit was successful.

It was not that Emily had no thought for her appearance, but she refused to give in to her desire to appear at her best before the detestable Mr. DeVere. She had no intention of making any extraordinary effort to attract his notice and was equally determined to cure herself of her unwanted attraction to him. This she was in a fair way to doing by Friday, the day of her aunt's dinner party, by the simple expediency of dwelling almost obsessively on every arrogant word he had spoken and recalling the dismissal and contempt which he had scarcely bothered to hide from her.

The pearl-colored silk gown she wore might not have been in the first stare of fashion, but she knew it became her. Yet when Galen arrived and bowed over her hand, his expression was one of polite indifference and gave no sign that he found her appearance at all improved. For all that Emily was determined that his opinion should not matter to her, she knew herself piqued. Mrs. Armitage had invited a few other friends as well, and Emily gave her attentions to the Rushes and the Hopkinsons, who were old friends, intending to pay Galen no more heed than he paid to her. She found comfort in numbers and felt easier in Galen's company. She spoke little to him but when she did, her manner was more poised, if still a bit retiring.

Emily had attracted Galen's notice more than she realized. He noted that she did not appear at such disadvantage as she had at their first meeting. Not only was she a bit more conversable, but she had pulled her hair into a more fashionable knot, allowing a few soft curls to dangle, and if her gown was not the most fashionable, it was of excellent cut and caressed her deeply rounded curves most flatteringly. He even acknowledged that he found her attractive, but purely in a physical sense; he neither wished nor intended to further his acquaintance with her.

But an innocent remark made by Mrs. Rush concerning the number of Englishmen who were leaving the United States since the declaration of war, began the discussion which ended with Galen irrevocably committed to giving Emily passage on the *Devon*.

"And you, Mr. DeVere?" said Mrs. Rush archly at the end of her comment. "Do you remain with us, or do you set sail for other waters?"

Casting her a quick, wry smile, Galen replied, "The latter, but I fear you will not believe me when I tell you it is not crying craven. It is no more than coincidence. I would be returning to England at this time if our countries were in perfect harmony. In fact, I would that they were; I am not political, but I believe that war seldom serves anyone except the politicians and the armaments merchants."

"How very republican you sound, Mr. DeVere," said Mrs. Hopkinson roguishly. "Your English friends will think you most odd if you espouse such sentiments. It is their militant notions, after all, which have brought us to such a pass."

Emily, already familiar with the faint sardonic curl of Galen's well-shaped lips, waited for an expected setdown at this provocative remark, but his answer was quite mild. "I have not set foot in England for better than twelve years, Mrs. Hopkins. No doubt my English friends, if I still may count them as such, shall think me odd whatever my sentiments."

"Emily shall be making the crossing to England as well," interjected Lucille Armitage, breaking off what she was saying to Charles Rush. "She has at last decided to visit her aunt, Lady Laelard, and is actually to sail on Mr. DeVere's ship. It is quite a settled thing, is it not,

Mr. DeVere?'' she added, punctuating her remark with a guileless smile.

Emily could not prevent herself from glancing up at Galen and she saw that his smile had frozen on his face. She stteled herself for an expected denial to her aunt's ingenuous assumption but once gain Galen surprised her.

''Yes,'' he replied after a pause that was not sufficient to be particularly noted by anyone else. The words repudiating Mrs. Armitage's assumption hovered on his lips, but breeding, which forbade him to embarrass his hostess, and honor, which reminded him of his obligation to his host, proved stronger. ''It is settled. That is, if Miss Hampton is determined to make the crossing.''

Emily quite understood the challenge in his words. It was her turn to commit herself to the voyage or deny her wish to make it. She felt an uncomfortable sinking sensation as she spoke, but she picked up the gauntlet and said with credible unconcern, ''Oh, it is quite settled. We are to sail in June, are we not, Mr. DeVere?''

Galen acknowledged that this was his intention. His lips curved in a half-smile, his expression was pleasant, but his eyes as they rested briefly on Emily appeared far darker than she remembered them and quite unfathomable. Intentionally or not, her aunt had outmaneuvered him, and Emily suspected that it was rage that lurked in the depths of those eyes, which fascinated her in spite of herself.

Emily could not be certain if her aunt had spoken innocently, but as the result of her remarks at the dinner table, the preparations for Emily's journey to England took on a more definite complexion and it appeared that barring some untoward event, Emily would find herself in a few short weeks aboard the *Devon* crossing the Atlantic. Emily, herself caught up in the numerous little matters that had to be seen to before she could leave for so extended a period, scarcely had time to think of the decision which had been virtually forced on her and whether or not she actually did mean to go through with it.

Her former indolence was a thing of the past; her books lay unopened and the pianoforte sat untouched. Mrs. Armitage insisted—and this time met no resistance—that Emily have several of her gowns refurbished for the journey, deciding that it would be best to wait to purchase new dresses until Emily had arrived in England and could patronize the fashionable London modistes rather than risk being a bit behind the fashion by the time she arrived. Her uncle saw to the transferring of funds for her sufficient for an extended visit and supplied her with letters of credit should she require any additional amount.

April passed into May and what had seemed an impossible task, to be ready for her journey by the first week in June, now appeared to be well in hand. Emily was not certain of the day they would sail, for Galen had indicated that the actual day of embarkation would depend on the weather and the timely arrival from Brazil of the cargo that the *Devon* would carry to Lisbon before going on to Portsmouth.

When at first there was no further word from Galen, Emily gave it little thought, but by the last week in May she found herself disturbed that he had made no effort to keep her abreast of his plans, which would affect her as well. Comments to her aunt and uncle showed them to be unconcerned, but Emily's anxieties about the voyage, which activity had made her forget for a time, returned to plague her and make her wish that she had never agreed to go to England.

It was the very last day in May when Galen did finally call at Chestnut Street again. Mrs. Armitage was out paying morning visits, as was her usual custom, and Emily was just putting on her bonnet for a walk to Asbury Dickin's Bookstore, the first opportunity she had had for visiting the renowned bookseller's establishment in several weeks. For the sake of civility, she knew she should put off her plans, but she decided that his lack of consideration for her merited none for him. Tying the ribbons of her bonnet with a determined little tug, she picked up her gloves and reticule and went downstairs to the saloon where he awaited her.

He was looking out the window onto Chestnut Street and he turned slowly as he heard her come into the room, a smile of greeting lightening his features. It was at that moment that Emily knew she could not underestimate the power of his attraction. She was vexed with herself for feeling what she did not hesitate to characterize as a schoolgirl's fascination for a handsome face, but nevertheless her heart beat faster merely at the sight of him.

She had hoped her reaction to him would be different, but she was able to meet him at least with the appearance of equanimity. "My aunt will be sorry to have missed you, Mr. DeVere," she said with quiet composure as he bowed over her hand. "We have been expecting you to call any time these past few weeks," she added pointedly.

He gave her his characteristic half-smile. "I have had no news for you before now," he said simply and without apology. Civility might have led him to call sooner with or without news, but he had not forgiven Emily or the Armitages for forcing his hand, and he had no intention pretending that he regarded his relationship to any of them as anything other than business. "But you are dressed for the street, Miss Hampton. Do I keep you from an appointment?"

"Yes," Emily replied, adding with relish, "but I can spare you a few minutes if you have something important to say to me." She quite deliberately did not suggest that they sit.

He met this handsome setdown with another smile. He saw before him a pretty young woman dressed in a dark blue walking dress which lent color to her eyes and flattered her complexion. She regarded him with cool dignity and perhaps even disapproval, a decided contrast to her shy awkwardness when they had first met. He wondered that he had ever regarded her as biddable and mousy.

But this alteration in his judgment of her did not reconcile him to having her in his charge. "I am afraid our plans to sail next week must be put off for at least another month and possibly longer," he said, watching her eyes for some reaction that would give him hope that she might cry off. "It is irksome, but, I fear, unavoidable. I have just learned that the cargo which was to arrive from Ceara last week will be delayed by at least that length of time."

Emily guessed that he hoped the delay would cause her to change her mind about making the crossing. "Indeed?" she said, allowing her skepticism to be heard. "Perhaps if the delay is indefinite it would be best if I sought passage elsewhere or gave up my intention to visit my aunt altogether."

These suggestions would have been quite pleasing to him if he had not recognized the sarcasm in her tone. "As you wish, Miss Hampton," he said coldly. "The *Devon* is a merchantman, not a passenger ship; and it sails to accommodate the goods it carries, not the passengers."

"Which you would as lief did not sail on your ship at all," Emily said plainly.

"In the circumstances, it would be uncivil of me to agree, Miss Hampton."

The sardonicism in his voice was sufficient to ignite her temper, which his arrogant manner had already exacerbated. "Oh, by all means, let us be civil, Mr. DeVere. We may also pay service to the fiction that we look forward to making a long voyage in each other's company."

"If you dislike my company, Miss Hampton, there is not the least need to subject yourself to it."

"You mean I might choose not to sail with you."

"That is your choice," he agreed.

"And it is what you heartily wish I would choose."

Their eyes met in an equally furious glare. "We are quite alone and you needn't have concern at offending my aunt or uncle, so let us have the tree without any bark on it, if you please. You don't at all want me on your ship, but you have agreed to take me, and I have every intention of sailing with you whenever that might be, even if you assure me that it is exactly the time of year when we are certain to be set upon by pirates, meet up with sea monsters, or be forced to ride out tidal waves. I have weathered storms before, Mr. DeVere."

"So have I, Miss Hampton, so enact me no melodrama," he said bitingly, his eyes alight with a rage to match her own. "Your uncle may find your shrewish manners and want of conduct engaging, but I do not. If this is a sample of the behavior we may expect during the vouage, I might best serve the interests of my crew and other passengers to revoke my promise to carry you to England."

Emily caught her breath at his audacious reading of her character but did not speak because she could not trust herself to give a temperate response. His eyes were the color and density of ice, and filled with such cold rage that for one horrified moment she thought that he would strike her.

Only a short distance separated them. Without warning, he pulled her into his arms and took her lips in a kiss that was surprisingly gentle. For a moment she was rigid in his arms, but she yielded to his embrace without conscious thought, powerless to prevent her instinctive response to the taste and feel of his mouth on hers.

Galen released her as suddenly as he had embraced her, as astounded as she by what he had done. He had no conscious amorous designs on Emily and could scarcely credit even an unconscious desire to make love to a female he had taken in dislike from almost before they had met. "Dear God," he said under his breath. "I beg your pardon, Miss Hampton. I should not have done that."

Emily, who was feeling weak-kneed, put out a hand to the back of the nearest chair. "No," she agreed with a tremor in her voice that she could not suppress, "you should not have. I am surprised that you would wish to," she added baldly.

He smiled, and it was a rare smile that touched his eyes, melting the ice she usually saw there. "So am I," he replied candidly. He still smiled, but his eyes became sober again. "I do beg your pardon most sincerely, Miss Hampton," he repeated. "I fear we have not made a very good beginning."

Though Emily was physically attracted to Galen, she could not like him, but for the moment at least she found him agreeable. His forbidding veneer had cracked, making him appear more approachable. "How could we, Mr. DeVere? You took me in immediate dislike," she said plainly. "You dismissed me as insipid and gauche."

His smile spread into a grin, making his features seem almost boyish. "If I did, it was an opinion which did not survive our second meeting," he said with equal frankness.

"No, you have revised it to regard me as a shrew who lacks conduct," she said with some asperity.

"Please, Miss Hampton, let us cry quits." He reached out and placed his hand on her arm in appeal, and Emily felt an unexpected current pass between them at even so simple a touch. "My manner toward you has not been that of a gentleman, and I am truly sorry for it. I felt I was having my hand forced in this matter and I disliked it to the point that I appear to have forgotten both breeding and address." He removed his hand from her arm, but Emily still felt the spot as if his touch had burned her.

It was a handsome apology and Emily acknowledged it as such. "My aunt and uncle had no wish to offend you, Mr. DeVere," she said, unconsciously rubbing the place where he had touched her. "Their concern has been for my welfare. But I understand that you would dislike having me foisted upon you in such a high-handed manner, and if you wish, I shall withdraw from my intention to sail on the *Devon*. You may trust me to think of an excuse that will satisfy my aunt and uncle.''

This was exactly what Galen had hoped for, Emily herself deciding against making the voyage; but perversely, he found himself refusing to accept her withdrawal. "That won't be necessary. I wouldn't go back on my word and there is not the least need for you to sacrifice yourself for my honor. We will make the crossing as planned.'' He walked over and picked up his hat and gloves from the table by the door. "I have already disposed of most of my assets,'' he said as he drew on his gloves, "but there are still a number of legal complications that keep me greatly occupied, so you shall probably continue to find me remiss in calling. But I shall see to it that you have ample opportunity to prepare yourself for the day that we sail.''

She bit back a tart rejoinder reminding him that since she had supposed that they were to sail in a week's time most of her preparations already were made, and instead politely thanked him for his consideration without any hint of sarcasm. But the moment of understanding between them had passed.

He took his leave of her, but Emily did not offer to see him out. She stood, still supporting herself against the chair, until she heard his footsteps retreat across the hall and the front door close. She walked to the window and looked down at him as he crossed Chestnut Street heading toward Market, where she knew he had lodgings. She leaned her head against the glass, which felt cool on her skin, and breathed the faint odor of starch and dust from the curtain she had pulled aside, watching him until he was out of her sight.

Her intention of visiting the bookstore was forgotten until she caught sight of herself in a mirror at the opposite end of the room and was surprised to see that she still wore her bonnet and gloves. She pulled one of these off and put fingers to her cheek, but it was cool and—the mirror told her—unflushed.

She allowed herself to hope for a moment or two that Galen had not noted the turmoil his embrace had caused in her or that her lips had become pliable beneath his, but she could not convince herself of it. It would be fatal to indulge in a *tendre* for him; her common sense forbade even the thought of it, yet her recalcitrant heart beat faster at the memory of his embrace.

4

It was not until the second last week in August that a definite date was set for the departure of the *Devon*. The Armitages had retired to their summer home on the Chesapeake to escape the heat of the city and it was here that Emily at last received word from Galen, the first she had had in a month when he had last written to tell her that he had no news at all.

Though he had promised her ample warning, he gave her little more than a week to return to town and make herself ready. Emily felt a wave of exasperation at this further proof of his highhandedness, and for a moment she toyed with the thought of not making the voyage after all. But she knew that she no longer even questioned her wish to embark on a journey that she had deemed too perilous even to consider just a few months earlier.

What doubts remained to her were of a very different nature. In spite of what had occurred between them on the last occasion that they had met, she knew Galen for a gentleman and had no fear that he would go beyond the line of what was proper once she had left the protection of her uncle and aunt. What she feared was the attraction she felt toward him that she didn't want but couldn't help. She did not like Galen DeVere, but paradoxically, she was afraid of falling in love with him—or at least imagining herself in love with him.

She found this prospect quite alarming. She had always assumed that if ever she met her ideal, theirs would be a meeting of souls, but it appeared that her nature was considerably more earthy than her ideals—a lowering realization. The most sensible thing would have been for her to delay her visit to England until passage on another ship could be found, but she knew she would not.

When Emily, accompanied by her aunt and uncle and Annie Lloyd, the young woman they had hired as her servant for the journey, came on board the *Devon* in the early morning hours of the twenty-seventh of August, Galen was too taken up with seeing to all the last-minute details of command for the start of the voyage to greet them in more than a perfunctory way. His features were once again set in forbidding lines and his manner toward Emily one of indifference. All traces of the approachable man, of whom she had had but a tantalizing glimpse, had vanished. Emily felt an odd mixture of relief and disappointment, but told herself that she was glad of it.

She had little opportunity to examine her ambivalent feelings toward Galen. A great many other things vied to occupy her attention as Jacob Farley, who had introduced himself to them and taken charge of directing Emily's baggage to her stateroom, offered to give them a brief tour of the ship before the Armitages returned to shore.

Mr. Farley was dressed in a manner similar to the ship's officers and Mr. Armitage begged him not to neglect his duties for their sake, but Farley laughed and assured him that he did not. "In the usual way I have many duties to occupy me, but on the voyage out, at least, I'm a passenger like yourself, Miss Hampton, with no rank and, fortunately, no responsibility. On the return journey it will be another matter though. When we reach Portsmouth, Captain DeVere will transfer ownership of the *Devon* to me and then I shall sail her home as her captain."

The ship was a scurrying mass of activity and Farley deftly led them about in an unobtrusive manner, pointing out various features of the ship and explaining many nautical terms that would otherwise have been incomprehensible to Emily.

Emily had heard so much about Mr. DeVere's fleet of merchantmen and of his great success in trade that somehow she had pictured the *Devon* as more impressive than she found it to be. In fact, it was a moderate-sized frigate, designed for optimum efficiency rather than impressiveness, but to Emily it seemed to have a fragile appearance that did not inspire confidence.

At first sight Emily felt intimidated by the largeness of Mr. Farley, but his smile was so reassuring and his manner so friendly that she could not but respond to him. She found herself feeling grateful that he would be a fellow passenger; his congeniality would be a most welcome foil to the captain's remoteness.

When Mrs. Armitage questioned him about the other passengers he told her that these were a Mr. Cooke, who had not yet come aboard, and Mrs. Wilard, who was already settling herself in her stateroom. He then offered to show them the stateroom that Emily would occupy, which proved to be larger than Emily had supposed it would be and which connected with a similar but smaller room for her maid.

By the time Mr. Farley escorted Emily and the Armitages on deck again, Mr. Cooke had arrived and proved to be an amiable dark-haired, dark-eyed man of about thirty whose openness of manner rivaled Mr. Farley's. Emily was encouraged to hope that at least as far as her company was concerned, she was sure to have a very pleasant crossing.

As the Armitages were taking their leave of Emily, Mrs. Wilard came out on deck and was made known to all of the others. Emily had hoped to find her as friendly and amiable as the gentleman, for it would be Mrs. Wilard toward whom she would most naturally look for companionship, with no other female of her own station aboard the ship. But Mrs. Wilard, a pretty woman of about Emily's age and a widow of less than a year, was retiring and reserved and said little beyond remarking that she hoped she would not be ill for the *entire* journey. As she spoke, a slight breeze stirred the soft blond curls that framed her delicate featured face. She paled and said, "I can feel the deck moving already."

"Actually, the deck is as still as ever it will be, Mrs. Wilard, until we are next again in port," Galen said, coming up to them. "It is only a matter of accustoming yourself to the motion."

Emily supposed she might have expected such an unfeeling remark from Galen and was pleased to hear Mr. Farley address him in a tone of familiar raillery. "Spoken by a man who has never been sick on the water in his life," he said, laughing. "We are not all blessed with your constitution, Captain."

Galen's smile was a bit thin, but his response was pleasant enough. "You only think so because you have known me since I gained my sea legs. It was not always so. My advice, Mrs. Wilard, is to eat even if you think you cannot. You are more likely to feel ill on an empty stomach."

Mrs. Wilard thanked him, but it was obvious that she thought little of his suggestion. Emily, though she wanted to think well of the other woman, feared she was a poor creature, of the sort that Galen had labeled her on their first meeting. Determined not to judge the other woman too harshly, she said with an engaging smile, "I do hope we shall become great friends, Mrs. Wilard. I know no one at all in England, you know, not even the relatives with whom I am to stay, and it would be a great comfort to be able to claim at least one friend."

"Two, I hope," put in Mr. Cooke with an engaging smile of his own. "I have been away from England for more than two years and have lost touch with many of my friends there, but my sister resides in town and enjoys a wide acquaintance. I know she would be very happy to introduce you to her friends."

It was Galen who responded to him. "I have no doubt," he said levelly, "that Lady Laelard, Miss

Hampton's aunt with whom she is to stay, will see to it that she does not want for friends.''

It was clearly a setdown and Mr. Cooke recognized it as such, for faint color stole into his countenance. Emily was both annoyed and amazed. She could not imagine why Galen would wish to snub Mr. Cooke on her behalf, and she resented his assumption that he had the right to do so. It was hardly the time or place for her to call him to account so she contented herself by casting Mr. Cooke her most enchanting smile and turning a frosty shoulder toward Galen to show him what she thought of his interference.

Mrs. Wilard returned to her stateroom and Mr. Cooke followed the affable Mr. Farley to be shown to his. Annie had gone to her mistress's room to begin to unpack the things she would need for the voyage and Emily at last exchanged somewhat tearful goodbyes and godspeeds with her aunt and uncle. When the Armitages were gone, Emily felt a moment of pure panic at the thought of the enormity of the step she was taking, fearing that she was not yet ready for such independence. She indulged for a moment in the wild fantasy of running after the Armitages and begging them to take her back with them to Chestnut Street. But the moment passed, and though she still felt some trepidation, she resolutely returned to her stateroom to help her maid with the unpacking.

Emily had not given much though to seasickness. Galen, during his recital of the more unpleasant aspects of sea travel, had informed her that dwelling on a fear of it might well turn it into a self-fulfilling prophesy. She was pleased then, as they at last left port and sailed beyond the Delaware Bay into the open sea, that she felt not the smallest twinge of queasiness. But by the following morning, she discovered that Annie Lloyd was not as fortunate. In fact, for the first week of their crossing, it was Emily who tended her maid, who was prostrate with her sickness and not even able to rise from her bed. Emily spent only brief periods on deck to take a bit of air and took all of her meals in her state-room to be near to the girl in case she was needed.

Mr. Farley occasionally came to inquire after the invalid and informed her that Mrs. Wilard was similarly stricken. "I had great hopes that this crossing would be considerably enlivened by the presence of ladies on board," he said to her on one occasion when they were several days out of port. "We are a sad male gathering at the captain's table with nothing to talk of but politics and sailors' jaw. I hope your girl is feeling better and you may join us tonight, Miss Hampton."

Emily thanked him, doubting that Galen had a similar wish to have her at his table, but she declined. "I hope Annie is a bit better. I persuaded her to take some toast this morning, and thus far she has kept it down, but she is too weak to be left alone, I think. In any case, if Mrs. Wilard is similarly afflicted, I am not sure it would be proper for me to join what you yourself describe as a male gathering."

"Stuff and nonsense," Mr. Farley said dismissively. "The captain's table isn't in a dowager's drawing room. And if you fear our conversation might be too free, you are fair and far off, Miss Hampton." He grinned conspiratorially. "The captain's an Englishman, you know, and his notions of propriety are rather stiff by our standards. He thinks we Americans are shockingly free in our ways—though he can be the devil of a fellow himself in congenial company. He'd come down hard on anyone offering an insult to a lady, so I promise you, we'd all be on our best behavior."

Remembering that swift embrace in her uncle's saloon, Emily found it difficult to think of Galen as a bastion of propriety. She thanked Mr. Farley once again for the invitation but again declined, promising only that she would consider joining the captain's table for dinner when her maid was better.

Whenever Emily was able to go out on deck, Mr. Cooke was almost certain to materialize beside her to take a bit of exercise with her and engage her in light conversation, for which she was most grateful. Emily was too kind-hearted to mind ministering to the sick serving girl, but it was a tedious manner in which to spend her first ocean voyage. Mr. Cooke's company was pleasant and undemanding, his manner, as familiarity between them grew, becoming slightly bantering. It was not long before they were on very easy terms despite the brevity of their acquaintance.

Emily caught only glimpses of Galen and had exchanged scarcely a word with him since she had come aboard the *Devon*. He had sent his first mate, Mr. Hatter, to inquire after the invalid and to ask if there was any way in which he or his staff might be of assistance, but he had not personally visited Emily's stateroom as Mr. Farley had.

Emily, always sensitive to any perceived insult from Galen, knew that the press of his duties might fairly excuse him from personal attention, but she could not help believing that his neglect was deliberate. It did not surprise her that he should wish to avoid her, and she told herself that it was certainly for the best for her own peace of mind. Yet, as before, her mind was at variance with her feelings.

Galen, occupied with his responsibilities as captain, gave Emily far less thought than she gave to him, but Mr. Hatter kept him apprised of her needs and the sick maid's progress, and his friend Jacob Farley reported that Emily was in good spirits and coping quite well with the responsibility of nursing her abigail.

Galen also noted her encounters with Mr. Cooke and on occasion had overheard sufficient of their conversation to be aware of the terms on which they stood. He did not particularly like Mr. Cooke, recognizing at once from his excess of gentility and patronizing manner that he belonged to a class that Galen did not hesitate to castigate as mushrooms.

But though Galen was aware of a disquieting sensation whenever he observed them together, he did not acknowledge that he had any personal interest in wishing to protect Emily from a man who was a social climber and possibly a fortune hunter as well; he regarded it as his duty as captain and as a part of the responsibility that he had taken on in his agreement with Mr. Armitage to see to Emily's welfare to put a spoke in Mr. Cooke's wheel. Accordingly, by the end of the week, whenever Emily was approached by Mr. Cooke as she strolled on deck, they were soon joined by Mr. Farley or Mr. Hatter and in such an unobtrusive manner that she never suspected that it was at the specific direction of the captain.

As Emily had feared, Galen had certainly been aware of her response to him when he had kissed her, and he had felt the surge of his own desire, but unlike Emily he placed no particular importance on it. He had still been at Harrow when he had embarked on his first successful love affair and since that time he had desired many women and even loved a few of them after a fashion, but none had ever left any lasting mark on his heart. He might be physically attracted to Emily but he did not regard his desire for her as anything more than passing. Had she been of the muslin company, he might have pursued her, but she was not and that was an end to it.

By the middle of their second week at sea, Annie was at last sufficiently recovered to be able to assume at least some of her duties and Emily was freed to enjoy the voyage. All fears of encountering any English ships which might challenge them proved unfounded and the weather was so glorious that spending time on deck was a pleasure that Emily enjoyed at every opportunity.

For the most part her companions remained Mr. Cooke and Mr. Farley, though on occasion Mrs. Wilard was persuaded by her dresser to take a brief turn about the deck. Despite that lady's languishing manner and die-away airs, her color was good and, Mr. Farley disclosed, her appetite was not as impaired as she claimed. "Either that or her maid is eating enough for two," he told Emily confidentially.

Whether or not Mrs. Wilard was genuinely ill, or

exaggerating her illness to make herself interesting, the result for Emily was the same; either she spent her time in quiet reading and reflection or she was cast into exclusively male company which, whatever Mr. Farley might say, she knew was improper for an unmarried woman in any circumstances. Yet despite her earlier penchant for quiet and solitude she found these things had lost their former appeal. When Mr. Farley next asked her to join the gentlemen for dinner at the captain's table, she did not again refuse, and after that night, joined them regularly, though only on a very few evenings did Mrs. Wilard also condescend to make one of the party.

Emily also discovered herself sufficiently lost to propriety to spend much of her days in the company of one or another of the gentlemen as well, strolling the deck, engaged in lively discussion, or playing games of chance for fabulous sums with imaginary markers, most of which were won by Mr. Cooke, who was a first-rate cardplayer and outclassed the others at every game they set their hands to. Even Galen, when his responsibilities permitted, would make a fourth for a game of whist or walk the deck with Emily after dinner.

At first their conversations were not easy, for Galen's reserve with her amounted to taciturnity. But Emily, since she could not avoid his company, was determined not to be intimidated by his forbidding manner. She took pains to draw him out and was eventually rewarded for her efforts. She asked him endless questions about the sea and his adventures and travels and he, with increasing ease, spoke fluently of his experiences.

At these times all was harmony between them and Emily, liking him very well, could almost forget that Galen could be imperious and overbearing. But she was yet in no danger of letting herself lose her heart to him, for in spite of a sense of intimacy that existed when they shared these confidences, at all other times he behaved toward her with a formality that kept the distance between them intact.

The amiable Mr. Cooke and the helpful Mr. Farley were both at pains to amuse her, and each day dawned lovelier than last, so the time passed so quickly that she could scarcely credit it when Galen mentioned one evening during dinner that they should be in sight of the Azores within a day or so.

"So soon?" Emily asked, her surprise evident.

"We've been a month at sea, Miss Hampton," Farley replied, looking up from his plate, "and with the weather we've enjoyed we're dead on course."

Mrs. Wilard, who had joined them that evening, said that she was heartily glad of it. "We are not far from Lisbon then, are we Captain DeVere? At least then we shall enjoy a day or two without this dreadful pitching while we are in port to unload the cargo."

Emily and Jacob Farley exchanged a smiling glance; with the exceptional weather they had enjoyed, there had been very little pitching or rolling, and even Annie Lloyd, once she had become used to the motion of the ship, enjoyed a hearty appetite.

"You gained your sea legs rather quickly, Miss Hampton," Mr. Hatter said, "You are made of stronger stuff than most of your sex."

Emily was not aware that seasickness had anything to do with sex, but she smiled at him and said in a bantering tone, "Many would say that other women enjoy a finer sensibility. A lady does not generally take it in good part to have her appetite complimented. Though in the circumstances, I am pleased to be able to say it it is quite true. My appetite has been unimpaired since we left Philadelphia."

"It would not do to be too confident about possessing your sea legs, Miss Hampton," Galen suggested dampeningly. "We have enjoyed particularly fine weather but it is unlikely at this time of year that it will hold indefinitely. A crossing such as this entirely without any rough weather is virtually unheard of."

"If that happens, I expect I shall be confined to my cabin again," Mrs. Wilard said mournfully.

"If we do encounter a squall, you would be well advised to stay in your stateroom as well, Miss Hampton," Galen advised. "I don't want to have to fetch you from the water if you lean too far over the side."

Aware that he was deliberately quizzing her, Emily said caustically, "It is at least comforting to know that you *would* pull me from the water, Captain DeVere. I was not at all sanguine about that." This won for her an appreciative smile which acknowledged the hit, but he made no rejoinder.

"We'd best find another topic or we may all be looking for our sea legs before long," Jacob Farley said and, picking up his glass, he saluted Emily. "To your continued good health, Miss Hampton. I hope this fine weather may hold for I've seldom seen more glorious days. When I first put out to sea with only twelve years in my dish I thought storms glorious and good weather dull, until more experience with an angry sea than I care to recall taught me my folly."

"Twelve years," exclaimed Mrs. Wilard with a dramatic gesture of surprise. "You were little more than a babe, I wonder your mother permitted it."

The ship's officers and Jacob Farley exchanged smiling glances. "I was near to old for an apprentice, Mrs. Wilard. Nine is not an uncommon age to begin and thirteen is considered a late start."

"Did you begin your career at such an early age as well, Captain DeVere?" Emily asked Galen with genuine curiosity. In spite of the discussions they had enjoyed, she knew very little about him beyond his more recent travels and adventures at sea.

"Younger," Galen replied readily, "but I didn't apprentice on a merchant ship like Jacob. My father taught me to sail and the lessons began when I was six."

"Was your father a naval man?" inquired Mrs. Wilard.

"No." The single word was spoken tersely and invited no further inquiry.

A small uncomfortable silence fell over the table which was manfully breached by Mr. Farley, who engaged Mr. Cooke in a discussion of the escalating war between England and the United States. Mr. Hatter was also drawn into the conversation and even Mrs. Wilard's opinion was sought on a particular matter. Only Galen and Emily took no part, each adopting an aloofness from the others for private reasons.

Emily's thoughts dwelt on Galen—as they all too often did. She was thinking that he was an anomaly; she had never before encountered a man whom she could both like and dislike in equal measure. Their eyes met across the table for a brief moment and a quizzing smile came into his which made them sparkle with blue light. Her heart fluttered in her breast, and she looked away in confusion, annoyed that he should have such power to discompose her.

Dinner finally drew to a close and the ladies left the gentlemen to their wine. Emily tried to persuade Mrs. Wilard to remain on deck for a bit but the widow, pleading queasiness as usual, declined and returned to her stateroom.

This was not to be a night of conviviality. As if to underscore Galen's warning about the weather, there was a perceptible difference in the motion of the ship and a sharp breeze had arisen that was not yet unpleasant but which hinted at something stronger in occasional gusts. Galen returned to the bridge shortly after the ladies had withdrawn and was followed by Mr. Farley.

Mr. Cooke, coming out onto the deck in their wake, offered to join her in a bit of exercise before they retired for the evening. "It would appear we are deserted by our friends, Miss Hampton," he said, placing her hand on his arm. "You shall have to make do with my poor company tonight."

As she assured him that she quite enjoyed his company, the breeze caught at her skirt and teased ringlets from the moorings of their pins. She had the thought that it might be as well to forgo a stroll of the deck this evening, but her companion seemed scarcely to notice the breeze and was already guiding her forward.

At first their conversation was much as it always was, a mixture of shared opinion and light badinage, but he directed it into channels that became more serious and, to Emily, a bit alarming. He spoke in a vague, but earnest manner of his future and his hope of finding someone who would share his aspirations. Though it seemed incredible to Emily that he would approach her on such short acquaintance, she feared that he was hinting at a proposal of marriage and hoped she was mistaken.

A side door leading into the galley was deeply recessed and several barrels were habitually stored there where they were not likely to topple or roll if the motion of the ship became unsteady. Just that happened as they were beside the opening; a strong gust of wind coupled with a sudden rolling motion of the deck nearly dashed them off their feet. Mr. Cooke drew her into the cavity and they braced themselves against the wall of the galley until the motion of the ship once again was stable. Emily was a bit shaken and realized that Galen was right when he suggested that the fair weather they had enjoyed had made her complacent. To have the surface beneath her feet suddenly heave and give way beneath her was dreadfully unnerving and the loss of balance did make her head reel for a moment.

Mr. Cooke had an arm about her waist and showed no disposition to release her once she no longer needed his support. Emily, fearing the worst, gently pulled away from him. "I think Captain DeVere must have the powers of a fortune teller," she said. "We are surely going into a storm. Perhaps we should go to our staterooms to get what rest we can. We may have little once we are in rough seas."

"Miss Hampton," he said in an intense way that showed he had not heeded her words, "I know you will think me precipitous, but I must speak while I have my courage in hand for I find that I cannot deny my feelings any longer."

Emily groaned internally. "Mr. Cooke, I wish you would not," she said quickly, disliking to snub him but preferring that to receiving an unwanted declaration. "I am quite tired and want nothing so much as my bed. If the deck were to move again in such a way, I am certain I should be sick and quite disgrace myself," she added, thinking that such flat unromanticism would surely put him off.

"Emily, I cannot wait," he said, proving her mistaken. "I am tortured by fears that once we leave ship you will be lost to me."

Emily managed to move a little further away from him. She was uncomfortably aware that there seemed to be no one else near to them, not even a seaman on watch going about his duty. "That is nonsense," she said with a slight forced laugh, hoping that lightness might answer where pragmatism had not. "I have told you that I hope you will call at my aunt's when we are in London."

"Oh, Emily," he said, his voice pleading and a little reproachful, "don't pretend to misunderstand me. You could not be ignorant of how my feelings toward you have grown. I knew the moment I set eyes on you that you were the loveliest creature I had ever beheld, but I am not your equal in fortune or connections and I fear you will think me beneath your regard. Yet in these past weeks I do not think it is vanity to say that I believe you have come to like me, at the least. For me it has grown to be so much more." He took her hand in his and placed a lingering kiss on her palm.

Emily withdrew her hand from his and said gently, "But not for me. I like you very well, Mr. Cooke, but it is nothing more than that. Your fortune and family are of no consequence to me; if I felt I could love you, I would not regard them. But I am simply not in love with you.''

"I feared this would be your response, but don't say I haven't any hope at all," he begged. "If you would but give me a chance to prove it, I promise you I would love you as no other man could and I would teach you to feel the same for me."

Emily was both vexed and dismayed that he did not accept her rejection of his offer. "Mr. Cooke, I have no wish to wound you, but there is not the least chance that I will return your feelings now or at any other time." Before she had even finished speaking, she found herself drawn into his embrace. This time there was no unwilling response as there had been with Galen. Emily was furious with Jeremy Cooke, and with herself for not having noticed that his attentions were becoming particular so that she might have guessed his intentions and avoided a declaration. She managed to get her hands between them and pushed against his chest, but his response was to hold her even tighter against him while his lips sought in vain for a response from hers.

Emily began to struggle in earnest and with a suddenness that nearly sent her backward, she found herself released. Emily steadied herself against a barrel behind her and saw that Mr. Cooke had not released her because of her efforts but because Galen had pulled him away. Galen, his expression set and stony, still had his hand on the other man's shoulder.

"What the devil do you suppose you're doing," Cooke demanded indignantly. "This is not your concern."

"No?" Galen said icily. "All that occurs on board this ship is my concern, Mr. Cooke. It was obvious that Miss Hampton did not welcome your attentions. You are perhaps unaware that it is customary for a gentleman to honor a lady's wishes in such matters."

The insult was deliberate and Jeremy Cooke's skin

flushed to an unbecoming shade. He turned to Emily and said stiffly, "Miss Hampton, I beg your pardon. I fear I misread your kindness to me."

The situation was so awkward that Emily had no idea what to reply, but Mr. Cooke did not wait for a response. Sketching Emily the briefest of bows and casting a curt nod toward the captain, he turned on his heel and left them.

Though Emily certainly had not intended to encourage Mr. Cooke, she did see that he might have mistaken her friendliness for something warmer. She found it particularly humiliating that Galen had been the one to discover her discomfiture. She forced herself to meet Galen's eyes, scarcely knowing whether she would find solicitousness or censure, but what she saw, surprisingly, was anger.

"It is not my concern, Miss Hampton, if you choose to engage in dalliance with a fellow passenger," he said, his voice clipped. "But I have given Mr. Armitage my word to see to your welfare. If you do not wish for the inevitable result of encouraging intimacy with a man who is barely known to you, you would be wise to behave with greater discretion. The next time you might not be fortunate enough to have someone at hand to save you from your folly."

Emily gasped with indignation, her chagrin forgotten. "You make it sound as if I courted Mr. Cooke's advances. You should know, Captain DeVere, that even without encouragement, a woman is not always safe from an unwanted embrace."

His eyes, so often cold, blazed for a moment and if she could have stepped back, she would have. "As you say, Miss Hampton," he said more temperately than she expected. "Nevertheless, I do not think you can say that Mr. Cooke received no encouragement. I have observed you in his company since we left port and cannot entirely blame him for misinterpreting the freeness of your manner toward him. If your behavior is indeed artless, then may I suggest that in future you spend less time strolling the deck with Mr. Cooke and more in your stateroom, where at least you will not find yourself cast into difficulties from which you require my extrication.''

She was glad that she stood in the shadows, for her face burned with humiliation. "I have no need for a duenna, Captain DeVere," she said furiously. "And if I did, I would certainly not choose you for the post. There was not the least need for you to interfere."

His half-smile was intentionally insulting. "I see. Then you did wish for Cooke's embrace. I beg your pardon, in that case. It did not look so to me, but then I am unacquainted with your tastes, Miss Hampton."

Her hand lashed out to strike him, but he caught it at the wrist so that her fingers just grazed his cheek without force. He drew her closer to him and their eyes locked for a long moment before he spoke. "When we arrive in England I shall hand you into the care of Lady Laeland and then you may cast out lures to every fortune hunter and captain sharp in England with my perfect goodwill, but until that time you are under my protection whether you choose to see it as a mantle or a yoke.''

"You have no right to order my behavior," she said, her voice tight with anger.

He smiled again in the way that was designed to bring her rage to the boil. "You are misinformed, Miss Hampton. As captain, there is no greater authority than mine on this ship. If I wish it, I can have you confined to your stateroom for the remainder of the voyage. If you cannot keep out of scrapes, I shall do so. I have too much to occupy me to play the nursemaid."

Tears of fury and humiliation stung at Emily's eyes and she could not trust herself to speak. She pushed past him, her eyes filling and blinding her. She didn't see the coil of rope until she tripped over it and was sent sprawling headlong into the deck. A seaman who witnessed her fall came rushing to her assistance, but Galen waved him away.

Looking up, Emily saw Galen approach her and tried to struggle to her feet without his assistance, but the ship gave another unexpected roll and she was caught off balance and fell to her knees again. Galen extended his hand to her. She wanted to reject his offer of help but her common sense reasserted itself and she reluctantly took his hand. As soon as she stood the ship rolled again and she swayed into his arms.

He steadied her and released her. In the fuller light outside of the alcove, she was even more certain that the emotion she read in his eyes was purely anger. Again this puzzled her, for though she might have expected condemnation or distaste for the situation he had discovered her in, she could not imagine why he should be angry with her. Unless of course it was because of the obligation he felt toward assuring her welfare for the sake of her uncle. But surely that would cause annoyance, not the cold, steely rage she had read in his eyes when he had pulled Mr. Cooke away from her.

After a moment, his lids veiled his eyes and he said without inflection, "We are heading into rougher seas, Miss Hampton. It would be prudent for you to go to your stateroom and remain there if we are in for a squall, which I fear we are."

A retort, engendered by her bruised vanity, rose to her lips but she bit it back. What he said was sensible and to disagree would only make her appear petulant. Murmuring her thanks to him for helping her to rise, she turned with an abruptness that was intentionally rude and went to her stateroom.

Galen understood his angry response to finding Emily with Jeremy Cooke even less than she did. It had taken all his considerable self-control to prevent himself from laying Mr. Cooke flat on the deck with a punishing right. In spite of his words, he did not believe that Emily had willfully encouraged Mr. Cooke, but if he acquitted her of coquettery, he condemned her for her naiveté. But this was insufficient explanation for his strong reaction, and he knew it. The truth teased at his consciousness, but he refused it admittance and was aided by the fact that they were indeed headed into stormy weather, and all his attention was needed to see to the securing of his ship.

5

When Emily reached her stateroom, she too faced difficulties that pushed her encounter with Galen temporarily from her mind. In spite of the earlier improvement in her health, Annie Lloyd was once again prostrated by sickness as the motion the ship increased.

Within another hour or so they were in the midst of the squall but by first light the winds had begun to abate and the motion of the ship became more steady. Annie fell into an exhausted but peaceful sleep and Emily, having had quite enough herself of feeling tossed about in her stateroom, ate a hasty breakfast brought to her on a tray and then went out on deck. She felt some qualms about meeting either Galen or Mr. Cooke after what had occurred the previous evening, but since in the close quarters of the ship this was unavoidable, she saw little point in denying herself the air and exercise she craved.

The weather outside was indeed calm, but the sky had an odd appearance. Toward the stern, the sky was bright and crisp and sunny, but in the direction of the bow, far to the east, it was still dark and lowering. Emily wore a spotted muslin morning dress that was quite suitable for the time of year, yet in spite of the bright sunshine that fell on the deck the air was dank and chill and the thin muslin dress too light for comfort.

As luck would have it, Galen stood talking to Jacob Farley only a few feet away as she came out on deck. The latter smiled at her, but the captain's eyes merely flicked over her in an assessing way that made her feel uncomfortable. "Feeling more the thing, Miss Hampton?" Farley said, approaching her. "It wasn't much of a blow by sailors' standards, but if you've never been on the water during a storm before, even a squall can be oversetting."

"I have been well enough," she said, favoring him with a sunny smile to match the improved weather, "but my maid has fared poorly. She is sleeping comfortably now and I thought I might leave her to get a bit of air."

Jacob complimented Emily on her devotion to her serving girl, but Galen came up behind him and cut him short. "You would do best to remain with your abigail, Miss Hampton. This gale has blown over, but it was sufficient to put us off course and I don't care for the look of the sky even if the wind is dying." He spoke with a cool indifference, as if the greater affinity that had been growing between them before their quarrel had never existed. With a curt nod, he turned and walked away again.

His brusqueness caused a return of her feelings of angry humiliation, as if she had been caught out again in some disgrace. She knew it was the attraction she felt toward him that made her respond to his words as if she had been reproved when in fact he had merely offered advice. It was as if she had a need for his unconditional approval. And that, she told herself savagely, you shall never have.

She quite forgot Mr. Farley, who was still beside her and who walked with her to the side of the ship to look down on the sea, which was far calmer but still tipped with white. "The captain is a bit abrupt at times, Miss Hampton," he said after standing beside her for a few minutes in silence. "You mustn't take it as a personal affront; he has much to occupy him and his shortness is no more than a reflection of his involvement in his duties."

Emily thought it exactly in keeping with Mr. Farley's good and generous nature that he should feel a need to defend his friend, but it also added to her mortification that her feelings were so obvious to him that he felt the defense necessary. She had never thought of herself as lacking in grace, humor, or aplomb, but Galen possessed the signal ability to reduce her to feeling like an unseasoned schoolgirl. "Your belief does you credit as a friend to Captain DeVere, Mr. Farley," she replied, allowing her anger with herself to be redirected onto Galen, "but I do not so easily excuse him. He is obviously a man possessed of education and breeding; he is perfectly aware when his words will or will not offend."

"He's damn high-handed at times, if you ask me," said Mr. Cooke, coming up behind them.

Emily saw Mr. Farley's face set in lines of disapproval, but she turned to Mr. Cooke, her desire for an ally for her point of view successfully overcoming any awkwardness that might have arisen between them. "He is certainly that," she concurred. "He informed me once that he disliked carrying passengers on his ships, but that is hardly an excuse to treat us as if we were just another more troublesome bit of cargo."

"You do the captain an injustice, Miss Hampton," Jacob said rather stiffly.

"Well, DeVere's not my idea of an amiable fellow," Cooke put in and then, turning a shoulder to Mr. Farley, asked Emily if she would wish to take a bit of exercise.

Emily accepted Mr. Cooke's arm and they left Jacob standing by the side of the ship. Emily was pleased that Mr. Cooke used the opportunity of their *tête-à-tête* to apologize for his ungentlemanly behavior and to express the hope that she would not only forgive but forget his lapse so that they might remain as friends. Emily was very ready to do this and by dinner that evening they were once again on the same easy terms they had enjoyed before his declaration.

The following day was overcast and there was a stiff breeze but it was not until two days later while the *Devon* was still off course as it approached waters north of Madeira, that the storm which threatened finally broke. This time it was no mere squall. It began in the early hours of the morning, and Emily was awakened by the piteous moans of Annie Lloyd in the next room.

More than once Emily was certain that she too would be sick, but remembering Galen's advice to Mrs. Wilard, she forced herself to eat the bread and butter and lemonade brought to her by a seaman with an apology and an explanation that fare would be simple until the motion of the ship steadied again. It did settle Emily's uneasy stomach, but she could not persuade Annie, who blanched at the mention of food, to follow her example.

Luncheon, such as it was, consisted of more lemonade and bread with a bit of hard cheese and arrived so late as to nearly qualify as dinner, and dinner was brought to her so long after the usual hour she had given up expecting it. When she saw the drawn, weary face of the seaman who brought her her tray, his clothes drenched and clinging to him like a puckered second skin, she felt the first real sensation of alarm despite the unabated tossing of the ship.

She asked him his name and he gave it to her civilly, though he was obviously impatient to return to more vital duties. But Emily, who observed that seawater rolled along the passage and trickled into her stateroom when she opened the door, stayed him a moment longer. "Is all well, Michaels?"

"As can be expected, Miss," the seaman replied with a brief nod. "It's a bad one, no mistaking that, but we've a good captain and a fine crew. If he can keep her off the rocks, I reckon we'll make it."

"Rocks?" Emily said with surprise and alarm. "In the middle of the ocean?"

"The Madeiras, Miss. The rain is so fierce you can't make them out, but Mr. Hatter reckons that if it were clear we'd be in sight of the shore."

To Emily the Madeiras were vague spots on her Uncle Walter's globe in his study. She had no notion of the tracherousness of these waters, but vague fears suddenly took on hideous shape as she imagined the *Devon* being dashed to pieces on great outcroppings of rock which she was not even sure existed. Thanking the seaman, who she was sure had simply answered truthfully with no thought to upset her, she let him return to the deck.

Though not plagued with seasickness, Emily slept poorly and awoke at an early hour dispirited by the realization that the storm was still in full gale. In this humor she found the stateroom stuffy and cramped and the prospect of another day confined to it almost unbearable. The motion of the ship made reading uncomfortable and writing impossible; there was little she could do for Annie besides making her as comfortable as she could. In fact, there was nothing at all to do but to listen to the wind and the sea, alone with thoughts that became increasingly disquieting as the storm continued.

She ate the usual ration of bread and butter and lemonade as it was brought to her but asked no further questions of the harried seamen who served her. She was not at all sure she wished to hear their answers. When she had eaten her dinner she composed herself for sleep for want of anything else to do, but sleep did not come and the harder she attempted to will herself to it, the more it eluded her.

Half in exasperation, half in despair, she got up and went into the other room to check on Annie. Finding the maid asleep, Emily redonned her dress and chose her most practical shawl and wrapped it about her. She stepped into the passageway cautiously. It did seem to her that the excessive motion of the ship had ebbed—or at the least that she had become accustomed to it—and she dared to go out on to the deck.

The rain had stopped but the wind was still strong and the seas high. As Emily stood there, her back against the wooden wall of the great cabin, half poised to scamper back into her stateroom, immense swells formed and occasionally lapped onto the deck. She was frightened, but she was also fascinated and more exhilarated than she could ever remember feeling before in her life.

Emily had not intended to leave the security of the cabin, but fascination overcame fear. Seawater washed the deck making footing uncertain and the constant roll of the ship as it rode the waves made balance for the unseasoned precarious. Somehow she made it to the side without mishap and without attracting notice. The sea in the throes of a gale was the most horrifyingly beautiful thing she had ever seen. She felt bewitched, entranced; and though a sensible inner voice warned her of her danger, she did not heed it. Nothing but the waves and the wind and the sharp taste of the salt spray existed for her at that moment.

A touch on her arm brought her out of her trance with a sharp intake of breath. Galen stood behind her, his expression incredulous and furious. "Are you mad?" he demanded, and she realized that he had to shout to be heard. She had been oblivious to the roar of wind and sea and to all activity about her. He put his hand under her arm and none too gently guided her back toward the great cabin.

A sudden wave, larger than any previous one, broke over the deck and deluged Emily and Galen as well, soaking them both to the skin, though in Galen's case it was redundant for he had been wet through since the storm had broken. The dousing took Emily's breath away and nearly brought her off her feet. Instinctively, she clung to Galen for support as the deck, in a motion that was becoming all too familiar, seemed to drop away from them. Yet another wave washed over them before they could reach the cabin and almost simultaneously, there was a horrible sound of rending and the entire ship seemed to shudder like a living thing.

They were cast against the outer wall of the great cabin, Galen managing to twist his body so that he took most of the force of the blow. Nevertheless, Emily gasped for air and slid to her knees from the shock. Galen pulled her to her feet and half dragged, half carried her to her stateroom.

The noise of the storm was less inside and he said more temperately in volume, but quite savagely in inflection, "If you want to die, there are pleasanter ways to go about it. If you attempt to leave this room again, I shall have you forcibly confined under a guard." With this he left her, pulling the door hard behind him.

Emily stood for a moment staring at the closed door. Little rivulets of seawater ran from her shawl and dress onto the floor. All at once she sank to the floor, not in a faint but in shock and exhaustion. Though her experience in the storm had lasted no more than a few minutes, it had thoroughly shaken her. For the first time she had an appreciation of the might of the ocean and a glimmer of understanding why so many men found the sea an alluring, if exacting mistress.

Annie, terror overcoming sickness, came into Emily's room and huddled beside her. "We hit something, didn't we, Miss?" she said in a horrified whisper.

Emily looked at the serving girl uncomprehendingly for a moment and then, recalling the terrible sound as she and Galen had been thrown against the wall of the cabin, she said dully, "Yes, I suppose we must have."

"Oh, Miss," the maid said in a high voice that was clearly on the edge of hysteria, "we shall go down, won't we? We're going to die here."

For all Emily knew, this was true. What she had seen in the few minutes she had been on deck convinced her of the possibility, but she said bracingly, "Nonsense. We have probably just scraped against some rocks. Captain DeVere is an excellent seaman and he has a fine crew," she added, parroting the assurance of the sailor who had brought her her meals.

With common sense and chivying, Emily convinced the serving girl to help her out of her soaked garments and changed into a dry blue cotton round gown. If there were to be problems with the ship, she wished to be ready to face them. She then dragged blankets off

Annie's berth to wrap around Annie and herself and settled them both in her bed.

Emily could not say when she finally drifted into sleep, but it seemed only a very short time before she was awakened by a loud knocking on the door. The sound was not inquiring but insistent. There was a feeble light coming through the porthole to indicate that dawn at last had arrived.

"Miss Hampton!" It was Mr. Farley's voice, and the urgency in it was unmistakable. Emily opened the door at once and he almost tumbled into the small room. "Miss Hampton, I beg your pardon if I startled you awake, but the captain wants everyone on deck."

Behind her Emily heard Annie scramble to her feet, uttering a small frightened moan. "What is it, Mr. Farley? We have struck something, have we not?"

Farley nodded. "Aye, rocks. We're that near to the coast of Madeira, but not close enough for our comfort. We thought the damage slight at first but the water below is rising steadily. I'm sorry to have to say it, but the captain thinks we may have to abandon ship, Miss Hampton, and the sooner the better. We've the launch and a few other boats. Enough to get us all into the water safely."

"In this storm?" Emily cried, too dismayed to hide it for the sake of the frightened maid. Another moan from Annie turned into a sob and Emily turned and said sharply, "Annie, do not! If you want to have hysterics, save them until you have the leisure to indulge yourself. Gather what you can into my bandbox and I shall wrap a few of our things into a blanket."

"I'm afraid not, Miss Hampton," Farley said regretfully, but in a tone that brooked no argument. "This ship is not really rigged out for passengers and our boats are little more than dinghies. The captain said you were to gather up your jewels and anything else you have of value you can carry in your pockets or reticule and come up on deck at once. The ladies and Mr. Cooke will be first off and the rest of us will follow."

Emily willed herself to be calm, but she was shaking inside. "We are going down that fast?"

"No. But we want to be as well away from the ship as possible so we don't find ourselves dragged into its undertow when it does go down. The captain has hope that we may be able to reach land before dark if we get an early start. The wind is down a bit and the sea is calmer, but it isn't weather we'd leave the ship in if we had any choice."

Farley left them to go to Mrs. Wilard and Emily told Annie to fetch her jewel case. Annie's face was so white that Emily was sure she would faint and have to be carried on deck, but the maid managed to keep herself in hand and she helped Emily pass the contents of her jewel case and the letters of credit into Emily's pockets and reticule.

Outside, the rain had stopped again, and the wind was more of a stiff breeze, but the swells were still alarmingly high. There were four small boats on deck and one slightly larger one which was being lowered to the water as Emily and Annie Lloyd came out on deck. Galen and Mr. Hatter were forward amid the men dragging tarpaulins off the boats and gathering casks of water and other minimal necessities. Mr. Farley had charge of the passengers and he led Emily and her maid to where Mr. Cooke and Mrs. Wilard, weeping and trembling, already stood.

Jeremy Cooke pointedly ignored the sobbing widow and turned to Emily. "They look so very small, don't they?" he said, with a nod of his head indicating the boats.

Emily could not but agree with him. The first boat touched the water and from the height of the deck seemed very small indeed. Two more boats followed it with seamen scrambling down the side of the ship to steady them in the heavy sea. Mr. Farley informed them that as passengers they would be first into the boats and extended his hand to Mrs. Wilard first. The widow shrunk away from him with a shriek. Containing his irritation admirably, Jacob turned to Emily and said quietly, "Will you show us the way, Miss Hampton?"

Emily was no less afraid than Mrs. Wilard, but she nodded, and gave him her hand. Mr. Cooke stepped forward. "Perhaps it would be best if I went first to reassure the ladies?" he suggested.

Emily saw Mr. Farley purse his lips, and he started to protest, but Mr. Cooke paid no heed to him and in the space of a minute or so he had made the treacherous descent down the side of the ship and was being assisted into one of the boats by one of the seamen. Cooke turned to call up to shout encouragement to Emily to follow him.

As Emily gathered her skirts and prepared to go over the side, Galen materialized beside her. "Have a care, Miss Hampton," he said with a faint, rallying smile. "Remember, I don't want to have to fish you out of the sea."

She knew he was quizzing her to lift her spirits and she smiled in acknowledgment, but it had begun to rain again and the smile was wan. "It's all right, Emily," he said in a warmer voice than he had ever used with her before. "Mr. Hatter will be with you and he's a good man."

Emily felt a keen stab of disappointment; though she knew it was Galen's responsibility to stay with his ship until all hope was abandoned, she wished that he might be with them in their boat. She knew instinctively that her anxiety would not be nearly so great if he were near.

It was terrifying to go over the side of the ship while a sharp wind tore at her skirts and rain stung against her exposed skin. The movement of the ship in the heavy sea seemed even more pronounced and the ropes, as drenched as everything else aboard the *Devon*, felt cold and numbed her fingers as she grasped them.

Mr. Hatter himself had gone before her and was waiting with his arms held out to her, but Mr. Cooke said something to him and pushed him aside. Emily, not really caring who received her as long as she was safely settled into the longboat, felt arms grasp her about the waist. For a moment she instinctively held on to the rope for security, but realizing she was hampering the effort to get her into the boat she let go all at once, not realizing that she was being pulled with some force. She fell into the boat with an abrupt motion and landed flat on the hard wooden bottom with a sharp thump. She could hear Mr. Hatter imploring Mr. Cooke to sit so that he might steady the boat but Cooke, determined to remain upright in the violently rocking boat struggled to maintain his own balance and ignored the first mate. The little boat pitched and nearly capsized. Emily, sprawled full length on the bottom, clung to the wood, but the two men in one swift motion were both cast into the sea.

There was suddenly a great deal of commotion, shouts that rose above the sounds of the rain and wind and sea. But the boat seemed to steady at last and Emily dared to sit up. She was quite alone in the boat; Jeremy Cooke was screaming that he couldn't swim and Mr. Hatter and another seaman swam toward the terrified man whose head and shoulders were alternately above and below the heavy swells of water.

All eyes including Emily's were riveted to this drama and at first no one, not even she, realized that the boat in which she sat was moving away from the ship. It was Galen who noted first that the rope that held that boat tethered to the ship had slipped free of its mooring. Jeremy Cooke was being half pushed, half dragged into one of the other boats and their efforts not to be dragged under by the swells completely occupied his rescuers and the attention of everyone else.

A particularly high swell lifted Emily's boat and in the space of a moment doubled its distance away from the ship. Emily, finally realizing her predicament, looked up with horror at the *Devon*. Galen made a swift decision and acted upon it. To the astonishment of everyone on deck, he kicked off his shoes and leapt into the water.

Emily, her eyes riveted on him, was torn between terror for her own predicament and the heart-stopping fear that Galen was sure to drown if he tried to reach her in a sea which was a churning froth all about her. One or two of the other seamen jumped into the water after their captain, but it was a sea that only the strongest swimmer could survive and after following him for a few yards they gave it up and turned back to the boats beside the ship.

Galen *was* a strong swimmer, but it was only the knowledge that both he and Emily would surely die if he failed to reach her that gave him the strength to go on despite the salt blinding his eyes and the immense power of the sea, which made him feel that he lost two feet for every three he gained. He was a natural athlete and he led a physically demanding life that kept his muscles taught and fit, but his body ached with the effort to reach Emily and when he finally caught the side of the boat, he could do no more than grasp it, his strength momentarily too sapped to make the effort to climb into the boat.

Emily clutched at his hands. Fear making her strong, she pulled at his arms to drag him into the boat, making it rock alarmingly again and to no effect. He was too heavy for her to lift. Horrified, she felt his grip slacken and watched with breath-catching dismay as he slid away from her back into the water.

For the first time she sobbed aloud, calling his name in a heartfelt wail. While her cry still carried on the air, mingling with the cacophony of wind and sea, the boat began to rock again and Galen catapulted himself into it beside her. Even knowing he was not drowned, she continued to sob, unable to stop.

Galen literally dragged himself upright and gently pulled her hands away from her face. "It's all right," he said, his voice so breathless his words were barely discernible. "It's all right now."

Emily continued to cry, her overwrought emotions needing the release. But she took the hand he offered her and held on so tightly that she hurt him, though she had no idea that she did so. Galen half-sat, half-lay against her skirts and waited until his breath and strength began to return and he was able to take stock of their situation.

The other three boats were filled and rowing away from the *Devon*, which now listed at a giddy angle. He felt a knot in his chest and swallowed hard, his throat parched by the salt water he had been forced to swallow. He had no choice but to acknowledge that the ship he had called the pride of his fleet would soon rest on the bottom of the sea, perhaps to be broken up by the same treacherous rocks that had brought her down.

Emily's breath still came in little gasping sobs, but she no longer wept. She looked toward the foundering ship and then at Galen. He was no longer looking at the *Devon*, but out over the water with an intensity that bespoke his emotions more than any outward display. Emily had the absurd feeling that it was somehow her fault because he had not wanted her on his ship.

Breaking out of his glum reverie, Galen sought for a pair of oars on the bottom of the boat and fitted them into the oar locks. He unbuttoned his sodden coat and waistcoat and stripped them off, and after a moment's hesitation removed his shirt as well. "You would be wise to strip down to your petticoat," he advised Emily. "It's warm and you're better off without all that wet cloth against your skin to chill you."

There was sense in this, for the soaking cotton clinging to her was cold and uncomfortable, but she looked at him in astonishment nevertheless. He gave a short mirthless laugh. "You could not be foolish or vain enough to imagine my intentions could be amorous at this time, Miss Hampton."

Emily flushed, but her mind was too dull to form a proper retort and the gratitude she must feel toward him would not have permitted her to utter it in any case. It was not easy to remove her gown, which was heavily weighted with water and the jewels which filled her pockets, and she was panting a little with the effort by the time she freed herself from it.

Galen was proven right; after the first shock of air against her bare skin, she felt far warmer and more comfortable without her dress. For several minutes she felt uncomfortable to be sitting in the company of a man, particularly this one, in just her petticoat, but Galen was intent on his rowing and paid her no heed at all, so the feeling passed.

Galen plied the oars steadily, carrying them further from the sinking ship. Emily wondered if she should offer to help with the other pair of oars but she felt so exhausted, she could not imagine even lifting them. It was an effort to remain sitting and she lay back a little against the side of the boat. In spite of the roughness of the sea and the obvious danger in which they stood, with Galen in the boat beside her she had a sense of security at odds with the reality of their situation. She fell asleep before she was even consciously aware that she would do so.

Emily was awakened by the change in motion beneath her as she had been many times in the past few days. When she opened her eyes it was dark, though not the full dark of night. It was not raining, but sprays of water washed over her and she realized that she lay in a pool of seawater. She sat up with a suddenness that made her dizzy. Galen still strained at the oars, but even Emily could tell that it was more in an effort to maintain control over the boat rather than to direct them in any way. She looked about and even in the failing light she could see for some distance and the ship was no longer in sight; more alarmingly, neither were the other boats from the *Devon*. The small boat heaved beneath her with far greater violence than the ship had ever done and Emily felt her stomach turn inside of her. Above all things she did not want to be sick in front of Galen, and she struggled for several minutes before she finally abandoned the effort and her pride and scrambled to the side of the boat. She felt more wretched than she could ever remember feeling in her life.

She had no idea how long she clung to the side of the boat but in her misery it seemed a very long time before the waves of nausea finally abated at least to the point that she dared to move away. Galen had stopped rowing and advised her to move as he returned the oars to the bottom of the boat. His tone was clipped and there was a tense grimness about it that sent a chill of terror through her.

"Are we going to make it?" Emily asked him, and had to repeat the question at a shout to be heard. It began to rain again in heavy stinging drops that added to their wretched predicament.

A sort of cupboard was built underneath the aft seat and Galen removed two pails from it, tossing one to Emily. "Probably not," he shouted in return. "Certainly not if you are going to just sit there and wring your hands. Bail." The last was a command and Emily obeyed, actually grateful to be doing something that might help them.

Between the rain and the spray it seemed to Emily that the boat filled with water as fast as they could remove it. Again time blurred and Emily could not say precisely when the rain had stopped and the wind had fallen, but as the first hint of dawn appeared in the clearing sky, Emily again found herself prone in the bottom of the boat, still panting a little from her efforts. But the boat had not capsized or sunk and neither of them had been cast into the sea and sure death, and she felt a sense of satisfaction for her hard labor.

6

The Madeira Islands, October 1812

Emily had fallen asleep again without realizing it, and when she awoke it was daylight and there was even a bit of sun shining through the clouds. She immediately looked about again for some sign of the other boats but still there was none; nor in the clearing weather could she see any outline of the islands they were supposed to be so near to.

Galen was rowing again and for a moment she watched him, fascinated by the fluid motion of muscle beneath his skin as he rowed. He met her eyes but did not smile or give her any sign of reassurance.

"Where are we?" she asked, feeling the question was somehow inane but not knowing what to say and needing to break the silence between them.

"Somewhere near Madeira," he replied easily enough, belying his stern expression. He glanced at the sky. "East of it, if I am any judge. Nearer to Porto Santo, perhaps—which means, for all the tossing we took, we haven't strayed very far from where the *Devon* went down. I hope the others have fared as well."

He displayed no emotion when he mentioned the loss of his ship, but Emily imagined she heard a subtle change in his tone. "I am sorry that the *Devon* was lost," she said impulsively.

"It is the risk every sailor faces whenever he puts out to sea. It isn't even my first time. It happens."

"You were rescued?"

"No. I did what I am doing now—I rowed to the nearest land. At least, I hope that is what I am doing," he admitted with a quick, humorless smile.

"Could I help?" she asked a little timidly, expecting that slight contemptuous upturn to his lips which she knew so well.

But he said with more kindness that she would have expected from him, "I doubt you could manage the weight of the oars, but perhaps you can spell me for a bit tonight when I tire, if we haven't reached land by then."

"Do you think we shall find land soon?"

"We have to, don't we?" he replied with a return to abruptness.

Galen was physically strong and up to the task of rowing, but he would still the oars from time to time to avoid utterly exhausting the muscles in his back and shoulders. As the day progressed so did the strength of the sun and though it dried them out at last, making it possible for Emily to redon her dress, it made Galen's labor even more difficult.

It was Emily who had the first sight of land and it was so near to dark that her heart sank rather than soared, for she feared they might lose sight of it in the dark or end up on outlying rocks like the *Devon*.

She pointed it out to him excitedly and Galen ceased his rowing to turn in the direction she indicated. For a moment his entire body sagged, and Emily was further afraid that his flagging strength would not be equal to carrying them the remaining distance.

"What is it?" she asked, pointing toward the island. "Do you know?"

"Not really. There are a few small uninhabited islands off the coast of Port Santo and Madeira. One of those most likely."

Emily found this less encouraging. She wanted people who would help them, and food and a warm bed and assurance that she would soon again be on her way to England. But she made no complaint, judging that it would not only be pointless but ill-received.

He corrected their course and then began rowing again with renewed strength. Without comment, Emily

picked up another oar and clumsily began to fit it into
the oarlock.

He stopped again and reached to put his hand on hers
to stay her. She met his eyes and said firmly, ''I want to
do this, Captain DeVere. I am not as helpless or weak as
you imagine and I am not going to risk not reaching that
island before night overtakes us because you choose to
think me useless. I am not.'' Galen did not reply. He
took the oar from her, fitted it into the lock, and
handed it to her. He did the same with the other.

Emily discovered that rowing a longboat in a sea that
was still a bit choppy was not a simple task. Her arms
and back fairly screamed with pain after a relatively
short time, but she would have paddled with her hands
if it would have helped them to reach the island even ten
minutes sooner.

The light was failing rapidly, and she could feel the
extra effort that Galen applied to his oars; she could
even hear his hard breathing over the sound of the oars
in the water. But at last the land loomed larger and
larger and finally the boat scraped against something
solid.

Galen cursed with feeling despite her presence and,
dropping his oars, he advised her to go over the side.
Emily stared at him in astonishment.

''We've scraped a hole in the bottom on some rocks,''
he said briskly. ''We'll be underwater in ten minutes in
any case.''

Emily looked down and saw that water was rapidly
filling the bottom of the boat. ''I can't swim,'' she said
wretchedly.

''You don't need to.'' He put on his shirt and coat
and dove into the sea, which proved to be barely
shoulder high. This was still too deep for Emily to wade
in comfortably and with surprising gentleness, he helped
her into the water and held her afloat until she could
stand unassisted.

The salt water stung her skin, which was slightly
burned by the strong afternoon sun, and got into her

mouth tasting horribly of brine. As they climbed out of the sea, Galen still held her by the waist and she clutched onto his shoulder for support. When they were at last out of reach of the water, he released her and collapsed at her feet. He half sat, half lay in the sand, supporting himself on one arm. Frightened, Emily knelt beside him. His breath came in gasps and a great shuddering heave wracked his body though there was nothing in his stomach, not even water, to vomit. The support of his arm gave out and he lay face down on the beach, looking to Emily more dead than alive.

Emily trembled in the cool night air, her dress once again heavy and chillingly wet. But she also trembled with fear. If he were to die . . . She could not even allow herself to think of it. Tentatively, almost afraid of knowing the truth, she touched his shoulder. He did not stir. "Captain? Captain DeVere? Are you unwell?"

To her relief he raised his head. "I am spent, Miss Hampton. Exhausted, worn out, used up." But he raised himself up again and even in the poor light she could see his eyes were sufficiently alert to allay her worst fears.

He rose very slowly, like an old man, and his steps were almost shuffling. He walked further inland and Emily followed him, feeling rather like a trailing puppy. The coarse sand gave way to a pebbly claylike soil and finally to thick scrub grass. When he reached this he stripped off his coat and waistcoat again and let himself drop once again to the ground.

Emily stood beside him uncertainly. She had supposed that he meant to continue on until they found a suitable place to rest until daylight, but they were still at the edge of the beach. He lay back on the grass and quite obviously composed himself for sleep.

Though physically weary from the rowing she had done, Emily had managed to sleep for a time in the boat and even during the height of the storm she had slept at least a little before Mr. Farley had come to tell them that they were to abandon ship. Her muscles ached, but her mind was alert and energetic and she wanted very much to explore and know more about this island which was to be their refuge. She did understand that Galen had probably had little or no sleep at all for several days, and even her short time at the oars, with him still carrying most of the effort, had taught her how taxing the labor was. But this was not a spot she would have chosen for a bed, however exhausted, and she could not but believe that they would find a more comfortable place if they continued on.

"Are you sure you are well?" she asked again.

"Perfectly."

"If we continued on . . ."

"By all means continue on, if you wish, Miss Hampton," he interrupted. "But do so quietly, if you please. I need to sleep."

"You can't be comfortable," she insisted. "The ground is so rocky. You will never be able to sleep here."

"Nevertheless, that is what I intend," he said crisply and with a clear warning in his voice that his patience was dissipating. "Provided, of course, that you will be still long enough for me to do so. If you think you may find a better place to spend the night, please do so. I have not suggested that we sleep together. In fact, in one sense, I would frankly be incapable of it."

His words were offensive, Emily felt deliberately so. "You are a horrid, vulgar man," she said, and then wished she had bitten back the words. However abrasive he might choose to be toward her, she owed him her very life.

"Go away, Miss Hampton," he said, sounding more weary than angry. "Find your comfortable nook among the shrubbery, but do it quietly."

Emily did not really wish to go further without him, but because she had made such a point of it, her pride forced her on. There was only a quarter moon and the night was quite dark. The grass gave way to an equally stunted, dense shrubbery and twice she stumbled over a rock or root and nearly fell. She had no idea how large the island was or how far inland she had gone. She had a sudden fear of not being able to find her way back to the beach and realized that she really had no intention at all of spending the night by herself even if she did find a suitable spot, which, as a matter of fact, she had yet to do.

Feeling foolish and a little panicky, she retraced her steps. Her fears proved groundless and she had no trouble at all finding her way back to Galen. She knelt beside him and his even breathing told her that he was asleep.

The night air was cool and she removed her wet dress, once again feeling better for doing so. She deliberately lay some distance from Galen, but when she awoke in the morning she found herself so close to him that they were touching. She was very nearly nestled in his arms.

She sat up abruptly. Galen stirred, but did not awaken. The sun was just rising, but it betokened another temperate day.

She went again into the shrubbery to relieve herself and to find the small stream of water she had stumbled into the night before so that she could wash off the salt water, which made her skin feel drawn and gritty. She could well imagine what the salt and sun had done to her complexion and hair and even if she had had a comb, she doubted her ability to draw it through her tangled curls.

In the light of day she saw that the low shrubbery and thick grass constituted most of the undergrowth of the island. She found what looked to her to be grape vines, and hunger made her dare to sample the fruit. It was bitter, but unquestionably what she supposed it to be, and a little further exploration led her to a small grouping of trees little more than shoulder height which bore a pearlike fruit.

This was also bitter, but less so than the grapes, and after eating two pieces of it she gathered several more and returned to the beach. Galen gave no appearance that he had moved while she was gone. She sat beside him and touched him, but he still did not stir. The sun was rising in the sky and soon would be as hot as it had been the previous afternoon. She shook Galen awake, informing him that if he did not find shelter he was certain to find himself sunburned.

The ice-blue eyes appeared glazed at first, but then focused on Emily and narrowed slightly. "Ah, the ever solicitous Miss Hampton is awake," he said sardonically.

Emily felt herself flush. "I am sorry," she said stiffly. "I shouldn't have disturbed you."

She made to rise, but he sat up and touched her arm. "It is I who beg your pardon, Miss Hampton," he said with no trace of irony, though she regarded him suspiciously as he spoke. "In spite of my fairness, I don't burn easily, but that is no reason to put it to the test."

He stood and stretched. Emily saw the powerful muscles in his legs contract beneath his form-fitting breeches and stockings and something inside of her stirred. She looked quickly away. "There is water fairly nearby if you walk straight ahead," she said a bit gruffly, "and I have brought you pears and there are grapes inland as well." She folded her legs beneath her and picked up a piece of the fruit and bit into it, tactfully making it clear that she would remain where she was while he went inland to attend to his own toilet.

He was gone such a very long time that she began to have some concern and was about to get up and search for him when she heard him returning at last. He sat down beside her and began to unbutton his shirt. "If I am any judge of the matter, we are on a small island —probably not more than a mile square—just off Porto Santo. I reached the opposite shore and there is a stretch of land in the distance which I am reasonably certain is that island. With luck, we may find ourselves rescued by a fishing boat before the day is out."

This was excellent news and Emily exclaimed joyfully at it, but she regarded him with puzzlement as he stripped off his shirt and began remove his stockings as well. The sun had already nearly dried out her petticoats and his clothes appeared to be in a similar state. "What are you doing?" she asked, unable to contain her curiosity.

He glanced at her and saw that her puzzlement was not untinged with suspicion. An impish light danced in his eyes for a moment before he returned to his task. "Undressing, Miss Hampton," he said in the patient tone of one forced to state the obvious.

"Why?"

"Because I am going into the water and I am tired of wearing wet clothes." He stood and began to undo the buttons on his breeches.

Emily almost gasped aloud. "You cannot mean to take all of your clothes off in front of me?"

His smile was nothing short of devilish. "Only if you insist on watching." He put his hands on his hips to push down his breeches and Emily caught a glimpse of the curling fair hair on his chest trailing down to meet his navel.

This time she could not suppress the intake of her breath as she turned quickly away from him, her heart hammering in her breast. She heard his laughter behind her as he went down to the water. It was several minutes before Emily dared to look again and when she did she saw only his shoulders and head above the water as he swam through the swells.

The sea was relatively calm again, and she had ample proof of his ability to swim, but Emily could not help feeling at least a tendril of anxiety for his safety—and her own, should anything happen to him. This grew considerably when he dove beneath the water and did not resurface for a longer time than she would have thought possible. He did this several times and then began to make his way to shore again.

Emily continued to watch him until his torso began to rise from the water and she realized that she would soon behold him in his nakedness. Some wanton part of her nature did not wish to look away, but her more conventional self won the battle and she turned and faced away from him.

She heard him come up beside her and he threw something on the sand nearly at her feet. It was a medium-sized fish, still very much alive. She looked at it in astonishment until his voice drew her attention. "I am respectably covered again, Miss Hampton," he said with his usual sardonic inflection.

"I would not have thought it possible to catch a fish without tackle or bait," she exclaimed. "How very clever you are." As she watched, he extracted a folding knife from his breeches pocket and with amazing rapidity gutted and scaled the fish.

He cut it into smaller pieces and offered one of them to Emily. She regarded it with distaste. "It isn't as bad as it looks," he said to encourage her. "Even if we are rescued today or the next, we can't guess when we shall have a proper meal again, and fruits alone aren't enough."

The fruit she had eaten had seemed only to increase the hunger she had felt since waking and Emily knew he was right. Hoping she would not be sick, Emily took the fish from him and tasted it. Neither taste nor texture were offensive as she feared—in fact, there was very little taste at all. She ate all that he gave to her and then between them, they finished the remainder of the fruit she had gathered earlier.

When this simple repast was finished, Galen lay back on the grass again and closed his eyes, but Emily felt restless and disinclined for rest. "What do we do now?" she asked, hoping she did not sound petulant.

He opened his eyes and regarded her for a moment. "We wait." Emily had gotten over her shyness at being with him in only her shift and petticoats and had no idea how much the thin material revealed her breasts and the seductive curve of her hips. Galen was very much aware of it. It was this as well as a wish to quiz her that made him add, "Unless you have some activity in mind." He spoke blandly and there was nothing in the words he used to offend, but Emily, always cognizant of the underlying attraction between them, understood him and her ready color rose. "Yes, I know," he said with a brief laugh. "I am 'a horrid, vulgar man.' It comes from having spent so much of my life with sailors. My sister used to tell me I was too fastidious. I wonder what she will make of me now."

This was the first he had mentioned his family to Emily and curiosity made her seize upon this to ask him about them. She noted that he hesitated before answering, but he did not snub her. He replied to her first question and one or two others but in a very few minutes, he had managed to turn the subject and it was Emily who was telling him of her life with her parents and how she had come to live with the Armitages. It wasn't until she began to describe her hopes for her visit with Lady Laelard that Emily realized that he had skill-fully diverted her from her inquisitiveness about his past.

After this a companionable silence fell between them and the remainder of the day was spent in exploration of the island with such snatches of conversation that broke out between them as one or the other had some subject brought to mind. Emily would never have supposed that she would spend such an agreeable day in the company of Galen DeVere. When later in the day as they shared a second meal of fruit gathered in their wanderings, he suggested that the enforced intimacy of their cir-cumstances made formality absurd, she had no dif-ficulty at all addressing him by his given name.

During the course of the day, several vessels appeared on the horizon, but none came within hailing distance and they were forced to resign themselves to another night on the island. Emily was more troubled by this than Galen. "What if no one comes close enough to see us," she said with a note of despair.

"How poor spirited," he said with mock reproach. By evening their intimacy had grown to the point that they addressed each other with the playful incivility reserved for friends. "It has only been one day. If not today, then tomorrow or the next day. If Jacob made it to Madeira—and pray God he did—he will set up a search for us, you may depend upon it."

Emily did not reply, but then she dared not say what was in her thoughts. Her greatest fear was not not being rescued at all, but not being rescued before she succumbed to her increasing attraction to him. Throughout the day, whenever he had touched her, to help her over a rocky bit of ground, to hand her a piece of fruit he had just picked, she had felt a current pass through her which she could scarcely believe him ignorant of. He acknowledged it openly no more than she did, but instinct told her that as the barriers of dislike and misunderstanding fell between them, the more likely it was that, with such enforced familiarity, restraints would soon vanish as well.

The first test of this theory came at nightfall. They had found a more comfortable and sheltered place to spend the night not far inland on the opposite side of the island. Tacitly, they retired there together when it became dark.

For a while they talked easily on a variety of subjects but gradually conversation became desultory and Galen lay down on the thick grass with his hands behind his head. Emily sat only a little apart from him, within touching distance; but she felt awkward about lying down beside him and equally so about moving farther away. She had put on her dress again now that it was dry and when the sun set and the temperature dropped, she was considerably more comfortable than she had been the night before, but still she shivered when a breeze came off the ocean.

She was not sure that Galen was still awake until she heard him say, "Come beside me if you are cold. I promise not to bite."

Emily was not certain what to make of this invitation. He might be offering her nothing more than simple warmth, or he might equally have something other in mind. Remembering his swift embrace in her uncle's house she felt a very different sort of shiver pass through her.

When she didn't reply, he raised himself on one elbow. "You aren't afraid of me, Emily?" he asked quietly.

"No, of course not," she replied and mentally added, I am far more afraid of myself. But she moved next to him and lay down with perhaps an inch or two to spare between them. She heard him laugh in his throat and he drew her near him. She stiffened, expecting him to kiss her, but as soon as they touched his grip relaxed and he bade her good night and said nothing further. After a minute or so, the tension seeped out of Emily and a day spent in the sun and salt air took its toll, sending her directly to sleep.

It was still dark when she awoke. Galen's arm was still about her, but his touch was very different. His hand possessively caressed the curve of her hip and thigh and she opened her eyes to see him looming above her. She started to speak but was silenced when he put a finger to her lips. In a moment this was replaced by his lips on hers. His tongue expertly separated her teeth and sparks of excitement shot to every extreme of her body. His hand found her breast and a moan she could not contain escaped her lips. But the sound of her own voice startled her into a realization of what was happening. "Galen. Galen, please. We must not," she begged, praying that he would heed her, for she doubted her ability to resist if he ignored her plea.

He raised his head and his voice was thick with desire when he spoke. "I want you, Emily. I've wanted you far longer than I've admitted even to myself." He lowered himself on her and she found his weight curiously light. She could feel every inch of his hard, muscular body stretched out against hers.

Finding more strength and willpower than she knew she possessed, she managed to place her hands between them and pushed against his chest. He gave in to the pressure of her hands and rolled off of her. He lay beside her, his chest rising and falling rapidly. He took in a deep breath and let it out again. "I'm sorry, Emily," he said, and sat up. "I'd better find somewhere else to sleep. I'll be nearby," he added, to allay any misgiving she might have about being left alone. When he was gone, Emily scarcely knew whether she was glad or sorry that he had heeded her protests so readily.

On the following morning, she found him on the beach before her. He had already been in the water and was cleaning a fish he had caught as she approached. His manner to her was so easy that she felt no awkwardness between them and almost forgot that only a few hours earlier she had nearly given herself to him as completely as a woman could give to a man.

There was little conversation between them that morning, but neither Galen nor Emily took any special note of the long stretches of silence. Emily pondered her inability to control her feelings for Galen in spite of being so determined to do so and only wished she dared to give in to them. But for Galen what had occurred—or nearly occurred—forced him to face a reality that he would as soon have avoided.

By birth he was a gentleman and a man of honor, and his many years at sea—where a code of ethics for officers was strictly adhered to—had served to reinforce the values which were a part of his breeding as an English gentleman of noble birth. It was not until the night before, when he had lain apart from Emily very much awake and staring at a sky liberally salted with stars, that he had admitted to himself what he had known to be inevitable from the moment the boat they were in had been separated from the others. Even if there were no physical attraction between them, even if he had never touched her or even wished to, this intimacy which neither had sought so completely compromised them there would be no other choice for them: as soon as they reached England they would have to be married.

Though he had told Jacob Farley that he expected he would marry when he returned to England, he certainly didn't want to be married in this way. He had disliked being forced to take Emily as a passenger on his ship; even less did he want to find himself forced to take her as his wife, however much he might desire her physically. Yet he could not in fairness blame Emily. It was the capriciousness of the sea and the vagueries of fate that had landed them in this scrape.

His opinion of Emily had undergone considerable change since the voyage had begun. In their conversations on board the *Devon* he had found her to be clever, intelligent, and possessed of a droll sense of humor not unlike his own. Yet to set against this, he had watched her encourage Jeremy Cooke and even after Cooke had made advances to her which she claimed were unwelcome, she had not discouraged his attentions entirely. Nor was Galen blind to the fact that though there was harmony between them now, they both had strong wills that all too readily clashed. Theirs was not likely to be an easy union.

The attraction he felt for her had not been instantaneous as hers had been for him. He had been as taken by surprise as she when he had kissed her that afternoon at the Armitages'; but the sudden desire to do so had been so overwhelming that he had not resisted it. And then today, in the musky darkness that preceded dawn, he had awakened and felt the warmth of her body next to his. He gave in to a desire to touch her cheek. Her skin was smooth and silken and he had been suddenly very aware of her as a woman. With complete unexpectedness, he had found himself aroused and wanting her so badly that it was nearly a physical pain. He had told himself a hundred times since then that it was nothing more than the usual sailors' complaint resulting from long stretches of enforced celibacy. But he had never before been affected with such intensity, even after a voyage of three times the duration of this one.

The suspicion that his feelings for her might go deeper than he acknowledged teased at him, but he would not give it credence. His thoughts unconsciously made him distance himself from Emily and when late in the afternoon they finally saw one of the fishing boats draw nearer, he responded to her excitement with more remoteness than he had shown toward her since they had reached the island. In the exhilaration of the moment, however, Emily took no notice of his coolness and after a few minutes, he found himself inflicted with her enthusiasm and high spirits.

The boat did espy them and when the fishermen had sailed as close as they dared, a dinghy put out from the boat to come to them. To Emily's surprise, Galen spoke Portuguese sufficiently to make himself understood, but then Brazil was a frequent destination for merchant ships, so it was not really so very unusual that he should be familiar with the language. To Emily, the rapidly spoken words were gibberish, but she guessed well enough that Galen was explaining what had happened to them through gestures and inflection.

As they were assisted into the dinghy, Emily felt an unexpected reluctance to leave the little island. She felt a curious sense of loss as the beach receded and became no more than a spot on the vast expanse of water as the fishing boat turned and headed away from the island.

As Galen had guessed, they were only a few miles from Porto Santo, which was the home of the fishermen who had come to their rescue, and it was there that they were taken. The fishing boat was not a third of the size that the *Devon* had been and even on the open deck it reeked of fish.

Emily discovered that if she stayed near the side of the boat looking out over the sea, the overpowering odor was lessened. While Galen conversed with the captain, whose name was Gomes, she effaced herself against the stern rail, staying out of the way of the men going about their duties as much as possible. Her thoughts were occupied with all that had passed between herself and Galen in the past few days and like him she was unsure of her feelings and even her perceptions.

The island of Porto Santo gradually grew from an ephemeral strip of land on the horizon into a solid mass with wide sandy beaches and an ocher tint to the land-scape that gave it the appearance of a desert. But to Emily, for whom the island was a return to the civilized world, it appeared as inviting as a tropical paradise. Galen had told her it was not a large island, but compared to the minute bit of land on which they had washed up, it seemed huge to Emily. The sun was dropping in the sky and they had nearly reached their destination when Galen sought her out.

"Are you well?" he asked, noting that she had not strayed from the side of the boat.

"Yes. But I would not be if I had to breathe the odor of fish undiluted. At least here I can smell the salt and the spray."

He held out a small cup to her. "Drink this. Gomes himself sends it to you."

She took the cup and gazed into it. "It is wine. But I don't care for wine except with meals."

"You needn't drink it all, just sip it. If you don't, you'll offend Captain Gomes, and since he has graciously offered to take us to his home for the night and promised to take us to Madeira to the English magistrate at Funchal tomorrow, we would be wise to court his goodwill."

Emily obediently raised the cup to her lips and tasted the wine, which was quite good, as good as any Madeira her father or uncle had in their cellars and perhaps even better. Galen saw her approval in her expression, and smiled. "I thought you might like it. What better place to sample the best Madeira?" He raised a second cup and drank deeply from it.

Emily regarded him suspiciously for a moment,

fearing that he was drunk, for they had neither of them eaten since the simple meal of raw fish and fruit they had shared in the morning. But when he put down his cup again and looked at her, his eyes appeared clear and alert and there were no other signs of inebriation.

He leaned against the side of the boat with his back to the sea. "There is something I must tell you, Emily. I have told Gomes that you are my wife."

Emily was startled by his words, but this was not the reason her heart began to beat faster. "But why?"

"It is for your protection. Gomes will warn his men that you belong to me and you will be treated with the proper respect given to a married woman, not only now, but until we are safely with the English in Funchal."

Emily gave a surprised little laugh. "You make these people sound like savages."

"No, of course they are not savages, but the peasants regard women in a way that being gently born you might not understand. If I did not say you were my wife, they would assume you were my doxy and you would not much like the way you would be treated if that were the case."

"Couldn't you have said I was your sister?"

"It wouldn't have answered as well," he said shortly. He gave her an oddly keen, swift look. "Is the prospect of regarding me as your husband so unpalatable, Emily?" he asked in quiet way that made the turmoil in her breast even greater.

"No," she admitted, looking away from him out onto the sea. "It is just . . . it might prove awkward. Later, that is."

"You are thinking we may be forced to sleep together again, and that I shall attempt to make love to you," he suggested, smiling faintly. "If I were the gentleman I claim to be I suppose I would give you my word that I would not even attempt to kiss you again, but I don't think I can."

These last words were spoken with such soft intensity that Emily was compelled to look up at him. The unaccustomed warmth she saw in his eyes made her catch at her breath. He bent his head and kissed her lightly. When she made no objection, he kissed her again, more lingeringly. He released her, but traced the fullness of her lips with a finger, sending shivers of pleasure through her as if his mouth still held hers. Their eyes met and held for several minutes in silence. "We have much to settle between us, Emily," he said at last.

Emily's heart soared at these words. Even though he had not asked her to be his wife in so many words, she believed that this was what he meant her to understand. She knew him as a man of honor; she did not for a moment suppose that he offered her anything less.

She was a little frightened at the strength of her desire, which rose so readily to meet his. The values instilled in Emily since birth stressed the importance and necessity of female virtue, but she knew that if they shared a bed tonight it would probably be as lovers.

Captain Gomes's house was a rambling cottage that seemed to Emily to be bursting full of people, all of whom converged upon them at once to exclaim over them and hear the story of the wreck of the *Devon* and their adventure on the deserted island. Emily, of course, was still reduced to communicating by facial expression and gestures, but Galen, who spoke their language enough to answer most of their questions, was the center of attention.

The captain's wife was a pleasant woman who made them welcome at once in her home and who fed them lavishly with delicious brown bread, sausage, and more of the excellent wine they had tasted on board the fishing boat. The adventures of the day coupled with the first substantial meal she had had since before they had been shipwrecked and the soporific effects of the wine, made Emily languorous and sleepy almost as soon as the meal was finished.

Galen sat beside her on a wooden bench drawn up to an immense rough-hewn table which dominated the room. Becoming aware of her drowsiness, he put his

arm about her and drew her against him. She felt an odd
stirring of delight at this public sign of his affection. For
a moment she lost herself in the fantasy that she really
was his wife. "The women will be leaving the men to
their wine soon, *menina*," he said into her ear. "Mrs.
Gomes will show you to the place she has readied for us
then and in a little bit I'll join you." His lips just
brushed against her ear in promise of more to follow.

Anticipation evaporated her weariness. However im-
probable, she had fallen in love with a man she had
declared detestable a little more than a month ago. She
supposed she had never really disliked him; she had
been attracted to him from the day they had met and her
enmity toward him had been in response to his coldness
and unflattering assessment of her. And now, in a very
short while, she would be his lover and soon, his wife.
Feeling the protection of his arm about her, she had a
sense of complete peace and security and she knew
loving him was exactly her heart's desire.

The room to which Emily was taken by the captain's
wife was little more than the size of a cupboard by
Emily's standards. A bed that looked too small for two
people to share filled most of the space, but Emily was
grateful for any decent mattress after two nights spent
with nothing more than grass to cushion her body from
the hard ground. Emily took off her dress, folded it,
and placed it with her reticule on the only other object in
the room, a small bench near the door.

The only light in the room was from a lantern on a
table outside the door and Emily left this open to let in
the light until Galen came to her. He did not keep her
waiting very long.

Without hesitation, he lay down gently beside her,
molding his length to hers. Emily felt her senses come
alive at his touch. Her breasts hardened and became
sensitive to the smallest caress; her thighs tingled with a
delicious sense of anticipation. She entwined her legs
with his and responded to each caress with eagerness.

Emily's heart was beating so wildly, Galen could feel

it beneath his hand which lay between her breasts. Her mouth was sweet, her flesh was firm, yet yielding; he found in her response to him everything he had hoped for. If marriage was to be forced on them, at least it would not be a cold, grudging coupling as were so many arranged or enforced marriages.

His physical need was intense, but he was too experienced in the ways of love to give in to it. He understood her inexperience and anxieties and meant to initiate her slowly into the art of loving, but his iron control began to slip away from him. He had drunk more wine than was his custom and had feared it would dull his senses, but instead it had heightened them and with each caress, he found it more and more difficult to contain his need for her.

Emily felt the quickening of his desire, which grew increasingly demanding. The intensity of it frightened her even as she responded to his every touch. His hands, his lips, his tongue left white hot trails wherever they met her skin. In a minute, in a very few moments, she would be his, incontrovertibly.

This realization sent an undefinable shiver of fear through her. She wanted to make love with him, but it was happening so quickly. Surprised at her own strength of will, she put one hand against his chest and gently pushed him away from her. "Galen, I am not sure . . ."

He put his hand over hers and said gently, "It will be all right, Emily. I would do nothing to harm you. We must be married as soon as we reach England. We are merely hastening our wedding night."

His assurance that they were to be married should have allayed her concern, but instead she felt as if a cold hand had clutched her heart and the desire that had nearly consumed her a moment ago began to evaporate. "*Must* be married?" she said, her voice rising a little.

He took a deep breath and let it out slowly. His own arousal abated a little with annoyance. He might understand her anxieties, but not a wish to discuss them in the midst of lovemaking. Frustrated desire and the freedom which wine can give to the tongue made him speak a bit sharply. "In the eyes of the world we are already lovers. If we did not marry, your reputation would be destroyed and my honor would be impugned as well."

"Therefore we might as well prove them right since we have no choice in the matter," she said caustically but with a catch in her voice. It wasn't love that fed his desire for her, but mere attraction freed from restraint by resignation.

He gave a short, soft laugh and raised himself on one elbow. "No, of course not," he said softly and bent his head to kiss her, but she turned her head away from him. "I've offended you, Emily. I'm sorry. I didn't mean to."

She turned to him again, though with the door closed she could not see him clearly enough to gauge his expression. "How do you feel?"

There was a perceptible hesitation before he replied. "I want and need you very much."

Was she the fool to even think that he might love her? Tears from a bitter ache that went beyond disappointment formed in her eyes. "Would you wish for us to be married if we were not in these circumstances?"

Again he was silent for several moments before answering. "How can I answer that? We were little more than acquaintances before we were cast together like this. I didn't think of it before we were shipwrecked, but from the time we were separated from the others it was inevitable."

He won no credit from her for his honesty. "I thank you for your flattering offer, Mr. DeVere, but I fear I must decline," she said jeeringly, pushing herself away from him as much as the limited space would allow.

He said with exasperation, "I think you wish to find insult in my words. It is not intended, but if I have expressed myself badly, I beg your pardon, Emily. It is the wine which makes me stupid."

"*In vino veritas*," she flashed back.

"How very clever," he said sardonically, and got up.

"Where are you going?" she åsked, not wanting him to make love to her, but yet not wanting him to leave her either.

"Back to the kitchen. I can hear Gomes and his brother still in there talking."

"I wish you would not. They will think we have quarreled."

"That isn't what they'll think," he said, with such an ironic inflection that she could not mistake his meaning.

When he opened the door, dim light spilled into the room and she watched his tall, lean silhouette go out. If only he had said he loved her, she would be filled with happiness now instead of this awful dull pain. She turned on her side with her back to the door and wept into the oversoft mattress. He would marry her, but according to the dictates of honor, not because he wanted her as his wife. How could she have been such a fool as to let herself love him? She had known from the beginning that it would be a horrible mistake.

She thought he exaggerated the danger to her reputation and she would not be held hostage for the satisfaction of his honor. If he could not feel for her as she felt for him, then she would not have him at all and damn the consequences. But her heart ached at the prospect of sending him away when she need only say one word to spend the rest of her life at his side.

Her inability to understand her own feelings for Galen added to the wretchedness of the pain in her heart. The only thing she knew for certain was that she longed more than ever to reach England where perhaps in the sanity of the English clime she would be able to sort out the muddle her life had become.

7

The following morning Galen and Emily were once again on the fishing boat, this time being taken to Funchal and Sir Richard Berry, His Majesty's Counsel and Magistrate for the English community that resided on Madeira while it was occupied by the English Navy.

There was perfect civility between them, but all intimacy was at an end. Their politeness was the politeness of strangers. In the sobriety of the morning Galen knew he had been clumsy and a fool and he meant to do what he could to repair the rift that had come between them, but Emily's cold, set features made it clear it would be no easy task.

He had felt a brief moment of relief when she had said she would not marry him, but with his own honor at stake as well as hers, he could not leave it at that. When he approached Emily on the boat, she turned her back on him and replied so frigidly that he supposed his timing was still at fault and that he would do better to let it be for the moment. But her rejection stung him more than it should have and he shied away from the pain of it while denying to himself that it existed.

At first sight, Sir Richard's servant was inclined to close the door on them, but Galen, used to command, persuaded the major domo to give them entrance and to fetch his master. When they were shown into the magistrate's study, there was another man with Sir Richard. Jacob Farley rose the moment they entered and exclaimed with astonishment and delight. "Gale! This is too wonderful." Farley embraced first his friend and then Emily, tears unashamedly forming in his eyes. "I have just this day hired a boat and completed my plans to begin a search for you."

"And we have saved you the trouble," Galen said, smiling, obviously as moved as Jacob to find his friend alive and well. "You must tell me at once what has become of the others."

Sir Richard proved to be a pleasant elderly man who bestowed a gentler greeting on Emily and sent his servant to fetch his wife who, he assured Emily, would see to her comfort. While she waited for Lady Berry, Emily sat gingerly in a small brocade chair near Sir Richard's desk, feeling very ragged and tattered in this elegant room. Galen seemed to have forgotten her existence as he listened to Jacob tell him that the other boats, which had managed to stay together, had been spotted before nightfall by an English seventy-four on its way to Funchal from Lisbon. If dark and the return of the wind and rain had not overtaken them, they would have gone in search of Galen and Emily at once, but by midday the next day there was no sign of them and the worst was feared.

Only Jacob Farley refused to believe that the sea had claimed his friend and when they had reached Funchal he alone had refused passage to London on another ship-of-the-line leaving Funchal the following day, determined to remain until he had proved to his satisfaction that Galen and Emily were not washed up on some outcropping, languishing for want of anyone to care whether or not they were still alive.

Emily noted that Galen did not speak of the small deserted island but implied that they had been longer in the water as well as longer on Porto Santo to account for the days that had passed since the wreck of the *Devon*.

Lady Berry was as amiable as her husband and her exclamations ranged from horror at all that had befallen Emily to delight that she had survived her ordeal and was come to her for assistance. "The first thing we must do is find you something to wear, my dear," she said, understanding Emily's feeling of awkwardness in her ruined dress. "You will want a hot bath as well, I expect, and a proper meal, and then bed. You must tell me everything, if it is not too difficult for you, but it can keep until tomorrow when you have had a good long rest."

Emily acknowledged that this program sounded ideal. While Emily ate a light but delicious meal brought to her on a tray in the comfortable bedchamber that Lady Berry had allotted her, Lady Berry's own dresser began the preparations for Emily's bath and Lady Berry herself rummaged through her wardrobe for something that would fit Emily and be suitable for her to wear.

"Mr. Farley is a most capable gentleman, and most mannerly, even though he is an American," Lady Berry said, unconscious that she might be giving offense to her listener. Her chatter had been incessant since she had greeted Emily in her husband's study, but after the anxieties of the past few days, Emily found the older woman's commonplaces soothing and, since no reply was expected of her, undemanding as well.

"We took in Mrs. Wilard and the maids and Mr. Cooke here," Lady Berry went on, "and Mr. Farley found lodgings for the officers and the remainder of the crew and by the next morning had arranged passage for them all to continue their journey the very next day. It is only two days since they have left, so you have only just missed them, you know."

She pulled out a blue muslin dress and held it up for inspection. She sighed. "I fear I can give you several pounds, my dear, so I am not at all sure how well I may outfit you, but my woman, Brently, is wonderful with a needle, so I am sure we may contrive something for you by morning and for tonight, we need only be concerned about a nightdress, which need not fit you to perfection. You needn't fear you shall be marooned here, though," she said without pause for the turn in topic. "Since our navy occupies both the islands and much of the mainland of Portugal, there is quite a bit of traffic between the two and passage to England is not impossible from Lisbon, which is what the others who left are hoping for when they arrive in Portugal.''

She decided definitely on the blue muslin and gave it to her dresser with instructions to work on it as soon as Emily was in her bath. "Was Mrs. Wilard a particular friend of yours? I hope not," she said confidentially as she helped Emily out of her sea-bleached cotton dress. "I think she was an excessively silly woman, though I suppose I should not so say. She told me she does not go into society much, which is just as well, for I am sure she would not take. There," she added as Brently poured the last of the hot water into Emily's bath. "Now you shall have the luxury of a hot bath and then you must go directly to sleep and have a nice long rest."

Emily feared that she was overtired and her mind too overstimulated by all that had occurred in the last two days for comfortable sleep, but the bath and a very comfortable bed proved excellent soporifics and she fell into sleep almost as soon as she crawled between the sheets. She awoke in the morning feeling truly rested and relaxed for the first time since the storm at sea which had brought them to grief had first begun to blow. In fact, if it had not been for the dull pain in her heart, which she feared was become part of her, she would have felt very good indeed. She tried on the altered blue muslin and found it fit to perfection.

Lady Berry was delighted to see her charge in such fine fettle and was pleased by Emily's assurance that she would prefer to eat her breakfast in the breakfast room rather than have a tray in her bedchamber. "Though I hope you will not think it neglect that we eat alone. Sir Richard had business to attend to this morning and was up and out of the house some time ago."

Emily knew Galen for an early riser as well and she asked, "What of DeVere? Doesn't he join us?"

"He did not stay the night with us," Lady Berry informed her. "Did he not send word to you before he left with Mr. Farley?'' She sighed. ''Men are like that, I fear. When they have much on their minds they are not likely to think of the little things that can mean so much to our sex.''

''He is gone with Mr. Farley?'' Emily asked a bit faintly. It distressed her that he had left her here alone—though she did not suppose that he would abandon her altogether until he saw her safely with her aunt in England.

But Lady Berry heard the faint anxiety in Emily's tone and gave her arm a squeeze as they entered the breakfast room. ''Only to Mr. Farley's lodgings. Even though you are betrothed, he did not think it proper for him to remain under the same roof when you had no female relative to attend you.''

Emily stopped in the act of unfolding her napkin and stared at the older woman in astonishment. ''He told you we were betrothed?''

''Is it not announced yet?'' Lady Berry asked, finding nothing peculiar in Emily's words. ''Well, you must not blame him. He would feel the need to tell us in the circumstances, you know. It is most proper in him to put your good name above convention. Your aunt will announce it when you are settled in England, I suppose. She must be delighted that you have made so excellent a match. Mr. Farley told us a little of Lord DeVere's history before you arrived and I gather it is quite an old name, though being from the north and being so much out of the country since my marriage, I am not familiar with it. You will like being Lady DeVere, I think. They say what is in a title, but it can be quite pleasant at times to be 'my lady.' ''

Emily, listening to this ingenuous speech, felt as if her wits had abandoned her. She was outraged that he would dare to tell anyone that they were to be married when she had told him that she would not have him, but her anger dissolved into confusion as Lady Berry spoke of him as Lord Devere. At first Emily thought she must be speaking of some relative of Galen's, but she realized it could only be Galen himself that the other woman spoke of.

Any wish she had had to avoid Galen was gone; now she very much wanted to speak with him. As the day passed and he neither called on her nor sent any word to her, she whipped her anger into a fine froth of fury. She berated herself that on the basis of a few days of congenial behavior, she had allowed herself to forget what an odious, overbearing man Galen DeVere was.

On top of his crime of supposing that he could force her to his will to marry him, was added the fact that he had not even thought enough of her feelings to inform her that he possessed a title. It was alarming to think of how little she knew of him and yet they had come so very close to being lovers. By his continued behavior as well as what he had said to her that night in the fisherman's cottage, he had proven that he had no feeling for her beyond a physical desire, and she was supremely grateful for whatever it had been that had made her withdraw from him before her surrender to him had been complete and irrevocable.

Galen and Jacob Farley finally came early the following day to inform Emily and the Berrys that Mr. Farley had convinced the captain of the *Bethia*, the ship that had rescued the boats from the wreck of the *Devon*, to give Galen and Emily passage on his ship when it would sail for Portsmouth at the end of the week for repairs incurred during the storm.

Emily was both pleased and relieved by this news, but it did nothing to soften her anger toward Galen. There was no opportunity for private conversation, but she made her feelings toward him clear by a coolness that bordered on incivility. Oblivious to what the Berrys must think of her, when the gentlemen returned that evening to take dinner with them she compounded her defiance by flirting openly with Mr. Farley, who appeared a bit disconcerted at first but was nothing loath to respond in kind.

"Are you trying to get me shot, Miss Hampton," he

said quizzingly when she drew him a little apart in the withdrawing room after dinner. "If you smile at me in that dazzling way one more time, Gale will be asking me to name my friends."

"It is none of his concern whom I smile at or how," she said darkly, her eyes snapping with combativeness.

Farley's brow knit. "But he told me you and he are to be married when you reach England."

"Did he also tell you why?" she said with a sardonic curl to her lips.

He colored a bit and said lamely, "In the circumstances . . ."

"In the circumstances, I would not have him were my only other recourse a nunnery."

Farley blinked a little at her vehemence. "But he said it was a settled thing."

"He is mistaken," she retorted, and lest Galen—should he be watching—suppose that there was other than flirtation to their discussion she smiled again in the way that Mr. Farley had made objection to.

Galen did notice her behavior, of course, but nothing in his manner or speech gave away his thoughts or feelings. Lady Berry from time to time regarded Galen and Emily with barely concealed curiosity, for they behaved nothing at all like a betrothed couple. She supposed there had been some lovers' quarrel which they would soon make up between them. It was, in fact, a quarrel that had yet to take place.

In spite of daily visits, Emily and Galen were never together without company and what conversation did pass between them was of a general nature and always exacting in civility. It was only from time to time when their eyes met unobserved by others that the cold fire in his blue eyes and the sparks that lit her gray ones gave promise of the conflagration ahead.

It was not until they were actually aboard the *Bethia* that they were finally able to speak freely, and this did not occur immediately for Emily shared a stateroom with the wife of one of Sir Richard's aides who was increasing and was returning to England for her confinement. Emily had thought that with the *Devon* wrecked, Mr. Farley might journey to England with them, but he had business matters to attend to in America, made all the more pressing by the wreck of the *Devon* and the loss of her cargo. Because of the war between America and England, he was more likely to find quick passage to America from Lisbon than from any port in England and so he bade them farewell from the shore as Emily and Galen along with Mrs. Swingletree left in the longboat that would take them to the *Bethia*.

Mrs. Swingletree proved to be a much more pleasing fellow passenger than Mrs. Wilard, for she was possessed of a lively temperament and was not sick at all in spite of her delicate condition. Lady Berry had not told Mrs. Swingletree of Galen and Emily's supposed betrothal, but she had hinted it to her broadly enough. After dinner on the second day out from Funchal, Mrs. Swingletree, who had not been married for so long that she did not recall how much moments of privacy had been cherished by her and her husband during their betrothal, tactfully found an excuse to remain on deck when Galen offered to escort the ladies to their stateroom.

Emily was indeed grateful to Mrs. Swingletree, but not for the reason that lady supposed. They went into the cabin and Galen followed her into the stateroom without waiting for invitation and closed the door, leaning back against it. "Make the most of your opportunity, Emily," he said with resignation. "You have been wanting to ring a peal over my head since I left you with the Berrys. Lady Berry is a charming woman, but a sad rattle, I fear. I suppose she told you that I mentioned our betrothal to her. What would you have had me tell her?"

"Need you have told her anything?" Emily said indignantly.

"Of course I had to tell her something," he said with

a patronizing smile that made her long to strike him. "With Jacob there to give us the lie, we could not pretend that we had not been days alone together on terms of the greatest intimacy."

"Not the greatest intimacy," she snapped.

He laughed. "No. Not quite." He laughed again when he saw belligerent sparks in her eyes. "If you want to hit me, Emily, you will never succeed in getting past my guard if you let your eyes give away your intention."

"I don't want to hit you," she said coldly and untruthfully. "I don't want anything at all to do with you. I meant what I said, *Lord* DeVere," she added with deliberate formality. "I will not be forced to marry you, whatever the consequences."

"I believe you told Jacob you would prefer a nunnery," he said with a sardonic smile. "That was not the impression you gave to me."

Emily colored both from the implication of his words and surprise that Mr. Farley had repeated their conversation to him. She took a deep breath and managed to say with a fair attempt at dignity, "I can neither deny nor defend what has occurred between us, nor can I account for it. It was shock or vulnerability or propinquity or maybe all of those things, but now that we are again in the world I have come to my senses and I wish you to understand that it is not just that I don't wish for a forced marriage. I dislike you, Lord DeVere, and would not have you for a husband in any circumstances. You are overbearing, arrogant, insensitive, ill-bred, self-centered . . ."

Galen paled slightly as each epithet struck him like a blow. His blue eyes hardened. "Enough," he said quietly, but with sufficient sharpness to make her end her recital of his shortcomings. "You have made your feelings completely clear. Now you shall have mine. If you find me such a monster, I do not wonder at your rejection of my offer, but I promise you, your aunt will be of a different opinion." She started to speak but he held up his hand and she was silent again. "The situation we find ourselves in is of your making, Miss Hampton. If you had not encouraged that fool Cooke so that he wished to impress you, the evacuation of the *Devon* would have gone smoothly and you would never have been set adrift from the ship nor I forced to come to your rescue.''

''You make it sound as if I arranged all that occurred,'' she said furiously. ''It was an accident. Mr. Cooke was trying to be helpful and merely lost his balance. He is worth ten of you. I wish it were he here now instead of you.''

''So do I.''

His accents were so heartfelt that it was Emily who now felt as if she had been slapped. ''Then consider yourself freed from any obligation of honor to marry me. There is nothing you or my aunt or anyone could ever say or do that would persuade me to be your wife.''

He made her a cold, mocking bow. ''As you wish, Miss Hampton. I leave you to your fate.'' His eyes were as hard and glittering as diamonds and even in her rage Emily felt a qualm that she had gone further than she meant to.

The moment he left her all her anger evaporated and, feeling like an abandoned child, she lay down upon her bed and wept. It was this way that Mrs. Swingletree found her several minutes later. She sat beside Emily and made soothing sounds and comments until Emily's sobs at last abated. Emily knew she must guess that there had been a quarrel, but Mrs. Swingletree was too well-bred to pry. ''You must not be so cast down,'' she said bracingly. ''Whatever it is, everything usually comes out all right in the end, you know.''

Emily made no reply but she had no doubt at all that for her nothing would ever be all right again. Without her anger to shield her from the reality that she had fallen in love with a man who did not love her, wretchedness returned in full measure, and only a fierce determination to put Galen DeVere from her life and her mind prevented her from sinking into complete despair.

8

England, November 1812

Emily had meant every word she had said to Galen as she spoke them, but when her bottled anger was finally released and spent, she wished every one of them back again. It was not that she had changed her mind about marrying him under duress, but knowing that she had said what she had deliberately to wound him. Yet, her common sense told her that it was for the best; he had finally understood that she would not accept his offer of marriage to save her honor or his.

There were no further overt quarrels between Galen and Emily, and Emily did not again indulge her unhappiness with tears. They were unfailingly pleasant to each other for the remainder of the time they were together, and Emily could almost forget at times that they had quarreled at all. But it was different now; an invisible wall had been erected between them. There was more civility between them than amiability and the distance that set them apart was not the distance of strangers, but of lovers who have lost the knack of loving. On the surface it was an agreeable, uneventful voyage, but to Emily it seemed endless.

Mrs. Swingletree kept Emily from being too downcast. She was of such a cheerful and considerate disposition, it was impossible to be dispirited in her company. It had been decided before they had left Funchal that Emily would stay with Mrs. Swingletree and her mother, who lived on the outskirts of Portsmouth, until she could inform her aunt that she had at last arrived in England.

Fortunately, Mrs. Arthur, Mrs. Swingletree's mother, proved to be as friendly as her daughter and ready to show Emily every kindness. She listened to the tale of Emily's adventure—severely expurgated—with a lively interest that was untainted by vulgar curiosity. Being the sort of woman who looks for and finds the silver lining in every cloud, she declared that at the least Emily would now have the pleasure of shopping for an entire wardrobe of new clothes when she went to London.

Unwittingly, she made Emily very conscious that besides her jewelry which she had saved from the shipwreck, her sole possessions were two dresses: the blue muslin that Lady Berry had first given her and another in green cotton with an embroidered hem which proved to be the only other dress that Lady Berry had which could be made to fit Emily without undergoing major and lengthy alteration. Emily gathered from the letters she had received from Lady Laelard that that lady was very fashionable and she dreaded to think of the first impression she would make on her when her Aunt Dorothea beheld her in her borrowed finery.

In spite of her liking for mother and daughter, Emily did not wish to trespass on Mrs. Arthur's hospitality for longer than necessary and she wrote to Lady Laelard on the day they arrived in Portsmouth. It was a bare two days later that Emily was summoned by a servant, who informed her that her aunt had arrived and wished to see her.

The woman sitting with Mrs. Arthur was as formidably elegant and fashionable as Emily had feared, but she had a little the look of Emily's own beloved mother, which put Emily at her ease. The smile she gave to her niece was quite open and welcoming and Emily was able to greet her with sincere pleasure. But it was not her Aunt Dorothea, it was her mother's youngest sister, Caroline, who welcomed Emily.

"Dora is in a dreadful pelter," Lady Caroline said as she warmly clasped Emily's hand and drew her onto the sofa beside her. "Her two youngest boys have come down with measles and she was summoned to Whistley and could not put off the journey, so she has asked me to come and fetch you. You are to come to town with me, my dear, and we shall go to Whistley for the holidays, by which time the illness will have run its course, I hope. I think you will enjoy seeing London. You will wish to shop a bit perhaps."

Emily smiled a little at her aunt's tactful understatement. She had said nothing in her brief letter to Lady Laelard about the shipwreck or its aftermath, and Lady Caroline must suppose that the ill-fitting green cotton day dress was a fair example of Emily's wardrobe. Mrs. Arthur was a tactful woman and after a few minutes of general conversation, she left aunt and niece to become better acquainted. Emily apprised Lady Caroline of all that had occurred since she had left Philadelphia, to that lady's complete astonishment.

The story she gave to her aunt was more detailed than the one she had told to Mrs. Swingletree and Mrs. Arthur, but still was not complete. She told her aunt of being set adrift from the ship, of Galen's brave rescue and how they were separated from the others, but she gave no hint at all of the fevered embraces that had passed between her and Galen or how nearly she had succumbed to her own desire and his.

But Lady Caroline was a shrewd woman, and she read much into Emily's carefully unemotional references to Galen DeVere. "DeVere," she repeated thoughtfully after Emily had finished and she had exclaimed suitably over each event in the recital. "Yes, of course. They are neighbors of Dora and Andrew—or nearly so. But I seem to recall . . ." She fell into silence and Emily, who in spite of herself was eager to know what her aunt knew of Galen and his family, said nothing to distract her.

"Robert DeVere," Lady Caroline said at last with an air of satisfaction. "That is the name. And there is a sister as well—Lady Haverton, with whom I am slightly acquainted. But this cannot be your captain. Robert DeVere died nearly a year ago. Drank himself to death, I believe, and from the point of view of whoever his heir might be, not a moment too soon. The *on-dit* is that the estate is quite wasted to nothing."

"I believe his heir must be Mr. DeVere, or Lord DeVere as he is called now," Emily responded.

"Well, he won't get much for his inheritance but an empty title," Lady Caroline said baldly. "It is too bad really. The poor man loses his ship and comes home to debt rather than a honeyfall. He may end by wishing he had stayed in America after all, or perhaps he will go back to see if he can make his fortune again."

Emily knew that Galen was far from needing to inherit a fortune, but she didn't bother to correct her aunt's misconception. The subject was turned then to the arrangements Lady Caroline had made for her niece's removal to London, which was to be on the following morning.

"I hope I shall not be burdensome to you, Aunt Caroline," Emily said diffidently. "It is very kind of you to take me in as an unexpected guest."

Lady Caroline Antrop opened her eyes a little in surprise. She was a small, delicately made woman, with wispy, somewhat frizzy blond hair, sharp features that were saved from looking pinched by a rose-pink complexion, and dark gray eyes that were habitually half closed with affected languor that had been a part of her so long it was now natural. "But, my dear, you are not a guest, you are a Harcourt and a part of my family. Besides," she added with a dimpling smile, "after a week or two of complete boredom, you shall probably find staying with me burdensome. The Little Season is dwindling to an end and town is becoming thin of company. But I think I can contrive one or two invitations for us—when you are ready to go out," she added with another oblique reference to the presumed deficiencies of Emily's wardrobe. "It is the greatest pity that your cousin Amanda chose to return to Whistley with her mother, for if she were with us at least you would have a companion of your own age.''

Emily quickly assured her aunt that she had no doubt she would be completely satisfied with her company alone. Emily was surprised that Lady Caroline had made nothing of the time that Emily had spent alone with Galen as he had seemed to think she would. In curiosity, she asked her aunt if she thought there would be any danger to her reputation because of it.

Lady Caroline pursed her lips and then sighed and said cautiously, ''That will depend. I do not know what manner of man this Lord DeVere may be, but the name DeVere is not an honored one. If it were generally known that he had compromised you, you could find yourself in a very difficult position. But need it ever be known? I did not like to say anything at once for I didn't wish it to look as if I meant to scold you at our first meeting for impropriety which, after all, you could not help. Will Lord DeVere tell anyone, do you think?''

''No. I think not. He was concerned that we have a care to our reputations.'' She had not mentioned his proposal of marriage and her rejection of it.

''What of Mrs. Arthur and her daughter?''

''They know only that Galen was the captain of the ship that was wrecked. I stayed with the Berrys until we were able to obtain passage on the *Bethia*, but Ga—Lord DeVere stayed at lodgings his friend Mr. Farley had obtained.''

''Good. And the others from the *Devon*? They know that you were separated from them and did not arrive in Madeira at the same time that they did.''

But Emily perceived no difficulty there either. ''Mrs. Wilard is to live with her family, who are merchants in Northumberland and do not come to town, and Mr. Cooke is a most kind gentleman who would have no reason to speak against me. All of the others are Americans and have gone to Lisbon in hope of gaining passage back to America.''

Lady Caroline nodded with satisfaction and began to

pull on her gloves. "Then I think we need not be overly concerned. The only thing which you must guard against is speaking of what occurred to you too freely to any friends you might make. In fact, I would speak of it as little as possible. Make it known from the start that the memory distresses you, which is hardly surprising, and then you may safely snub anyone ill-bred enough to be inquisitive. I include your Aunt Dorothea and your cousins as well."

"You do not wish me to tell everything to them?" Emily said, surprised that her aunt would think the subterfuge necessary within her own family.

"I would advise against it," Lady Caroline said, her eyes lowered as she turned to find her reticule on the table beside her chair. "The fewer people who know all of the truth, the less likelihood there is that it will ever become an *on-dit*, and that, my dear, would be fatal."

Emily felt she had been given some sort of warning about the Laelards, though of what she was not entirely certain. Then Lady Caroline smiled her delightful, wholehearted smile again and seemed so completely guileless that Emily wondered if she had read more into her words than intended.

Mrs. Arthur, returning to the sitting room, urged Lady Caroline to spend the night, but Lady Caroline assured her that she would be most comfortable at the Ship and Anchor, where her dresser and major domo, who had made the journey with her, were already securing all that was necessary for her comfort. She also mentioned that she always traveled with her own sheets and china, and Emily, listening to this display of consequence, felt a little daunted and was glad of a night's respite to adjust herself to this change in circumstances, so different from the simplicity and even privation she had known most recently.

9

Galen spent barely an hour in Portsmouth after their arrival. He hired a horse with the funds loaned to him by Sir Richard to tide him over until he could reach London and establish himself at the bank where his own funds had already been transferred in expectation of his arrival. It took him some minutes to accustom himself to the motion of a horse beneath him again after so many weeks at sea, but once he had, he was glad that he had decided to ride instead of drive himself to London. Being a passenger on a ship was very different from being captain and the inactivity had chafed him, all the more so because it had given him far more opportunity for thought than he wished to have.

He told himself that he was glad to be able to accept Emily's absolute rejection of his proposal, which after all he had not wished to make, but it was all too often in the forefront of his mind. Emily was not at all the usual sort of woman to attract his notice and he could not comprehend why any effect she might have on him should be more than ephemeral. Once she had refused his advances and rejected his compulsory offer of marriage that should have been an end of it for him, but it was not.

Like Emily, he had decided that propinquity had had much to do with the attraction that had grown so strong between them. Now that he was returned at last to England he had a great deal to occupy him and with relief he put all thoughts of her firmly from his mind as he went about the business of establishing himself as the rightful heir to the barony and saw to the many small legal details necessary to claim his funds and put a final period to the disastrous episode of the last voyage of the *Devon*.

He was master of his thoughts during those hours claimed by activity, but in the quiet of the night not even the comfort to be found in the arms of an exceptionally pretty and quite obliging member of the demimonde was sufficient to banish the memory of Emily lying beside him that last night on the deserted island, so soft, so fragrant, and so desirable that he had been unable to resist making love to her.

At the end of a sennight he gave up the unequal struggle, but ony partially. It occurred to him that if he saw Emily again in a commonplace setting he would view her stripped of the romance of their shared adventure and might once again be able to regard her with the indifference he had felt when they had first met in Philadelphia. Breeding dictated that he should in any case make at least one call on her at her aunt's to assure himself that she was well settled. Then at last his obligation to Mr. Armitage would be satisfied.

He was surprised to discover that the knocker was off the door of Laelard House in Berkeley Square and supposed that he would have to wait until he went into Sussex to accomplish his intent, but on impulse he went to the service door to inquire if the Laelards were to be found at their estate in Sussex. A rather young and obligingly voluble underfootman answered his questions readily and volunteered the further information that Emily was not at Whistley with the Laelards but residing in Upper Mount Street with Lady Caroline Antrop.

Lady Caroline was as unknown to Galen as were the Laelards, but he obtained her exact direction from his informant and redirected his steps to Upper Mount Street. Like Emily, he had been forced to borrow clothes and since his arrival in town he had given no more than cursory attention to his appearance, being far more concerned with the business matters that had to be seen to at once. It was only the previous day that he had finally visited the shop of the fashionable Mr. Weston and had ordered all that was necessary to properly outfit a gentleman of means and pretensions to fashion, and the clothes he still wore were ill-fitting and of no fashion at all. Lady Caroline, as she greeted her unexpected guest in her receiving saloon, could be excused for feeling that her assumption that Galen was not plump in the pocket was confirmed.

"It is very good of you to call, my lord," Lady Caroline said as they were seated in two spindle-legged chairs. If Lady Caroline had meant to encourage future visits, she would have led her guest to a more comfortable seat on the sofa or one of the chairs grouped about it, but she did not. It was a fine distinction, but it was not lost on Galen, who was faintly amused by it and wondered what Emily might have told her aunt of him and of their time together.

"I know Emily will be sorry to have missed you," Lady Caroline continued. "She is having a fitting with Madame Celeste this morning, but I fear you will find her seldom at home, Lord DeVere. If it is not the modiste it is the maunta-maker, and I think she is quite determined as well to see every sight that London has to offer before we retire to my sister's estate in Sussex for the holidays. We spent the entire day at Cornhill yesterday viewing the Royal Exchange and the Bank of England and I confess myself quite worn out with the effort, which is why I have sent Emily along to Madame Celeste with only a maid. Though I admit that it is interesting to view the things one has always taken for granted through new eyes, it is also rather wearing."

Galen listened to this speech and decided—correctly—at the end of it that it was also designed to warn him away. If he were to call again he would probably not find Emily there to receive him then either. He was not sure what to make of this. "I too am sorry to have missed Miss Hampton. I wished to assure myself that she has taken no harm from the misadventure we suffered on our crossing from America.''

''She is in excellent fettle,'' Lady Caroline replied, and then gave him a chilly smile. ''Actually, it is as well that you have called when Emily was from home. There is a matter of some delicacy concerning my niece which ought to be discussed but which she might feel awkward mentioning to you herself.''

Galen was not surprised by this. He had been wondering what Emily had told her aunt of the aftermath of the shipwreck. ''You may rely on my discretion, Lady Caroline,'' he said guardedly, giving away nothing until he knew the extent of her knowledge.

Lady Caroline was quite straightforward with him and he was surprised that Emily had revealed as much as she had. But he was even more surprised by Lady Caroline's assessment of the situation. ''Emily felt a little concern for her reputation if it should be known that you spent so much time alone with her,'' she said in summation, ''but if we are careful and discreet, I see no cause for anxiety. We have decided that even my sister and her family need not be told of your separation from the other boats and the delay before you reached Funchal.

''You are a gentleman, Lord DeVere,'' she added with only a faintly discernible trace of condescension. ''However much you might dislike dissembling, I know you would put the honor of a lady ahead of any scruples you might have about telling untruths.''

Galen bowed his head in mechanical acquiescence. ''Of course. But do you think it will answer?''

''Well, it has to, doesn't it,'' Lady Caroline said briskly.

From what she had told him, Lady Caroline was clearly in Emily's confidence and no doubt Emily had told her aunt that marriage to Galen was not to be considered. He knew he should be glad of it. ''As I have said, Lady Caroline, you may rely on me,'' he said blandly.

Lady Caroline gave a small sigh that might have been relief and got up to ring for her butler. "You will take a glass of Madeira with me before you leave, I hope," she said to him, and because her back was to him did not see the small ironic smile that touched his lips at the mention of the wine.

He stood also to take his leave of her. "I thank you, Lady Caroline, but no. I have business to attend to in the city and I am already late for an appointment."

"Do you go into Sussex soon?" Lady Caroline asked politely. "Perhaps we shall meet during the holidays. I believe your home is not far from Whistley Lodge, my brother-in-law's estate."

"Perhaps," he agreed noncommittally. "But I am not acquainted with the Laelards that I recall."

Now that matters were so satisfactorily settled, Lady Caroline's conscience pricked her a little for her cavalier treatment of a man who had after all saved her niece's life. "That must be remedied, my lord," she said with a gracious smile. "If you go to Sussex any time soon, you would do me a very great favor if you would call at Whistley to assure my sister that Emily is well and looking forward to our visit next month. Emily and I have both written, of course, but it will be much more reassuring to Dora if she hears that all is well first hand. She was greatly disappointed that she could not be here herself when Emily arrived."

Galen was not certain what he thought of this turn-about, but he murmured vague assent to the charge laid upon him. He doubted that he would carry it out, but in the end he did. Not because he felt bound by any promise to Lady Caroline, but because his ambivalence toward Emily was such that he found he could not completely sever the last tenuous connection that existed between them.

Before Emily could return from her visit to the modiste, she had a second caller, Jeremy Cooke, and Lady Caroline's reception of him was far more cordial than the one she had given to Galen. When on their arrival in London Lady Caroline had learned that Mr. Cooke had called at Laelard House in Berkeley Square to inquire after Emily, she deemed it prudent to send a message to Mr. Cooke inviting him to call to assure himself of Emily's safety.

"It is the wise thing to do, I think," she had said to Emily, who supplied her with the information that Mr. Cooke planned to live with his sister until he found suitable lodgings. "I have never heard of him or his sister, but that does not mean they do not move in *ton* circles. It is best to be sure. After all, he has no notion at all what has become of you after the ship was wrecked. He may make a nuisance of himself trying to discover what he can and start just the sort of unnecessary talk that we wish to avoid. When he arrives you shall tell him exactly the same as you mean to tell your Aunt Dora. I only hope he does not inquire too closely into the chronology of your story, or we shall be dished," she added, filling her niece with trepidation.

But there was no need for concern, Mr. Cooke accepted her version of the events without so much as a flicker in his expression to suggest that he suspected evasion or untruths. In fact, he was so delighted that Emily had come to no harm that he scarcely seemed to heed the tale in his pleasure that all was happily resolved.

Lady Caroline was not taken in by Mr. Cooke's well-bred air of prosperity; she judged him by the same standard that Galen had done and reached much the same conclusion. But she saw at once that though Mr. Cooke might be a fortune hunter on the catch for a rich wife, Emily was in no danger of succumbing to his charm. Emily appeared to accept him uncritically, but there was nothing in her manner toward Mr. Cooke that suggested to her aunt that Emily held him in deeper regard.

Lady Caroline thought it was no bad thing for Emily to have at least one acquaintance in town who had been known to her for more than a few days and so Mr. Cooke was encouraged to call, which he did with a nice sense of propriety: often enough to make his interest clear, but not so frequently that his attentions appeared too particular.

On this occasion, though, Mr. Cooke found himself given encouragement beyond what he had dared to hope for. Lady Caroline, partly on impulse and partly because she was feeling a little guilty that she had discouraged Galen without Emily's knowledge or consent, invited Cooke on her sister's behalf to spend the holidays with her and Emily at Whistley. Whatever his sister's claims on him might have been, he accepted with alacrity and by the time Emily returned to Upper Mount Street, it was a settled thing.

Emily was pleased that Mr. Cooke would be making the journey into Kent with them but unsure of the wisdom of the invitation. She would be glad of Mr. Cooke's company but she did not wish to offer him any unintentional encouragement to renew his unwanted advances toward her. When he had gone she said to her aunt, "It was very kind of you to include Mr. Cooke, but I am a little afraid that he may read more into the invitation than is intended."

"He may," Lady Caroline agreed, unperturbed. "But you are a sensible, clever girl, Emily, and I am sure you will be able to hint him away if his attentions do become particular. I asked him along because I thought it would be less daunting for you to meet nearly the whole of the family at once if you had someone you knew a little along."

Emily agreed that this was so and said nothing more about it. Lady Caroline was grateful that Emily did not question her further and turned the topic by asking Emily how her fitting had gone. Emily, delighted at the prospect that she would soon be the possessor of several pretty, fashionable new dresses and gowns, responded with enthusiasm and, for the moment at least, Mr. Cooke and the visit to Whistley were forgotten.

Lady Caroline regarded Mr. Cooke as no threat to her niece or her fortune, but Galen DeVere was another matter entirely. Lady Caroline was an astute woman and guessed that whatever Emily might say, more had passed between her and Galen than she had admitted.

The DeVere family was not personally known to her, except for Lady Haverton, who had been a DeVere before her marriage, but she knew of them by repute. The father had been a gamester, the mother a suspected suicide, the elder son a sot and libertine, and Lady Haverton had skirted the edge of ruin a number of times by engaging in *affaires* with several notable men of the *ton*.

She knew nothing of Galen, and discreet inquiry had garnered her nothing except the information that he had left his home and family and gone off to sea a number of years ago. While that was not precisely to his discredit, based on what she had observed of his appearance, it had not added to his consequence. He had risen to be captain of his ship and he was now Lord DeVere, but the ship was sunk and the title was an empty one. It might not be fair to visit the sins of a father on his son or of an elder brother on a younger, but Lady Caroline dismissed the DeVeres as having bad blood rather in the manner of the Barrymores and there was not one of them that had come to any good end.

But Lady Caroline knew that by a vulnerable young woman—and that was how she thought of Emily in this regard—an attractive and personable man would be judged with little thought to his lack of fortune or the encumbrance of a difficult family. Having met Galen, Lady Caroline had gauged for herself the degree of danger he might represent to her niece and it was high. She did not underestimate him for a moment.

She said nothing at all to Emily about Galen's visit and trusted that he had taken the hint that he would not be welcome to call again. Emily might wonder that he would not even make a civil call to inquire after her health, but it was all to the good if she thought him neglectful of her. Lady Caroline was not without a twinge of conscience for these machinations, but she assuaged it with the justification that she owed it to the memory of her dead sister to keep her daughter from forming an attachment to a man who was hopelessly ineligible.

It was less than a fortnight later when the letter arrived for Emily. Lady Caroline did not recognize Galen's hand, of course, but he had franked it so there was no doubt of the sender. All of the post was brought to Lady Caroline first thing in the morning with her cup of chocolate, so she knew Emily could not have seen it before her. At first she thought only to destroy the letter, but deciding that it would only be a temporary measure—for if he received no reply he might only write again—she opened and read it, though not without a guilty hammering of her heart.

Her very worst fears were confirmed. Galen had too much sense and discretion to be explicit in a letter, but Lady Caroline knew that she had been right in her assumption that there had been more between them than Emily had told her. His apology alone was very nearly a declaration and the terms of regard with which he addressed her erased the last of Lady Caroline's lingering doubts. This was the letter of a man in love—or at least professing love.

She refolded it thoughtfully when she was finished reading it and placed it in a concealed drawer in her writing desk until she had decided what she would do. She had to do something, there was no doubt of that. If Emily read the letter Lady Caroline was certain she would respond to it as its sender intended.

By the end of the day she had made up her mind. Going up to her room not long after dinner pleading the headache, she took the letter out of the drawer and reread it. Then she took several clean sheets of foolscap from another drawer, mended her pen, and began to write.

* * *

Galen's expectations of what he would find when he returned to Landsend were met and then some. The gates were hanging off their hinges and the drive was overgrown and pitted. The house and park were so untended and dilapidated that the place had a look of abandonment. After his mother's death his father had not bothered to keep up the estate, preferring to spend his money on horses and highflyers, but Galen had no recollection of his home's possessing such a desolate air in those days and something inside of him hardened with determination.

A slovenly dressed footman opened the door to him and appeared singularly unimpressed that his master had at last come to claim his inheritance. He led Galen to the library at the back of the house and nodded him into the room with an insolent jerk of his head. A man in a half-undressed state was seated in a leather chair that had more than one tear with the stuffing showing. He glanced up at Galen, first with indifference and then with amazement.

"Damme," he said, "I almost didn't know you. It is you, Gale, isn't it?" He swept a tray which held the remains of a meal that looked as if it had been consumed several days ago off the chair next to his and offered the chair to Galen.

Galen eyed it without enthusiasm, but a brief survey of the room gave him no hope of a better place to settle. There were more dirty glasses and crockery gracing the surfaces of several pieces of furniture and clothes, newspapers, and other less identifiable flotsom were strewn about the room as if a vortex had settled there and then moved on leaving chaos behind.

"It is I, John," Galen replied, electing to remain standing. "Though I gather I am not expected."

"Oh, we knew right enough," said his brother-in-law, Viscount Haverton. "Eugenia had your letter the day after we got here from town. You mean the state of the place, I suppose. Made no difference whether you were coming or not—been like this for years. Not much Genie or I could do about it."

"Except use it as a place to rusticate when your creditors start knocking at your door," Galen said dryly, and saw from Haverton's expression that he had scored a hit.

"Robert always told us to consider Landsend as our own," the viscount said defensively.

"Being so often in dun territory himself, he could not but be sympathetic," Galen remarked.

Letting this pass, Haverton commented, "You're looking prosperous yourself, Gale. If you've managed to repair the family fortune, you're a welcome sight, and there is no gainsaying that."

"I have repaired my own fortune, John. The family must see to itself. Where is Eugenia?"

"With the cook—if you can call the slattern that rules in the kitchen that. Hog's swill is what we were served last night, I give you my word on it."

Galen repressed a sigh. He had known that he would have some work ahead of him to bring Landsend back to a tolerable estate, but he had not envisioned quite this degree of discomfort while he did so. "Who is bailiff? Or is there one? What I have seen so far in and out of the house does not encourage me to hope."

John Haverton answered this and all of Galen's subsequent questions, however caustically posed, with unimpaired amiability. Whatever Galen might say about looking to themselves, it appeared that he meant to take an interest in his sorry inheritance, which was bound to reflect to the Havertons' good.

Before coming into Sussex, Galen had collected his coats from Weston and procured the remainder of his sartorial needs, so the appearance he presented was quite other than that which had caused Lady Caroline Antrop to summarily dismiss him as unfashionable and impecunious. He was dressed with understated elegance in a coat of dark brown superfine that was perfectly molded to his broad shoulders; his linen was perfectly white despite the long drive in his recently acquired open carriage; his neckcloth was tied with style, and his boots glowed with the touch of an expert hand. Everything about him bespoke taste, but more to the point, it bespoke money. When Lady Haverton joined them several minutes later, her impression of her brother was identical to her husband's and so was the speculative gleam that came into her eyes.

Eugenia Haverton was as fair as her younger brother, but with eyes of a more vivid shade of blue. A buxom, well-made woman, she had a comfortable, almost matronly appearance that belied her reputation as a well-born highflyer who had somehow managed to maintain her position in the *ton* despite a lifelong flirtation with incipient ruin. She had an air of serene self-assurance the result of so often getting what-ever—or whomever—she had set her sights upon. The only check to an otherwise successful career was her marriage to John Haverton, an inveterate gamester, and he had not been her choice but her father's.

Like Galen, she was fashionably and elegantly dressed and completely out of place in such unpre-possessing surroundings. As Galen dutifully bowed over her hand, he was reasonably sure that the diamonds that graced her fingers were quite genuine and the pearls at her throat had a luster that was never made by human hand. He had little doubt of the source of these trinkets; what he did wonder was how she managed to keep them out of her husband's grasp.

"It is a pity you could not have come back before Robin stuck his spoon in the wall," she said to Galen. "He was wont to ask for you from time to time, though usually while in his cups so you needn't refine too much upon it."

Galen was in no danger of this. "What specifically did he die of?"

She shrugged with an unconcern which would have been thought callous by anyone other than another member of her family. "Good living, I suppose, or rather, too much of it. And why not? He was bred to intemperance. The only thing dear papa was ever extravagant with besides his temper and his own pleasures was Robin. I thought you'd shaken off the dust of this place, Galen," she added without pause. "You've come back for the title, I suppose."

"I doubt you'll believe it, Eugenia, but I have not," he replied.

Eugenia sat in the chair that Galen had scorned. "You're right, I don't believe you. You're not so great a fool that you don't know the value of a title if you have the money to back it up, and you look as if you do have it."

"I am well enough to pass," he said repressively. "I wonder, though, if my funds are equal to putting this place in order. Is what I've seen a fair example of the whole?"

"I don't know what you've seen," Eugenia said with a slow smile not unlike his own, "but I can still answer your question. Yes, a very fair example. It would suit me very well if you mean to put your blunt into making Landsend and the DeVeres respectable again, but I wonder if it will suit you?"

"So do I." On the whole, Galen was not as discouraged as he seemed to be. It was not, in fact, much worse than he had expected and already plans were formulating in his mind for measures which could be taken at once to make the house, at least, more habitable.

John regaled him with an account of the state of the home and tenant farms, which was equally grim but not unexpected, and Eugenia seemed to find relish in informing him of the shortcomings of the staff he had inherited along with the house.

Galen at last gave in to weariness after his long drive and perched himself at the edge of a chair which was otherwise covered with an assortment of cast-off clothes and books. "You must tell me whom I can pension off and whom to dismiss. If there is anyone worth keeping, I see no sign of it," he added as he looked at his hand where it was now streaked with gray from touching the arm of the chair. "At least I needn't fear ennui. Are you acquainted with the Laelards of Whistley Lodge?"

Eugenia was surprised by this abrupt change in topic and her brows went up. "The Grand Dorothea? The Laelards are very high in the instep, though why they should be is a puzzle. She was a Harcourt before her marriage, but the viscountcy is a fairly recent creation and of no great distinction. Nor is theirs any great fortune. Laelard has a competency and nothing more, with a daughter and three sons to settle respectably."

"I called at Whistley at the behest of Lady Laelard's sister, whom I met in town. I am invited to dine on Friday," Galen informed her.

"Does she know who you are, dear boy?" asked John in some surprise.

"No doubt my prosperous appearance assuaged her doubts about my respectability," Galen said, smiling. "Either that or the imploring looks and broad hints her daughter sent her to invite me to return to Whistley did the trick."

"The Exquisite Amanda," said the viscountess contemptuously. "If you really are prosperous, you'll want to watch your purse with that one, though I doubt your suit would succeed unless you're as well-heeled as Golden Ball. Dora Laelard has nothing less than a duke in mind for her darling girl."

"Which duke?"

Eugenia gave a dismissive wave of her hand. "Oh, any duke will do. The only requirements are that he be unmarried and rich and that he not read the marriage settlements too closely."

"It may not be impossible," Galen said musingly. "Miss Laelard is a diamond of the first water. Quite breathtaking, in fact."

"Only on first acquaintance," Eugenia said waspishly. "There is always a reason when a girl that lovely makes it to a second Season unattached. They will have to bring something off this Season, though there is always Edmund Timmons as an ace in the pocket. His father's estate marches with Whistley and he has been dangling after the beauty since he got out of short coats. Won't his nose be out of joint if Miss Laelard is casting out lures to you. But you aren't really interested there, are you, Gale? I can't believe you would imagine yourself in love over a pretty face."

"My dear Eugenia," Galen said with a deliberately patronizing air, "the last time we met I had not even attained my majority. You know nothing of me at all."

"Well, you are a DeVere," she retorted, rising to the bait, "so I daresay you may also be a fool."

"The eldest boy's not a bad sort," John intervened before a quarrel at the schoolroom level could erupt between brother and sister. "He fancies himself a poet and acts and dresses the part, but he's no man-milliner. Does it to set up the maternal back, if you ask me. Lord Laelard is something of a recluse; never sets foot off his own land if he can help it. Gave up the unequal struggle against trying to keep his wife from stealing his breeches years ago."

"You make Lady Laelard sound a veritable dragon," Galen complained. "She was not so with me."

"Hedging her bets," Haverton said without hesitation. "How she goes on from here depends on the extent of your bank account and what she can find out about it."

"By all means go to Laelard for dinner on Friday," Eugenia said, rising. "It's the best meal you're likely to have this week if you mean to stay here. After dinner tonight, I am not at all sure that you will. Mrs. Morgan does not agree that the mutton she plans to serve us this evening is rancid, but it smells as if the dogs wouldn't eat it unless starving."

Galen stood as well. "I certainly intend to stay. I have traveled thousands of miles at significant cost to return to Landsend and I don't mean to be routed by a bad joint of mutton. I think it is time I became acquainted with my staff." He proffered his arm to his sister. "Would you care to accompany me to the kitchens, Eugenia? I think you will enjoy this."

After years of dealing with able seamen from every quarter of life, possessing every manner of caprice and vice, the ragtag staff of Landsend were not really worthy of Galen's steel, but he put on a fine display of quiet but ruthless authority that achieved almost instantaneous results. By the end of the first week he deemed it necessary to let go only two of the servants: the insolent footman and a slatternly maid called Nancy. The remainder of the staff, who recognized that they at last had a master who meant to restore order to Landsend, went to work with a purpose.

He gave his sister virtual *carte blanche* to clean up and restore whatever could be salvaged of the furniture and hangings, and much of his time was spent with Mr. Reynard, the bailiff, who proved not to be incompetent but merely discouraged. Like the house servants, when Mr. Reynard saw that Galen was serious about bringing Landsend back to what it had been in his grandfather's time and possessed of the means to do so, he proved himself tireless in his service to his new employer.

But Galen's hope that all of his activity would banish Emily from his mind was not realized. Even when he was with Mr. Reynard inspecting the estate his thoughts would turn to recalling all that had passed between them. However firmly he would put such thoughts aside, in the next unguarded moment they were almost certain to return.

Far more upsetting to his peace of mind was that he saw her everywhere like a gentle spirit. When he was in the house, he could imagine her there, gracing and brightening the shabby rooms; when he rode about the estate he envisioned her beside him revisiting the haunts of his childhood. It occurred to him, to his complete dismay, that he thought about her all the time.

His intellect told him that a few days of enforced intimacy could not result in a lasting attachment, but he could not dismiss his feelings as mere physical attraction any longer. He distrusted the idea that he had fallen in love with her and was a little afraid of it, but by the end of that first week he could not deny it: Emily was necessary to his happiness.

But Lady Caroline's cold reception had made it clear to him that Emily had not forgiven him for the hard words they had spoken to each other aboard the *Bethia*. He could not think of the graceless way he had informed her that he felt obliged to marry her against his will without castigating himself for a fool.

He thought of returning to London to try to see her again, but hesitated to put the thought into action. She might refuse to see him or insist on the presence of her aunt at any meeting, and he meant to use more than the power of words to persuade her to forgive him.

But even if he had been more certain of Emily's response, it proved to be an impossible time for him to leave Landsend for plans for alterations inside and outside of the house were being drawn up and required his personal attention in every aspect. In the end he settled for the half measure of writing to Emily, hoping to soften the heart she had hardened against him.

He was not the sort of man to agonize over each phrase, writing and tearing up draft after draft. He sat at a small writing desk that had been his mother's and wrote steadily until the letter was finished. His words were more restrained than they might have been had he spoken them to her in person, but his apology was humble and sincere and he hoped she would be left in no doubt of his feelings for her. If she cared for him at all, she must surely forgive him.

He franked it so there would be no risk of it being

refused for postage. He had an almost superstitious concern that it would somehow go astray and even took it into the village himself to see it safe in the bag for the mailcoach.

10

Emily stared at her reflected image in the cheval glass in her well-appointed bedchamber at Whistley Lodge and decided that she had never looked better. Her hair had been cut and curled into a style known as the Artless but which was anything but unstudied. The gown she wore was silk and the color of forget-me-nots with an overdress of gauze shot with golden threads which brought out gleaming golden highlights in her hair. Unbidden, the thought came to her that she wished Galen could see her looking so lovely. She resolutely banished it at once, though not before the familiar ache surrounded her heart.

Despite the heat of their words on the *Bethia* and the coldness of their parting in Portsmouth, Emily had not supposed that it would be so final. It would have been no more than courtesy demanded for him to have called to assure himself of her welfare after her arrival in London, or if he had gone at once into Sussex, he might have written, but she had had no word from him at all.

His neglect made it painfully clear to her that his regard for her had not extended beyond the obligation he had felt for her welfare. He had told her once when they had first met that he would gladly wash his hands of her once they had safely reached England, and that was exactly what he had done. She had the satisfaction of knowing she had been right to refuse his offer of a loveless marriage, but she could not prevent the unhappiness she felt whenever she thought that she might never see him again and knew that it was because she had deliberately sent him away.

A maid from Lady Caroline's household had been elevated to serve as Emily's abigail, and she fussed about her new mistress, murmuring praise for Emily's appearance. The deep neckline of the blue silk gown gave Emily some concern, but she was assured by her aunt, maid, and modiste that the cut of the gown was not likely to be thought even daring by the standards of current fashion. Emily could not deny the striking effect of the soft drapes of silk, which showed her figure to advantage, and her confidence was buoyed by knowing she looked her best. Never in her life had she felt more attractive.

Emily and Lady Caroline, escorted by Mr. Cooke, had arrived at Whistley only the previous afternoon and tonight was to be the first of a number of parties that were planned for the entertainment of the guests at Whistley during the holiday season. They were not Lady Laelard's only guests; they had sat fourteen to dinner on the previous night and of these only Lady Caroline and Mr. Cooke were known to Emily, but Emily had not felt at all daunted by this, as she had feared she would be. She had attended a few small parties with her Aunt Caroline before they had left London and after the very first one her nervousness at being presented to the *ton* had left her as she realized that there was little difference between *ton* parties and the fashionable entertainments she had attended in Philadelphia and New York.

Emily's feelings about her new-found family, though, were mixed. She had come to regard Lady Caroline with some affection, though she was a bit put off by her aunt's occasionally managing ways, such as her insistence when Emily was choosing dresses and gowns to bring to Whistley that she knew better than Emily what would best become her.

Her Aunt Dorothea was quite taken up with her

duties as hostess and Emily had spoken no more than two dozen words with her since her arrival. Lady Laelard had treated her niece with every condescension and kindness, but Emily felt a cool reserve behind her aunt's overt friendliness that she suspected was Lady Laelard's truer nature.

Lord Laelard had done little more than acknowledge her presence at dinner before retiring to his study where, as far as Emily knew—for she had not set eyes on him again—he still remained. Her two youngest cousins William and Edward, aged nine and twelve, were high-spirited young gentlemen who had no more than a passing interest in an older cousin, and beyond asking her several naive questions about America, paid her no more heed than their father had done.

Emily's cousin Amanda was an Accredited Beauty and deserved the title. Amanda was exquisite, a genuine diamond of the first water with naturally curling hair the color of flax and wide blue eyes that held the dual appeal of gentleness and innocence. She had greeted Emily with a wholehearted delight that Emily could not but respond to. But Emily's hope that there would eventually be closeness between them did not outlive the day, for in conversation Emily discovered they were quite unalike in temperament and ideals. The only member of the Laelard family toward whom she had no equivocal feelings was her cousin Robin.

Robin Laelard was a young man of about her own age, possessed of a lively, if somewhat caustic, sense of humor and an artless manner of laughing at himself as well as his surroundings that Emily found endearing. He and Amanda had taken Emily about the large rambling Jacobean manor house in the morning so that Emily could become acquainted with its many eccentricities in design—the result of additions and alterations by succeeding generations. While Amanda in all serious-ness pointed out particular features, Robin had some cryptic comment for each which annoyed his sister and delighted Emily.

Robin's manner of dress was studiously unconventional. It was the fashion for gentlemen to wear coats and breeches that fit them to such perfection that not a crease could be discerned, but Robin's coat was quite loose fitting and the pantaloons which he wore even in the country draped his limbs with unusual fullness. Instead of a high, intricately tied starched neckcloth, he wore a striped silk neckerchief loosely knotted over his shirt, whose points wilted gracefully with no pretension to being starched. His hair was guinea gold and worn in long, loose, deliberately disordered locks that brushed the collar of his coat.

"Robin disdains all things fashionable," Amanda confided to Emily. "He is a poet, you see." This last was uttered with a curious mixture of reverence and contempt. As if to live up to this image, Robin frequently punctuated his remarks with an applicable couplet, but since Emily recognized most of these as belonging to other well-established poets, she had no notion how much of the excuse for his pose was legitimate and how much pure affectation.

"I knew blue would suit you as it does me," Amanda said when she came to Emily's room before going down to dinner. She was also dressed in blue, but of a richer, periwinkle shade. "I hope you do not mean to spoil the effect of the gown with a fichu. Aunt Caro told me you thought the neckline too revealing."

Emily smiled, turning away from the mirror. "No, I am quite resigned to displaying my bosom in public. The night Aunt Caroline and I went to Mrs. Aderley's card party, I felt certain that one of the ladies present would lose her bodice altogether, but she did not, and it seemed that no one, not even the gentlemen, regarded it."

Amanda dimpled. "Oh, the gentlemen regarded it well enough," she said brazenly, standing in front of the mirror to admire her own swell of white flesh over the delicate lace that rimmed the neckline of her overdress. "But a *gentleman* will not indicate it to a lady in an obvious way. It is all a delightful game. Surely ladies and gentlemen flirt in Philadelphia as well?'' she added naively.

''Occasionally,'' Emily said dryly, and sat down at her dressing table.

Taking her eyes off the mirror with reluctance, Amanda took a chair near to her cousin. ''In the first circles of the *ton*, flirtation has been perfected to an art. When a certain gentleman arrives tonight, you shall see a fine example of it,'' she said archly.

Emily did not immediately respond to this, pretending to be absorbed in deciding between a pair of diamond teardrop earrings and another of rosettes made of sapphires, a part of the jewels she had rescued before the wreck of the *Devon*. Amanda, she had discovered, was particularly fond of discussing the topic of her admirers, and though Emily felt no response of envy, she did find such self-congratulation distasteful and the younger girl's continual arch reference to a ''certain gentleman'' a bit tiresome.

Amanda was not merely an insipid beauty, but it might have been more to the point to say she was clever rather than educated. She had no particular interest in music beyond her limited ability to sing and play the least demanding popular airs and she confessed to Emily without the least self-consciousness that she never read books—even the fashionable ones—because they put her to sleep. Her conversation, when it was not about her social successes, appeared to be limited to the latest fashions in general, and which of these best became her in particular. But Emily thought her less vain and selfish than merely self-absorbed; it simply did not occur to Amanda that others might not find her as interesting as she was to herself.

But for all her successes, Amanda had yet to make the splendid match her family had hoped for, and Lady Caroline had confided to Emily that there had been no superfluity of offers for her beautiful niece's hand. Young men of large fortune and impeccable breeding might write poems to Amanda's eyes and lips, but so far she had received only two offers of marriage from gentlemen who had not passed Lady Laelard's exacting standards for an acceptable match for her only daughter.

Emily felt little curiosity about Amanda's latest admirer, who in Amanda's estimation was a paragon. Amanda teasingly refused to divulge his name and Emily, supposing that knowing it would mean nothing to her in any case, had no objection to playing her cousin's game.

"Oh, you look delightful," Amanda said as she assisted Emily to put on a sapphire collar to match the earrings she had chosen. "I quite adore sapphires," she added, touching the modest pearls that she wore. "They make my eyes bluer than ever. They make yours seem less gray as well, I think. You quite cast me in the shade tonight, cousin, but I shall not mind. There is only one gentleman on whom you must not cast your eyes, but I concede the rest to you with resignation."

Emily smiled, for they both knew it was rather unlikely that Amanda's court would abandon her in favor of Emily. But Emily didn't covet Amanda's admirers; she felt quite confident of her own appearance. It was only in comparison with the exquisite Amanda that she felt she suffered, and that did not trouble her in the least.

It was the evening before Christmas Eve and all of the guests who would be spending the holidays with the Laelards had already arrived. There were three or four other young people in the party: Lord and Lady Amerand, a young married couple who were friends of Robin's, Mr. Stanton-Gore, the son of one of Lady Laelard's particular friends, and a young man presented as Sir Edmund Timmons, whom Emily at first thought might be Amanda's "certain gentleman." Sir Edmund, whose breeding was too fine to permit him to sit in Amanda's pocket, was not quite able to keep his gaze from straying in Amanda's direction whenever she was in the room, but the beauty, though she was not averse to flirting with the baronet, gave no indication of a greater interest and Emily supposed that Amanda's favorite admirer was not among the house guests at Whistley.

Mr. Cooke was not indifferent to Amanda's loveliness, but having been given the hint by Mr. Stanton-Gore, with whom he found himself in instant rapport, that there was no fortune to sweeten the creampot, he paid her only compulsory court and reserved most of his attention for Emily. When Emily and Amanda entered the saloon where the company was gathered to await the announcement of dinner, he reserved his sweetest smile for Emily and attached himself at once to her side.

Emily was sitting with Mr. Cooke on a small sofa across from the door, listening with polite interest to an anecdote he was relating when Galen, in the company of an elegant older woman, came into the room. Emily felt as if her heart had stopped, so still did she become. It was only another moment before he saw her and their eyes met and held, and then he looked away without any acknowledgment that he had seen her.

Emily let out her breath slowly and realized that Mr. Cooke was staring at her expectantly. She supposed he had asked her some question, but she had no idea at all what response was required of her. In the moment she had seen Galen come into the room, everything and everyone else had faded from her consciousness. She had no choice but to beg his pardon and admit that she had not been attending.

"There is no need to beg my pardon," Mr. Cooke said handsomely. "I saw Captain DeVere come into the room. I don't wonder that you were startled; so was I. I wonder what he can be doing here?"

"He has succeeded to his brother's title and is Lord DeVere now. I believe his family's home is near to here," Emily replied, astonished at the calm control of her voice, so at odds with the turmoil inside of her. She had known, of course, that Landsend was only twenty miles or so from Whistley, but Galen himself had told her that he was unacquainted with the Laelards.

She was in for a further surprise. In spite of herself, she followed his progress into the room with her eyes. He parted from the older woman almost at once and went directly to speak to Amanda. Amanda blushed rosily as he bowed over her hand and her delight was clear to be read in her features. It was impossible, but it seemed to be true; Galen was Amanda's "certain gentleman." Emily suddenly felt hollow inside.

"No doubt Lady Laelard imagined she was doing you a service to invite him," Mr. Cooke said, misinterpreting Emily's stricken look. "She could not know, of course, how unpleasant he often was during the voyage."

Emily felt an unexpected urge to defend Galen, but realized the folly of doing so. "Since he is a neighbor, that is likely the reason he is invited," she replied, still with unimpaired outward calm. Mr. Cooke would not know that there was no previous acquaintance. But Emily, as she at last forced her eyes away from the painful observation of Amanda flirting outrageously with Galen, who obviously responded in kind, could not but wonder what quirk of fate had caused Galen to become acquainted with the Laelards.

Emily quite deliberately turned the topic and in a short while dinner was at last announced. Emily almost sighed aloud with relief. Unless she was unlucky enough to be placed near to Galen at dinner, she would be able to avoid a meeting with him until she had time to compose herself, for she doubted her ability to maintain her surface serenity if she had to speak with him at once.

But Emily's assumption that she had escaped an immediate meeting proved hasty. While the others in the room were forming into pairs to go in to the dining room, Amanda and Galen turned away from the door and met Emily and Jeremy Cooke as they approached it. Galen's eyes flicked over them and Emily felt his cool assessing glance like the lash of a whip.

Galen's features were composed in an expression of polite interest, but in his eyes which seemed to glitter a little in the candlelight, Emily read disdain. She knew well his opinion of Mr. Cooke, but he had no right to condemn her choice of partner when he had clearly made his own choice for Emily's beautiful but vapid cousin.

"I have a delightful surprise for you, Cousin Emily, as you can see," Amanda said. "There is a *certain* gentleman who is quite anxious to renew his acquaintance with you."

Emily didn't need the hint to know that Galen was the admirer Amanda had spoken of, and Emily could now understand her cousin's teasing refusal to divulge his name. Galen bowed over Emily's hand and as he raised his eyes to hers his expression was unreadable, but not, though he smiled, very pleasant.

Emily's response was no more than a polite murmur. Her heart had begun to hammer in her breast and she felt a weakness in her knees. She had made up her mind to forget him, but if Galen was paying his addresses to Amanda it would be impossible to avoid him or put him out of her mind and every encounter would be a painful reminder that she had been fool enough to fall in love with a man who did not love her. There would be no easy escape for Emily until she could return to Philadelphia, which she meant to do as soon as she decently could.

Galen's greeting to Mr. Cooke was cool but Amanda's prattle kept constraint from developing. "I vow, cousin, I am quite envious," she said to Emily with a pretty pout. "You and Lord DeVere have shared such an exciting adventure. Nothing of interest ever happens to me."

"A shipwreck is not an adventure to be envied, Miss

Laelard," Mr. Cooke said with some severity. "It was not exciting, but quite frightening to experience."

"Yes. And some kept their heads better than others," Galen said caustically.

Mr. Cooke could not mistake his meaning and his color began to rise, but this time it was Emily who found her voice and prevented any awkwardness by saying dismissively, "Oh, Lord DeVere has had many interesting adventures at sea. With a bit of persuasion, he is fond enough of relating them."

Something flashed in Galen's eyes which might have been annoyance or even appreciation. When he spoke his tone was too even to judge. "A sailor is always fond of his yarns, Miss Hampton. The wreck of the *Devon* was a harrowing experience, which always makes for an interesting story, as you have no doubt discovered."

"No," Emily said, conjuring up a brief, cool smile. "As Mr. Cooke has said, it was an unpleasant occurrence from start to finish and I do not really care to recall it." She turned and smiled at Mr. Cooke. "We shall keep everyone waiting for us if we do not go in to dinner." There was no opposition to this sentiment and all four repaired at once to the dining room.

Galen was placed beside Amanda at dinner, and Mr. Cooke was seated to Emily's right. On her left was the older woman who had entered the saloon on Galen's arm and who now introduced herself to Emily as Eugenia Haverton. "I am DeVere's sister, made respectable again by a sudden change in the family fortune," she said cryptically, and seeing that Emily did not comprehend her remark added with a dry laugh, "Did Galen never mention me? I suppose I must not be surprised. We are not a family to be proud of. I wonder if I should be flattered or insulted by his reticence. He has spoken to me of you on more than one occasion, Miss Hampton."

Emily felt her cheeks grow warm. She was uncertain how to understand this. She already felt some anxiety for what Galen might have said to the Laelards which could contradict her own version of the shipwreck and aftermath. Now to add to this there was a greater fear that with his sister Galen might have been even more forthcoming. It had seemed a simple, sensible thing to agree with her Aunt Caroline to practice the deception of omission, but now she feared the web of deceit they had woven would yet entrap her. "I have found Lord DeVere to be a reticent man," she replied cautiously.

"Yes," agreed Eugenia Haverton after a thoughtful moment. "He is inclined to keep his counsel. But he is not taciturn, or at least I have never found him so."

"Lord DeVere was mostly occupied with his responsibilities during the crossing and had little time for idle conversation," Emily responded a bit repressively, hoping to bring an end to this dangerous topic.

"However have you managed to survive such an ordeal as a shipwreck and still maintain your composure?" Eugenia said with a faint shudder. "I should be having hysterical fits until next Michaelmas at the least."

"There are times when recalling the experience still makes me feel quite vaporish," Emily acknowledged with a wry smile. It was rather how she was feeling at the moment. As dinner progressed, though, Eugenia's friendliness gradually put Emily at her ease.

Though she knew it would be wisest not to express any particular interest in Galen to his sister, her curiosity got the better of her. A chance remark made by Eugenia gave Emily an opening to inquire into Galen's life before he had gone to sea, for it was a thing he had never discussed with her, not even in the intimacy they shared on the small deserted island.

Lady Haverton had none of her brother's reserve, and Emily learned more of Galen through his past in those few minutes than she had in all the months that she had known him—including the interesting fact that even as a small boy, maintaining his honor had had some importance to him. Mr. Cooke, disliking her neglect, finally claimed Emily's attention, bringing Eugenia's reminiscences to an end.

Eugenia's interest in Emily was no more than polite, but as Emily turned away, Eugenia glanced across the table and saw that her brother was staring intently at Emily. As Galen became aware of his sister's interest he looked away without haste to make a remark to Amanda. But Eugenia's curiosity was engaged.

Galen had actually said very little about the voyage and the shipwreck. His references to Emily had only been in passing and Eugenia had not found in these any cause for interest until now. Emily's faint blush when told that Galen had spoken of her and her curiosity about Galen's past took on greater significance in light of the look Eugenia had surprised in her brother's eyes.

Lord Haverton had already returned to London, claiming that he would rather be obliged to dodge a few tradesmen than put up with the carpenters and plasterers who he declared had taken over Landsend. Eugenia agreed with her lord and remained only because she thought it would be too shabby to leave her brother alone for his first Christmas back at Landsend, but she intended to join her spouse in town on Boxing Day. After subtle surveillance of Galen and Emily during the remainder of dinner, however, Eugenia Haverton, whose celebrated repute stemmed more from ennui than innate lubricity, thought that perhaps she would not be too quick to leave Sussex after all.

When dinner was ended and the ladies had withdrawn, most of the men chose to linger over their port, but Galen, in the company of Robin Laelard, with whom he seemed to be on very good terms, entered the withdrawing room in less than a quarter hour. Emily was speaking with Lady Amerand but looked up at their entrance. Involuntarily her eyes went to Amanda, whose expression was a mixture of delight and smug self-congratulation. It was obvious Amanda thought herself the lure that had taken Galen away from the congenial company of the gentlemen, and Emily acknowledged unhappily that Amanda was probably right. As Amanda left her mother's side to greet Galen with a triumphant little laugh, Emily forced herself to give all her attention to the recipe for dried herbs that Lady Amerand was discussing.

Galen had better control than Emily and did not so much as glance at her as he came into the room, though he was quite aware of where she sat. He smiled at Amanda's chatter with practiced ease, but with a faint air of abstraction which Amanda, sensitive to the least competition for attention, noted. "I vow you are not attending to me, my lord," she said with an adorable pout, tapping him lightly on the arm with the edge of her fan. "I asked you quite plainly how long Lady Haverton remains at Landsend and you gave me not the smallest hint that you knew I had spoken."

Galen gave her a half-smile that was designed to tantalize. "Actually, I was trying to decide if your eyes were the color of the sky on a glorious summer day or that of a deep still pool," he replied without a blush.

It was exactly what Amanda wished to hear and she came perilously close to simpering. "I only wish I might believe your flattery, Lord DeVere," she said with her lovely, bell-like laugh. "But perhaps I should not, for you quite turn my head."

"No young woman of sense ever allows herself to become puffed up with conceit for a few pretty words, my dear," said Lady Caroline, coming up to them. "The more practiced the compliment the less it is to be believed." As she spoke her eyes met Galen's and held them in a steady gaze.

She had been even more astounded than Emily when Galen had entered the saloon, for she had not supposed her suggestion that he call at Whistley would be heeded or if it were that it would lead to anything more. Dorothea was a high stickler and given the reputation of the DeVeres and their renowned impecuniousness, it was incredible that DeVere and his sister should be invited to Whistley.

She was equally surprised by Galen's appearance. Gone were the ill-fitting clothes and air of indigence. He was superbly clothed in a black silk evening coat and breeches which unquestionably had been cut by the hand of a master tailor; his linen was dazzlingly white and expertly arranged. She supposed there must be enough revenue even from an impoverished estate like Landsend for him to decently outfit himself, though she wondered that he would choose to waste what little there was in such an extravagant fashion.

This might have puzzled her more if she had not noted his attentions to Amanda. It was not impossible that he was unaware of Amanda's meager dowry, for Dorothea Laelard was at considerable pains for it to be known as little as possible, and it might well be that he had reason to hope the Laelards would not be aware of *his* circumstances. It was hardly a secret in the family that Dorothea was on the catch for a well-heeled and titled husband for Amanda. It would be a rich joke if Galen and Amanda were each pursuing the other in hope of a nonexistent fortune.

But Lady Caroline could not afford the luxury of seeing out the jest. The arrival of Galen DeVere at Whistley while she and Emily were there was not just unfortunate—for Lady Caroline it was dangerous. She had never doubted that she had done the right thing to write to DeVere as if at Emily's behest, and she felt this was confirmed by the alacrity with which he had transferred his regard to Amanda. But Emily knew nothing of Galen's letter to her or her aunt's reply to him, and Lady Caroline had more sense than to leave it to chance that Galen would not make mention of it to Emily in some way.

She linked her arm in Galen's and said, "Even we older ladies have some claim to hearing pretty speeches. Will you take a turn with me about the room, my lord?

The tea tray will be brought in soon and I know
Amanda will want to help her mother.''

From Amanda's mulish expression it was quite
obvious that she disliked being shorn of her prize and
dismissed. She managed a light comment, but in such a
tight voice that her feelings were transparent. She then
turned to Sir Edmund, who had just come in to the
room, and bestowed on him a degree of attention that
he had not enjoyed since Galen's arrival in the neighborhood.

Lady Caroline sighed to see her niece expose herself in
such a manner, but it suited her purpose well enough for
Galen to observe Amanda in a less than attractive light.

The size of Lady Laelard's withdrawing room was
equal to accommodating so many guests and Galen and
Lady Caroline walked the perimeter of it exchanging
polite nothings until they reached the farthest end near
large windows. That portion of the room was too far
removed from the twin hearths that gave warmth to the
room to be other than chill, and they were quite un-
disturbed.

It was Lady Caroline who brought them to a halt, but
Galen had been expecting it and he turned to look down
at her with guarded expectation. She gave him a chilly
smile and said with a hint of condescension, ''I thought
I might do you the favor of putting a little word in your
ear. I hope you do not mind a little plain speaking, my
lord, for I dislike roundaboutation. You may be
thinking that because Emily is an heiress, that her
cousin is equally well dowered, but that is not the case.
Laelard is no pauper, but nearly all that he has is tied
into the entail and will go to Robin. With William and
Edward to provide for as well, Amanda cannot hope for
more than two or three thousand which, I think you will
agree, amounts to virtually no dowry at all.''

Galen listened to this speech a bit nonplussed. It was
not what he had expected. Emily knew that he was a rich
man and so did the Laelards; it did not occur to him that
Lady Caroline suspected him of being a fortune hunter

and was warning him off. If anything, he supposed she must be warning him of the Laelards' designs on his fortune, though he could not imagine why she would choose to do so. In any case, it was redundant.

From almost the first meeting, he had noted the faint glint of calculation in Lady Laelard's eyes which was echoed in Amanda's as she had preened at his flattery. By the time he had dined at Whistley on the Friday after his arrival in Sussex, the whole neighborhood from Hastings to Rye was well aware that Galen had returned home a bona fide nabob and was already drawing up plans for the restoration of Landsend. There is a world of difference between an impoverished barony and a rich one, and Galen's half-serious wish, expressed to Jacob Farley, that he could restore the honor of the family name by his own exemplary behavior was actually accomplished with no greater effort demanded of him than the openhanded expenditure of his money.

Dorothea Laelard was never behindhand with the news, and Galen found himself treated with every condescension. To his surprise—and later his sister's astonishment—when Lady Laelard learned that the Havertons were also at Landsend, she quite insisted that Galen bring them to call as soon as he could, for she declared it was really a great shame that they should live at no great distance and not be well known to each other.

Eugenia had snorted in an unladylike fashion at this intelligence. "The only reason La Laelard has never cut me dead in town is because we do not move in the same circles and seldom meet."

But Galen, after his hopes were dashed by the cold, brutally to-the-point letter he received from Lady Caroline on behalf of Emily, persuaded her to go with him to Whistley. He was in need of diversion and it gave him a perverse satisfaction to pay court to Emily's beautiful cousin, who gave him every encouragement. An acquaintance of no greater duration than a sennight convinced him that Amanda Laelard had no heart which he might unintentionally break, and he amused himself—reprehensibly, perhaps—by watching her and her family employ every art and artifice to bring him up to scratch.

"I suppose I must thank you for the warning, Lady Caroline, but it is unnecessary," he said at length. "My attentions toward Miss Laelard are not serious."

Lady Caroline raised disbelieving brows. "Yet you must be aware that Amanda is apt to have her head turned a little if those attentions are of a particular nature."

Galen regarded her quizzically and gave her a wry smile. Lady Caroline appeared to be the family guardian of her nieces' virtue and prospects; a sort of matchmaker in reverse. "I don't think I endanger Miss Laelard's delicate sensibilities, do you?" he asked candidly.

"She hasn't any," Lady Caroline said, equally forthright, not at all surprised that Galen had taken Amanda's measure. "But Emily does."

His smile grew, but it was not an expression of amusement. "The wounding there, I think, was not done by me."

"Emily had no wish to give you pain, Lord DeVere," Lady Caroline replied quickly, for she felt a little uncomfortable at his words, which were spoken unemotionally but in a tone which she thought was designed to hide, not deny feeling. "She felt it best that you understand unequivocally exactly how she felt. Surely you would not wish it to be any other way."

"She left me in do doubt at all of her feelings," he said levelly. "Or rather, you did. Miss Hampton did not choose to extend me the courtesy of replying to me in her own hand."

"Emily is a kind-hearted girl," Lady Caroline said carefully, wondering if she detected in his voice any hint of suspicion. "She found it difficult to write as plainly as she wished and was grateful when I offered to write on her behalf."

On the whole, Galen was a straightforward man, and though not naive or overly trustful, he was not quick to suspect deviousness in others. He had never doubted that the sentiments expressed in the letter had come from Emily and the unexpected sharpness of the pain he had felt when he had read it had prevented him from examining it too closely. In fact, he had read it through only once before putting it into the fire.

He was not a man to wear his heart on his sleeve and the pain he bore—dulled to an ache until he had walked into the room and seen Emily—he bore within himself. Not even Eugenia had guessed that there was anything amiss with him. This was certainly not the first disillusionment he had known in his thirty-two years, and experience had taught him that brooding availed him nothing.

"Quite," he said in a voice totally devoid of inflection. He would have moved on, but Lady Caroline again detained him.

"Emily had hoped to be spared a further meeting with you, my lord," she said. "She was quite surprised and upset to discover that you were among the company tonight."

"An unfounded hope which hints at naiveté," he replied with a faint, humorless upturning of his lips. "She knew my home was near to Whistley."

"She had hoped you would have sufficient delicacy to avoid a meeting," Lady Caroline said waspishly.

Galen's smile became more genuine. "Another unfounded hope, I fear."

Lady Caroline had to bite back a smile. There was something about Galen DeVere that she could not help liking despite the fact that she regarded him as a gazetted fortune hunter. "Emily is in a taking that you mean to confront her about her reply to you," she said. "I know you would not wish to be so ungentlemanly as to put her to the blush."

"Since once again you are Miss Hampton's emissary, you may assure her that I will make no mention of it. I would not for the world wish to cause her a moment's discomfort," he added so blandly that Lady Caroline detected no irony.

Lady Caroline inclined her head in acknowledgment of his promise. "Very nicely spoken, DeVere. I was certain you would feel just as you ought, but there are times when emotions get the better of one, do you not agree?"

"I find I do, Lady Caroline," he said with more truth than she guessed. Disengaging her from his arm, he excused himself perhaps a bit curtly, and went to speak to Lord Amerand.

Galen was too self-contained for emotions to overcome his iron control, but seeing Emily again—and in the company of Mr. Cooke—affected him far more than he had supposed it would. He meant to keep his promise to Lady Caroline that he would not discomfit Emily by any reference to the letter he had sent to her or her reply, but he could not just dismiss her from his mind as he wished to do.

Gradually, all of the gentlemen joined the ladies, though few of them took tea. Small groups formed for conversation and a few tables were set out in a quieter corner of the room for whist and piquet. Galen declined an invitation to make a fourth at whist and also managed to escape Amanda's attempts to include him in a game of lottery which she herself had suggested, thinking to put him at her side. Instead, despite the fact that he knew it would be best to avoid her, he slowly and indirectly made his way over to the pianoforte where Emily sat, idly playing the melody of a rather melancholy popular air.

"I had no notion that you played," he said, coming up behind her.

He startled her a little, for her thoughts had been far removed from the present. She glanced up at him, hoping her confusion did not show in her face. "No. How should you?" she said, returning her gaze to the music in front of her to avoid meeting his eyes.

"Is that a reproach?"

"Oh, I think it is rather late for reproaches," she said as lightly as she could.

He stood silent and staring for so long that she stopped playing and looked up at him again. He held her eyes with his for only a moment, but it was sufficient for color to tint her cheeks and her heart to begin to hammer within her again though she furiously willed it to be still. His expression was inscrutable, but it sent a little frisson through her. "I expect you are right," he said in a quiet but incisive tone, and turned away from her in as abrupt a fashion as he had approached her.

It took several minutes for Emily to regain her composure, but by the time Mr. Cooke had come up to her to beg her to play his favorite song, she was able to smile at him in her usual way. She had a very real headache to plead an escape, but she would not allow herself to be intimidated by Galen or her own wayward emotions.

On the return drive to Landsend, Eugenia made several unexceptional remarks concerning the evening they had just passed, but Galen was unresponsive, replying with monosyllables and making conversation impossible. Partly due to annoyance with him, partly to amuse herself, Eugenia said with exaggerated casualness, "Emily Hampton is quite a handsome young woman. I wonder you did not say so when you mentioned her to me."

"Did I mention her to you?" he said with no outward sign of interest. "I don't recall."

"Do you agree?"

"With what?"

"That Miss Hampton is a very attractive woman," Eugenia said patiently.

"I suppose."

"Next you will tell me you have not noticed. I am not deceived, dear brother."

"Of course not. There is nothing for you to be deceived about."

A coolness that was clearly a warning had come into his voice and Eugenia congratulated herself silently; she knew she had scored a hit. She shrugged with credible unconcern. "Perhaps not. Not on your side, that is. I suppose you may have inspired a passion in Miss Hampton of which you are quite unaware."

Galen was leaning against the side of the carriage looking out of the window onto the moonlit landscape, but he sat up and turned his attention to his sister at last. "What the devil are you about, Eugenia?"

"I? Not the least thing in the world, dearest. I was merely commenting on an observation I made tonight."

"What observation?" he asked sharply.

"The girl is in love with you."

To her astonishment, he began to laugh. "You have the wrong horse, Eugenia. You could not be more mistaken."

"I am not mistaken," she replied quietly. "You did not see the way that she looked at you when you were flirting with that spoiled child Amanda Laelard. I did."

He laughed again, this time with more sincere amusement. "I did not recall that you had a penchant for romantic fantasy, my dear. It is no more than that, I promise you."

There was a finality in his tone which Eugenia respected, allowing the subject to drop. But the reason she did so was because she felt she had received the answer she sought.

Galen dismissed his sister's words, but he could not so easily dismiss his thoughts. The early morning hours were well advanced before he found sleep.

11

Lady Laelard was hoping for snow, for the Whistley stables boasted a large sleigh which would have provided entertainment for a number of her guests during the day, but the weather was uncooperative. It had been bitter cold for several days but dry, and though Christmas Eve dawned with lowering clouds, the air warmed considerably and by breakfast a faint mist had come in off the ocean which coated the landscape a dull gray rather than an inviting white.

Few of the visitors to Whistley made haste to leave the comfort and warmth of their bedchambers and many had breakfast brought to them on trays in their rooms. When Lady Caroline entered the breakfast room it was quite empty save for her sister and her eldest nephew and the latter excused himself as soon as he had drunk the last of his coffee.

Lady Caroline particularly wished to speak with her sister and decided to take advantage of the opportunity before Dorothea—with her usual store of restless energy—was enmeshed in her duties as hostess. There was never any quarrel between the sisters, but neither was there a great deal of affection. They seldom sought each other out for private conversation and were indifferent correspondents unless talking or writing was to some purpose.

There was a brief exchange concerning each other's activities since their last meeting in town in October and some discussion of Emily, her outfitting, and modest presentation to the *ton*. "I must say that Emily is a pretty behaved sort of girl," acknowledged Dorothea Laelard. "I own I feared what to expect. She does not possess the town polish one might like to see, but growing up in such an outlandish place it might have been much worse. Nor is she an antidote, which I also suspected. Imagine to be an heiress of the first order and still be on the shelf! What can Regina have been about not to have found a proper husband for her?"

Lady Caroline helped herself to a piece of toast from the rack, smiling at her sister's pomposity. "What a shocking snob you are, Dora. From what Emily has told me, I would say that Philadelphia society is quite as refined as our own. And, she has told me as well that she is unmarried because she has yet to meet a gentleman who touched her heart."

"Her heart?" Lady Laelard's expression was one of extreme distaste. "I suppose we might have expected Regina to fill her head with such nonsense," she said, unknowingly echoing the sentiments of Lucille Armitage. "Well, I hope *I* know my duty toward my sister's daughter."

"Are you thinking of Robin?" Lady Caroline asked baldly. The viscountess cast her sister a baleful glance and in a quelling tone begged her to pass the marmalade pot at her elbow. But Lady Caroline was impervious to her sister's snubs. "Confess, Dora. You know you invited Emily here in the hope that all that lovely money would find its way into the Laelard coffers."

"I invited Emily to come to us because she is my dead sister's only child and it was my clear duty to do so," Lady Laelard replied with icy hauteur, and then spoiled the effect by adding a bit pettishly, "I do not think it can be counted a fault to want the best for my children. It is not only Robin I must think of but the others as well."

"I only mention it, Dora," Lady Caroline said between bites of succulent ham. "I hope they may take to one another. Emily is a charming young woman, but not, I think, a very happy one, and Robin has a sunny disposition and would make her a good husband—if he could be persuaded against dressing like a peddler.''

"God knows I have tried," Lady Laelard said in long-suffering accents, "but his father will add no weight to my strictures and I am not heeded. Why do you think the girl is unhappy?"

Lady Caroline ignored this and said, "I was quite surprised to see DeVere and Lady Haverton present last night. I thought you did not meet, despite the nearness of Landsend.''

The diversion was successful. "Why should it surprise you? According to DeVere, you asked him to call here on his way to Landsend. I should thank you for that, I suppose. He seems quite taken with Amanda, which is only natural, she is so lovely. If only she will not treat him to one of her tantrums before he comes up to scratch as she did with Benderly, which quite put him off. I am certain he was on the point of speaking to Laelard before that.''

Lady Caroline was so astonished that she heard nothing beyond her sister's expression of gratitude. "Thank me? Oh, Dora, can it be that you are deceived? I own it occurred to me last night that something like that might be the case. It is a very good thing that I had a word with DeVere, though it would have been better than a play when you discovered the truth of each other's circumstances.''

Lady Laelard regarded her sister in freak puzzlement. "Deceived! What is there to be deceived about? He is DeVere, is he not? And even if he were not, I am not certain it would matter. I have always wanted a title for Amanda, but a husband who is as rich as Croesus would more than make up for a title.''

Lady Caroline put down her cup and said a bit smugly, "It is no more than a pose; he is a fortune hunter. If you had set eyes on him when he first arrived in England you would have no doubt of it. He was dressed like a valet." Lady Laelard's response to this was to go into peals of laughter, which disconcerted her younger sister, who was expecting dismay. "It is amusing, I suppose," she continued, "for he doubtless thinks that Amanda is an heiress like Emily. I doubt there will be any further interest from him, though. I informed last night how matters stood with Amanda's expectations."

Lady Laelard's mirth came to an abrupt halt. "You did not! Caro, if you have ruined everything, I shall never forgive you," she said, outraged. "I have told you, he *is* as rich as Croecus. He has in his employ half the county putting Landsend to rights and I had it from Eugenia Haverton herself that he has fifty thousand a year at the least of it."

Lady Caroline regarded her in puzzled disbelief. "How could he? Everyone knows that none of the DeVeres have a penny to bless themselves with and he was the captain on the ship that brought Emily here from Philadelphia."

"He owned the ship," her sister replied caustically. "That ship and many others like it. A whole fleet of merchantmen, in fact. He has sold everything and come back to take up his proper position in the world."

Lady Caroline opened her mouth to deny her belief in what her sister was saying, but her certainty was shaken; Dora seemed so positive. With a sort of creeping horror she realized that if it were true, her interference had caused a wretched mull. If Emily had cared for Galen and he for her and there was not the least impediment to their attachment, then she had done both the greatest disservice imaginable.

"I—I don't think he is very serious in his intentions toward Amanda," Lady Caroline said numbly.

"No, I don't think so either," Lady Laelard agreed without concern. "But Amanda is a very fetching child and I mean to see to it that she is cast in his way at every opportunity, and always on her best behavior when he is at hand."

Lady Caroline knew it would have no effect; Galen's affections were already engaged—or at least they had been. Memories of the hopeful phrases in his letter which she had responded to so unfeelingly nearly made her wince with shame. "I would not hope too much, Dora," she counseled. "I have reason to think he is already attached."

The viscountess's face fell almost comically. "To whom?" she demanded.

"Someone he met before he arrived in England," Lady Caroline equivocated.

Lady Laelard waved a dismissive hand. "Then it does not signify. He has told me himself that he is here to stay. If he is heartsore for some chit he left behind in America, it is all to the good—a man looks to a new love to comfort him for an old one he has lost." Sir Edmund came into the room and she turned pointedly away from her sister.

Sir Edmund paid no more than cursory heed to Lady Caroline, but if he had he would have noted that her eyes were anguished. Her own mother had often said to her that her managing ways, however good-intentioned, would one day prove her folly, and she believed the prophesy was finally realized. Her conscience urged her to go to Emily and Galen and admit to them her crime, but she shrank from the very idea of it. The prospect of such humiliation was unbearable and they would hate her, which was no more than she deserved. And Dora would hate her, and so would Amanda, for being the cause of their falsely raised hopes. If her family cast her off and the truth became generally known, the whole world would hold her in contempt.

A smaller unheeded voice informed her that she was just being cowardly, but she truly could not imagine herself facing up to her transgression. She left the breakfast room and went to her own bedchamber, where she spent a wretched morning until she was finally able to convince herself that perhaps what she had done was for the best, after all. There *was* some misunderstanding between them—Galen had referred to it in his letter—and perhaps that was an indication that they were not well-suited in any case. By the time Lady Caroline joined the rest of the company for luncheon, she was in a fair way to regaining her usual equable humor and her last thought on the subject before she dismissed it from her mind was that if she had acted wrongly a kindly fate would surely take the matter in hand and put it to right without further interference from her.

At about the time that Lady Caroline had entered the breakfast room, Emily, who had taken toast and tea in her room, let herself out of a small side door just off the main receiving saloon which Amanda had pointed out to her on the previous morning. It was not a day to invite a walk about the grounds, but Emily felt too restless to remain alone in her room and too out of sorts to wish for company.

She was used to frequent long walks, which she had enjoyed almost daily in Philadelphia, and after her long voyage and the restrictions placed on young women for walking about in London, she longed for the exercise and thought it would be just the thing to restore her spirits in spite of the drear of the day.

She feared, though, that her aunts would object to her going out alone and into the damp, so she left the house as unobtrusively as possible, avoiding the formal gardens which were overlooked by the main wing of the house and going out into the park beyond the kitchen garden. Heedless of time and distance, she continued to the end of the park, crossed fields, and eventually came to a small wood which she entered without hesitation.

Most of her thoughts, not surprisingly, centered on Galen and their meeting the previous night. She was not certain what she had expected; he was as icily controlled and distant as ever and that he spoke to her at all was probably due to the odd appearance it would make if he did not when the Laelards knew them to be acquainted.

For Emily, all her happy anticipation for the coming holiday was spoiled. She had looked forward to the diversion of her first English Christmas, but now the fear that Galen would be a frequent visitor to Whistley made her regard the entertainments of the holiday season with dread. She chided herself for a fool for the heartache she felt, but she felt it nevertheless.

She was so lost in her thoughts she scarcely noted her surroundings, and was surprised to find herself at the end of the wood and brought to a standstill at the edge of a road. The mist had thickened to a light fog and the warm merino pelisse she wore felt slightly damp, allowing the chill to reach inside. She glanced about her and realized she had no idea where she might be, nor even a definite conviction of how she might retrace her steps to return to the house. The fog curling among the trees gave all her surroundings a gray sameness that increased her uncertainty.

She felt a moment of anxiety which she dismissed at once. The road, very likely, was the one that had taken them to Whistley and she need only follow it to return to the house. She climbed onto the road and with resignation began to walk along the side of it. It was likely a longer way back and she would probably be gone long enough to be missed and would be in for a scold on her return. She knew, without her Aunt Caroline to tell her, that it was not at all the thing for her to walk along the road unescorted, leaving herself open to the ogling stares of any passersby.

As if to punctuate this thought, Emily heard, in the enhanced stillness brought on by the fog, the distant approach of a light carriage. She thought for a moment of hiding in the bushes until it had passed but dismissed the idea as beneath her dignity. She continued on, her gaze fixed ahead, determined not to be put out of countenance.

The sound of the carriage came nearer and as it drew abreast of her, came to a halt. She had expected it to slow, but not to stop; she was even more surprised when she heard her name spoken. At the sound of Galen's voice, she felt as if her heart had stopped beating. She wanted to continue on, ignoring him, but she halted and looked up.

His countenance was unsmiling. "What the devil are you doing here?"

"Walking," she replied coolly.

"So I perceive. In a common road and unescorted. I'm on my way to Whistley. Get in and I'll take you there."

"Then I should be driving with you—unescorted," she replied in the same tone. "I thank you, my lord, but I shall continue to walk."

She began walking again and after a few seconds, the curricle began to move forward. He walked his pair beside her for several minutes before her rising anger got the better of her and she stopped and turned to him again. "Please do not let me keep you from your appointment at Whistley. Miss Laelard no doubt waits eagerly for your call." As soon as she said these words she wished them unsaid. Not for the world did she want him to know that his attentions to Amanda concerned her in any way.

"So, no doubt, does Mr. Cooke wait for you," he said with a faint mocking smile. "Let me take you up and we shall save them both unnecessary anxiety." She started to turn away and he leaned forward and held out his hand to her, his smile growing. "Even if you don't like me, have pity on my horses, Emily. They shall come down with chilblains standing about on a day like this."

Emily wanted to turn her back on him, but there was something in his smile she could not resist. She allowed him to hand her into the carriage. In a vehicle designed for two, it was impossible to keep any great distance from him, but Emily did her best by hugging the side of the carriage. "Be careful you don't fall out," he advised dryly, and gave his horses the office to start.

She kept her eyes on the road ahead, her features set

and unresponsive. They were silent for a minute or two and then he said, "I was not aware that Mr. Cooke was acquainted with the Laelards."

"Nor was I aware that you were acquainted with them," she said frostily. "I believe you told me in Philadelphia that you were not."

"I suppose you'd hoped you had seen the last of me."

"I thought it likely."

"And have found yourself disappointed," he said with spurious concern. "I told you I have come home to repair my family name and fortune. I am making a beginning by being agreeable to the neighborhood."

She darted a quick, contemptuous glance at him. "You told me Landsend is twenty miles from Whistley, which does not precisely put my uncle's estate in your neighborhood."

"No," he agreed, "but it is no great distance either."

"Particularly if one has sufficient purpose for becoming a regular caller," she said acidly as once again her feelings got the better of her sense.

He said nothing for a minute or so while he digested this remark. He had thought of little other than Eugenia's comments on Emily since she had made them the previous night, weighing these against the things Emily had said to him on board the *Bethia* and then her merciless reply to his attempt to make amends for his part in the discord that had come between them. It seemed impossible to reconcile the two and he had all but dismissed Eugenia's observations as imagination. But the comments Emily had just made showed that she was not indifferent to his attentions to Amanda, which surely must mean she was not indifferent to him. He said leadingly, "The Laelards have extended every consideration of hospitality to me. Miss Laelard in particular has been all kindness."

Emily turned involuntarily toward him at this provocative remark. "Amanda is kind to all the rich and handsome young men who make up her court," she retorted. She saw it once that it was a mistake. His eyes were appraising and she realized too late that she had risen to a deliberately set bait.

"In fact, she is quite unashamedly hanging out for a rich husband," he said with a short laugh. "Well, that, of course, explains her interest in me. I thank you for the compliment."

His attention was forced back to the road as they approached the gates of Whistley. Emily continued to regard his profile. "Even if I found myself destitute I should maintain a certain standard," she retorted.

He smiled. "Yet," he said, letting his eyes rest on her again for a moment, "for one night, at least, you did not hold me in such distaste, I think. You can pretend to your family and the world that we are no more than acquaintances, Emily, but not to me."

"Why should it matter to you?" she said, the faintest tremor in her voice. "Since you are set on fixing your interests with Amanda, you will hardly wish to recall that you once made love to her cousin."

"You are wrong. *I* have no wish to forget it."

"I do," Emily said with conviction, "and if you are the gentleman you claim to be, you will allow me to do so." With relief she saw the house come into view.

He was silent until they turned into the wide sweep in front of the house. "Must we always come to cuffs when we meet, Emily?" he said quietly.

"It is not my wish that we do so," she replied, but her tone was not conciliatory.

"Nor mine." He pulled up his pair in front of the portico.

In spite of how it would look, Emily was about to jump down from the carriage without even waiting for the assistance of the footman who had come out of the house as the carriage drew to a halt. But Galen's hand on her arm arrested her.

"Not all that we experienced together was unhappy, Emily," he said. "But let us put it all behind us, the good as well as the bad, and make a new beginning."

She met his eyes for a long moment. He had spoken similar words to her once before but it had availed them nothing. "I suppose it would be more comfortable since it is likely we shall continue to meet," she conceded, though she wished with all her heart that she might not see him again at all.

His smile was swift in acknowledgment of her grudging acquiescence. "Then let us begin at once." He waved the footman to the wheeler's head and leapt down himself to hand Emily to the ground.

Christmas Eve at Whistley was observed *en famille*, but on Christmas Day there were many callers and once again Lady Haverton and Lord DeVere dined with the Laelards. On Boxing Day there was a ball at another neighboring estate and for the next several days—until New Year's Day, in fact, when a heavy snow fell closing all roads for two days—there seemed to Emily to be one party after the other and at each of these Emily found herself cast into Galen's company whether she willed it or not. But this did not cause her the distress she had imagined it would.

Whenever Galen was present, Amanda still coquetted and cast out every lure in her repertoire and Galen responded with the sort of teasing flattery that so intrigued the spoiled beauty, who was never as sure of him as she wished to be. But despite Amanda's continuous efforts to attach him to her side, he refused to live in her pocket and spent much of the time, as he had told Emily he meant to do, reestablishing himself with his neighbors. This did not prove difficult, and not only because he had returned home with a fortune in hand. Galen exerted himself to be amiable to all, as willing to please as he was to be pleased.

He did not often single Emily out for his attentions as he did Amanda, but when he did he took pains to make himself pleasant to her and when they spoke, his obvious interest in her raised both her pulse rate and her hopes—momentarily at least. She knew better now than to read more into his words or manner than was plainly discernible.

If Amanda noted Galen's increased attentions toward Emily, Emily saw no sign of it. Amanda continued to treat her as a confident despite a lack of encouragement from Emily. The truth, Emily supposed, was that Amanda considered Emily as no more than passably pretty and did not regard her as a rival.

Of all the young gentlemen Emily met at the various parties and balls, only Mr. Cooke and, of course, Amanda's brother Robin seemed completely impervious to Amanda's exceptional loveliness and both of these attached themselves mostly to Emily, though for very different reasons. Robin, frank as always, confided to Emily his mother's purpose in inviting her to England and Whistley, which plainly disconcerted his cousin.

"Nothing to fear, Em," he said hastily, misreading the dismay in her expression. "I quite think of you as another sister. I suppose I shall have to settle down and set up my nursery one day—the title and all that—but I have no more intention of being led by Mama's match-making schemes than I daresay you do. Besides, now that Amanda appears to have attached DeVere, Mama is not likely to be as keen on bullying me to marry a fortune."

Robin had not the least idea how his ingenuous speech affected Emily. In the first place, she was mortified to discover that her Aunt Dorothea had acted not from a sense of affection or responsibility toward Emily's mother but out of pure self-interest. In the second place, it was like a knife thrust in her heart to hear how certain the Laelards appeared to think it was that Galen would eventually offer marriage to Amanda.

Robin's words were a confirmation of her own dark imaginings and when her Aunt Caroline, who was never content long away from town, decided to return to London in mid-January and invited Emily to come with her to complete her wardrobe, Emily accepted her invitation with alacrity. Lady Laelard at first seemed inclined to object to Emily's leaving Whistley so soon after her arrival, but after observing Emily and Lord DeVere deep in conversation on several occasions when they met in company, she withdrew her protests on the grounds that she would soon be reunited with her niece when she and Amanda came to town to open Laelard House for the Season early in March.

Mr. Cooke was also agreeable to an early departure from Whistley and within a sennight they were on the road bound for London. Emily again found herself cast into the hustle of shopping and fittings, which she rather enjoyed, particularly as more of the dresses which had been commissioned before she had gone to Whistley began to arrive and she had the pleasure of watching her wardrobe fill with lovely, fashionable dresses and gowns. Though the company in London was thin, enough people disdained the rustic delights of their large, drafty manor houses for their far cozier London residences to make up a number of select entertainments, and most evenings found Emily and her aunt from home.

Toward Mr. Cooke, Emily maintained a light, friendly manner that effectively kept him at arm's length. On occasion there was something in his expression or tone of voice that told her that he still entertained ambitions of attaching her more deeply, but he received no encouragement for his hopes and Emily gently, but firmly set him at an even greater distance whenever she feared he was about to overstep the bounds of friendship or propriety.

Emily supposed, in fact, that she would never marry at all. She had found the great love that her parents had urged her to seek, but for her there would be no storybook ending.

It was little more than a sennight before Robin Laelard also made the journey to London, pushed to do so by his mother, who, he admitted candidly to his aunt and cousin, had still not abandoned the hope that he might yet attach Emily and her fortune. This did not really surprise Emily; what did surprise her was that he came to town in company with Lady Haverton and Galen, who had made the journey, Robin informed them, to attend to legal business in the City.

Eugenia Haverton made no secret of her preference for town. Galen claimed not to share this taste and had told Emily only a day or so before Lady Caroline had made the decision to return to London that he expected to be settled in Sussex for some time. But according to Robin, the day after Emily and her aunt had left Whistley, he had sent instructions ahead to his man of business to hire a suitable house in town, which indicated that his stay there was likely to be protracted.

Emily hardly knew whether she was sorry or glad to see Galen again so soon. And it seemed that she did see him everywhere. There was not a card party or rout at which they did not meet Lord DeVere. For a man who had put himself out of society for so many years, he reclaimed his position with remarkable ease.

Emily could not deny that she enjoyed his company, but this gave her as much concern as it did pleasure. They were in a fair way to becoming very good friends, but she could not quite convince herself that on his side it was anything more, and she would not allow herself the painful luxury of harboring false hopes again. It did not occur to her that his pursuit was as cautious as her response, and for much the same reason.

It was about a fortnight after Galen's arrival in town that Emily and her aunt attended a musicale at the home of Lady Compton, a cousin of Lord Laelard. It was a small party, almost a family party, and Emily had not looked to see Galen present, but just before she entered the principal drawing room where the recital was to take place she saw him speaking with one of the other guests.

"I did not think we would see Lord DeVere tonight," she said to Robin beside her, impulsively speaking her thought aloud.

"Had dinner with DeVere last night at Watier's," Robin replied. "He mentioned that he had a taste for music of this sort so I asked him along. Knew my cousin wouldn't mind.''

They entered the drawing room, which was already well filled with guests, and found seats to one side near the back of the room. ''I suppose most hostesses are happy to include another personable young man in their numbers,'' Emily said with apparent indifference.

''Particularly the matchmaking mamas on the catch for a tidy fortune,'' Robin said with a bark of cynical laughter. ''Once the Season begins, DeVere will never know a moment of peace to call his own.''

Galen came up to them in time to overhear this remark. ''And you, Robin,'' he said as he sat beside him, ''being such a sad rattle, will doubtless tell each of your acquaintances of my circumstances—in confidence, of course—and thus seal my fate.''

Robin responded with a smile. ''I should be able to dine out on the strength of our acquaintance for the better part of the Season, I should think. Unless, of course, you tip me the double and find yourself leg-shackled before then.''

''Thus rendering us both uninteresting,'' Galen said dryly.

''I think that's Johnny Talbert over there with those fellows by the pianoforte,'' Robin said, his attention diverted. ''He has a pair of grays I've been trying to persuade him to sell me. You won't mind if I have a word with him, will you, Em? I daresay DeVere will bear you company for a bit.''

Emily had no objection. She gave Galen a welcoming smile that evoked a response in him that was far greater than she would have imagined.

Musically, the evening was something of a disappointment. The soprano was quite celebrated and indeed her voice was lovely and her technique flawless, but her choice of program was predictable and uninteresting. The applause afterward was sincere, but more polite than enthusiastic.

When the recital was ended, the musicians hired to

accompany the soprano continued to play for the entertainment of the guests who gathered into the usual small groups, with a number adjourning into an adjacent saloon to play at cards. Emily was rejoined by her aunt and cousin and did not speak with Galen again until after supper.

She and her aunt and several other people stood talking in the supper room after most of the other guests had returned to the drawing and card rooms, while the servants cleared up the remains of supper behind them. Galen came to stand beside Emily and soon they were engaged in a lively discussion of their own, oblivious of the others, who one by one drifted out of the supper room. Even Lady Caroline returned to the drawing room without her niece, and the servants, their work swiftly and efficiently completed, withdrew, leaving Emily and Galen entirely alone in the room.

It was Emily who first became aware that they were alone, or rather, if Galen noticed this, he said nothing. The realization made her feel oddly uncomfortable. "Oh dear," she said with small, uneasy laugh. "I think we have been abandoned by our friends, my lord. We had better return to the drawing room before we find ourselves the latest *on-dit*."

"It may already be too late," he said with an answering half-smile.

The smile faded from her eyes and her expression became alarmed. "What do you mean?"

"Last night at Watier's a friend gave me the hint that there has been some speculation about my intentions toward you."

Emily looked at him with disbelief. "How could there be? We have been friends, nothing more. Unless . . ." Her eyes were dark with suspicion.

"Unless I opened my budget about Porto Santo?" he said sardonically. "Do you really believe that, Emily?"

Emily did not believe it, but neither did she wish to believe that she had in any way given away her true

feelings for Galen to anyone, particularly to him.
"No," she said, and added with an edge in her voice,
"And I wish you will not call me by my given name. It is
that sort of thing that gives the gossips grist for their
mills."

"I don't except when we are alone. But it is how I
think of you."

His voice was caressing and his words reminded
Emily that they were quite alone. "My aunt will be
missing me," she said shortly, and was about to turn
away from him.

"Are you afraid to be alone with me, Emily?" he
asked quietly.

Emily might have ignored him and continued out of
the room, but she turned back to him and said with a
frankness that surprised even her, "Perhaps. A little, I
think."

"Why?"

"You know why," she replied almost angrily. He put
his hand on her arm and a tiny shiver of anticipation
went through her.

"But you say we are no more than friends," he said,
gently quizzing her. "What is there to fear?"

Emily found it difficult to look into his eyes, for the
expression she found there was familiar to her and too
seductive to be risked. She looked away from him. "I
beg you will not distress me, my lord, by speaking of
anything that ocurred between us before we arrived in
England. I have done my best to put it from my mind."

He ran a finger along the curve of her cheek. "Am I
really so little to your taste, Emily?" he said, his voice
silky and seductive. "Did I so misread you in Porto
Santo?"

There was a dangerous aura of intimacy growing
between them. Emily dearly wished to succumb to it but
was terrified of doing so and once again giving him the
power to pierce her vulnerable heart. "I admit I have
felt attracted to you," she said, her voice as steady as

she could make it with his touch still warm on her cheek. "But we could never be more than friends. We are too ill-suited to be more."

"Rubbish," he said succinctly, and drew her into his arms. Her mind protested, but her body had a will of its own. With remarkable intellectual detachment, she told herself she was a fool even as she entwined her arms about his neck and tilted back her head for his kiss. He demonstrated his mastery of that art and in a very short time rendered them both breathless.

He held her head in both his hands and looked at her as if he would devour her. "Emily, if you knew how much I have wanted you." He kissed her again as if he could not help doing so. "I don't know how I have contrived to keep my hands off you."

"It is as well that you have," she responded with a shaky laugh. "The gossips have had enough to say as it is."

Emily's response to his lovemaking was all that he had hoped for. He was feeling ebullient and perhaps a little triumphant. "If you had agreed to marry me in Funchal, you need never have feared the gossips. I think you had better do so now before your ruin is complete in a much more tangible way."

Emily felt the warmth inside of her fade. It still was not love that he offered her. If she married him she would have the protection of his name and her desire and his would at last be satisfied, but Emily knew that for her it was not enough.

If she married him without love, in time familiarity would dampen his ardor and then there would be nothing for her but emptiness and the daily humiliation of loving a man who did not love her. Choking back a sob she said as coolly as she could, "You flatter yourself, my lord, as you have before. I am not in the least danger from ruin in any quarter."

Galen was taken aback by her abrupt withdrawal, she had kissed him with a passion to match his own and he had been sure that all misunderstanding between them was resolved. He silently cursed himself. It had always been so easy to say the right words when his heart had not been engaged. "Emily, I didn't . . ."

But she would not allow him to say anything more. "I would not have permitted a return of easier terms between us, my lord, if I had supposed that you would misconstrue my feelings. I have told you that I have no wish to marry you and my mind is not changed. I beg you will never mention the subject again, for I shall always find it objectionable."

Emily's voice was emotionless and carried far more conviction than she would have guessed. Galen felt as if she had slapped him. "You are right, Miss Hampton," he said levelly. "The fault is mine. You have made your wishes in this matter clear—repeatedly." He essayed her a brief, formal bow. "Shall I return you to your aunt?"

She did not raise her eyes to his and did not see his expression, but the ice in his voice told her what it must be. "No. I shall manage on my own," she said with equal formality. He turned and left her, but she did not follow. She sat down on the nearest chair because her legs were trembling dangerously beneath her. She felt devastated, as if she had suffered some great loss. But how could she have lost his love when it had never been hers?

It was several minutes before she had herself sufficiently in hand to return to the company. Galen appeared to have left and for this she could only be grateful. Though no one, not even Lady Caroline, was aware that there was the least thing troubling Emily, the pretense took every ounce of her energy and concentration and so enervated her that instead of spending a wretched night recalling all that they had said to each other, she fell into a merciful sleep almost as soon as she got into bed.

12

When she awoke, the unhappy memory flooded over her, but she would not allow herself to dwell upon it. She kept herself as busy as she could throughout the morning and banished any thought of Galen the moment it occurred. Her remarkable discipline was the result of her resolve to speak to Robin that very day about arranging passage for her to return to Philadelphia as soon as possible. It was the only solution, she believed, that would give her peace, and having come to this conclusion, she felt at least a surface composure which she supposed would carry her through whatever might occur in the days remaining to her until her departure.

But this spurious serenity did not outlast the day. It was late afternoon and Emily sat with her aunt in her sitting room sorting silks for a chair cover the older woman was embroidering when Amanda entered into the room without ceremony, surprising both Emily and her aunt into staring at her.

"Have I a smudge on my nose?" Amanda demanded caustically as she bent to place a dutiful kiss on her aunt's cheek. "Anyone would think a ghost had come into the room." She pulled off embroidered ivory kid gloves which matched her cambric walking dress and settled herself in the nearest comfortable chair.

"My dear, you must forgive us," Lady Caroline said with a belated welcoming smile. "But we did not think to look for you or your mama for nearly a month yet. I hope nothing is amiss a Whistley?"

"No, of course not," Amanda said crossly, and then her tone and expression changed to one of uncomplicated delight. "Mama has decided to come up to town early this year. I am to have new gowns."

"I can scarcely credit it," Lady Caroline said frankly as she put her work aside. "Dora has always said that she counts it a stupid excess to waste money living in town while the company is still so thin."

"Mama also says that there are times when it is more wasteful to be pinchpenny," Amanda countered. "My gowns are to be made by Madame Celeste, and she is always so busy once the Season starts. One might go to a less fashionable modiste, but Mama says that it is false economy to be dressed in any but the latest kick of fashion."

"I have always preferred the work of Mademoiselle Henriette," Lady Caroline murmured, but her niece paid her not the least heed.

"At least one of my new gowns is to be celestial blue to match my eyes," Amanda proclaimed warmly, well launched on her favorite topic. "Lord DeVere feels that blue becomes me best of all colors," she added with a trace of smugness, "though he said he thinks me lovely in them all."

Lady Caroline had no doubt that her sister's sudden decision to come to town had little to do with new ball gowns. In the last few days before Lady Caroline and Emily had left Whistley, Dorothea had been quite as smug as her daughter in her growing assurance that it would require only a bit of skillful manipulation to bring Lord DeVere up to scratch. It must have dealt a considerable blow to her schemes when Galen had left Sussex so unexpectedly.

Whether or not Lady Laelard suspected the truth, Lady Caroline had no difficulty guessing why Galen had come to London so hard on their heels. She was not of a temperament to endlessly berate herself for her high-handed meddling, but she felt a profound relief to see Galen and Emily on easy terms. It suited Lady Caroline very well not only because it helped to expiate any lingering guilt for her interference, but also because it would doubtless wipe the silly, smug smile off her sister's face when she learned that Emily had quite cut Amanda out.

But if Lady Caroline had been privileged to know Emily's thoughts, she would not have felt so hopeful. Galen had seldom spoken of Amanda since he had come to town and Emily, enjoying his exclusive attention, had been all too willing to forget her beautiful cousin. After her quarrel with Galen the night before, though, Emily supposed she had removed any lingering impediment from Amanda's successful pursuit of Galen.

Amanda continued to chatter, blithely unaware of the inattentiveness of her aunt and cousin, until she at last talked herself to a standstill. "Oh, I very nearly forgot," she said suddenly as she began to draw on her gloves again, "Mama has sent me here to fetch you, Cousin Emily."

"To fetch me?" Emily said surprised.

"To Laelard House. You have only been visiting Aunt Caro. It was always intended that you would live with us at Laelard House for the Season and now that we are in town, there is no longer any need for you to stay here."

"But I like it here," Emily said and then realized that her words, meant as a compliment to Lady Caroline, reflected in an opposite way on the offered hospitality of the Laelards. "That is, if Aunt Caroline does not object, I am very well fixed here."

"Oh, but you must come, Cousin," Amanda said with a gamin smile. "Mama wishes us to become bosom bows above all things, and this way we shall be always together. You do wish that, too, Cousin, do you not?"

There was no polite answer to this but an affirmative, however insincerely meant. Emily half hoped that her Aunt Caroline would press her to remain, but Lady Caroline, thinking it might be no bad thing for Emily to be at hand so that Amanda could not steal a march on her, merely said, "Whatever you wish to do, my love," leaving Emily with little choice but to accept the invitation.

That very evening saw Emily established at Laelard House in Berkeley Square, which was far larger than Lady Caroline's house but not nearly as comfortable. Emily could well understand why her Aunt Dorothea preferred not to open the house before April. To make it at all habitable in the chill of early February it was necessary to have fires in most of the ground floor rooms and in a number of those on the first floor, as well as in each occupied bedroom and sitting room. And even with several of the Whistley staff brought from Sussex, Lady Laelard was obliged to take on another footman and maid for the Season to keep up the large mansion.

Emily's practical American sense told her it was silly to keep a great barn of a house that one could not afford to maintain properly, but a diffident and more tactful comment to this effect in response to her aunt's constant spate of complaints met with such a solid rebuff that Emily wished she had not spoken. Within a few days she also wished she had not been so biddable and had remained in Upper Mount Street, for in addition to the cold and various other discomforts of the house, she found daily shopping trips with the voluble and capricious Amanda and her exacting mother wearing and she had not even the luxury of escape from their constant company when they returned home.

Nor was she successful in carrying out her resolve to put into effect immediately her plan to return to America. Robin, she learned the night she went to Laelard House, had left that morning for Horley to attend a prize fight and was expected to remain several days with friends. Emily had not the least idea how to go about making the necessary arrangements herself and the one person who might have told her with ease was the last person she would ask, so she had no choice but to keep her patience in check and await Robin's return.

Galen had begun the habit of calling at Lady Caroline's two or three times a week, but it was not surprising that after his encounter with Emily at Lady Compton's he ceased to do so. He was, in fact, exceedingly bitter, his anger directed as much at himself as it was at Emily. He castigated himself unmercifully for having yet again left himself open to the stinging lash of her rejection.

He still had business to attend to in the City and this kept him well occupied for several days. For his evening entertainments he chose activities where he was not likely to encounter Emily, or for that matter, any female of gentle birth. He was not aware that Lady Laelard and Amanda had come to town or that Emily was now at Laelard House until his sister informed him of these events at the end of the week.

DeVere House had not been a part of the entail and Robert DeVere had sold it almost the moment he had come into his inheritance, but Galen, like Emily, preferred a trim town house to a great mansion and the house his agent had rented for him was small by the standards of the *ton* but elegant and well-appointed. Eugenia Haverton, whose London residence was not nearly as snug, thoroughly approved. "You ought to make the owner an offer for it, Gale," she said as she walked about the drawing room casually inspecting its accouterments. "Though I suppose you would rather wait to see what your wife may like before making such a commitment."

"That is not a thing that need concern me any time in the near future," he said with just a hint of dryness in his tone.

"No?" Eugenia said with apparent surprise as she turned over a porcelain shepherdess on a table near the pair of tall windows overlooking the street. "I made sure I would be wishing you happy soon."

"Why? Not because of the nonsense you spoke of

before Christmas, I trust?'' He sat in a comfortable wing chair before the fire watching his sister's languid progress.

"Partly," she said, putting down the shepherdess and moving on to a particularly pleasing landscape on the near wall. "And it was not nonsense. When you decided all of a sudden to come up to town so soon after Miss Hampton left Sussex, I thought perhaps you had discovered the truth of it for yourself."

"You could not have been more mistaken."

At these words, Eugenia turned to her brother, but what she saw in his face kept her from asking the questions that formed in her mind. Instead, she shrugged and went back to her examination of the painting. "It isn't Turner, of course, but it is rather good, don't you think?" She went back to her chair across from Galen's, where a glass of sherry awaited her on a nearby table. Picking up the glass and looking at Galen over the rim of it, she said without emphasis, "Well, if it is not to be Miss Hampton, perhaps you will offer for her cousin Miss Laelard. Dorothea Laelard will play every card in her hand to carry the trick. If you just go along quietly to Berkeley Square and pop the question, you will save yourself a deal of trouble making counterplays."

Galen's smile held no amusement. "She is welcome to play every card in the deck when they come to town, much good it will do her. Miss Laelard is undeniably lovely, but I am not a green youth to be dazzled by a beauty."

"How cruel you were to raise false hopes during the holidays, then," Eugenia admonished.

"I never gave the smallest indication that my regard for Miss Laelard surpassed admiration of her fine eyes. It won't do, though, for me to continue in that vein. A country flirtation is one thing, singling her out in town quite another."

"When I visited Lady Caroline yesterday she hinted that the Laelards live in hourly expectation of your call.

They have been in town since Tuesday," Eugenia informed him, then added in an offhanded way, "Miss Hampton is to live at Laelard House now as well. But if you do not care for either Miss Hampton or her cousin, then I suppose there is no reason for you to call, except once perhaps out of courtesy. We did spend rather a lot of time at Whistley to escape the carpenters."

"No doubt I shall call in time," Galen responded indifferently, and turned the subject. But despite his words to his sister, Monday found him in the principal saloon at Laelard House and he accepted an invitation to dine later in the week.

To the intense gratification of Amanda and her fond mother, Galen called as regularly at Laelard House in the weeks that followed as he had before at Upper Mount Street, and whenever they met at any social event, he was certain to join their party for at least a portion of the evening. Since Emily was now under the chaperonage of her Aunt Dorothea, it was inevitable that she and Galen were frequently in each other's company, but whenever he was near, Galen found her as quiet and passive as he had at their first meeting when he had so misjudged her.

Eugenia, never one to mince words, asked her brother frankly what he was about when he had himself declared that he had no serious intentions toward Amanda, and he found that he could not give her a direct answer. He thought he had made up his mind that there was nothing but unhappiness to be gained from continued pursuit of Emily, but to his chagrin, he discovered that he could not resist the opportunity to see Emily that his spurious flirtation with Amanda gave to him.

He also noted that while Emily had her own share of admirers, many of whom could be acquitted of hanging out for a fortune, she smiled on all equally, favoring only perhaps Jeremy Cooke, who had the advantage of longer acquaintance. Mr. Cooke, through the amiable sponsorship of Robin Laelard, was invited everywhere and sure to attach himself to Emily's side whenever he was permitted to do so. Galen found that he could not view Mr. Cooke laughing and conversing with ease with Emily without experiencing a strong desire to draw his cork.

By early March, Lady Laelard was dropping broad hints about the expected arrival of Lord Laelard within a fortnight or so. Galen realized with wry self-amusement that if he didn't have a care, he might just find himself maneuvered into parson's mousetrap by the determined Laelards. The solution, of course, was for him to withdraw from the beauty's court of admirers, and he made plans to return to Sussex only to find himself putting these off not once, but several times. He called himself every kind of fool, but the bittersweet lure of seeing Emily again still held power over him.

He did call less frequently at Laelard House—Emily did not always join her aunt and cousin when there were callers, in any case. But one late morning in mid-March when he did call he found Amanda and Emily hemming linens with fine stitches in the brightly sunlit morning room. Or rather, Emily was so engaged; Amanda was absorbed in *La Belle Assemblee*, her sewing put aside and quite forgotten. Robin Laelard was also present. He sat on the wide sill of the window overlooking the garden, perusing the latest copy of *The Sporting News*.

Amanda jumped up at once to greet Galen and declared that he was just the remedy she needed for her mopes. "Do you drive your curricle today, my lord?" she asked. "You know that you promised to take me up in it on the first fine day. Madame Celeste sent word that my gowns are not yet ready for fitting and I have been hoping all morning for something to divert me. I enjoy driving in the park above all things and I need only fetch my bonnet, pelisse, and the new muff Papa gave me for Christmas to be ready."

She looked up at him, her lovely smile confident of his response. Galen had no recollection at all of such a promise to Amanda but he said gallantly, "It would be an honor to take you out in my curricle, Miss Laelard, but though the sun shines, it is a raw day and I doubt you would enjoy it as much as you think. In any case, I fear that it would be an uncomfortable squeeze for three and it would be shockingly ill-bred of me not to include Miss Hampton in my invitation."

"Oh, Emily doesn't care for such things," Amanda said quickly, with a dismissive glance cast at her cousin.

Galen's eyes met Emily's and though his expression was grave, she could not mistake his amusement. "Is that so, Miss Hampton?"

"Apparently," Emily said flatly as she lowered her gaze again for her sewing.

"There, you see?" Amanda said, clapping her hands together like a happy child. "You need not be concerned for Emily and I assure you I find cold weather invigorating."

Galen laughed and abandoned all opposition. "Then by all means, Miss Laelard, fetch your new muff for me to admire." Casting Galen an alluring smile, Amanda did as she was bid.

Robin asked Galen what horses he fancied at an upcoming racing meet and Emily turned a little away from them as if concentrating on her stitches, but she was conscious of every word Galen spoke, as she always was. The last few weeks had been the most difficult of her life save for those she had borne after the deaths of her beloved parents. It was all very well to reason that she and Galen were ill-suited and that she would be a fool to marry him unless she could believe that he loved her, yet every encounter with him since Amanda's arrival in town left her with the agony of regret.

She knew she had no right to object to Galen's flirtation with her cousin. It was an impossible situation: she could not be happy with him and she was wretched without him. She wished with all her heart that she had never decided to come to England or met Galen DeVere. Her principal hope for peace lay in her early return to Philadelphia, but Robin, though he was willing to be of assistance, had had little success in his attempts to obtain passage for her on a ship that could take her to America. The difficulty was that the war between the United States and England had escalated to the point that trade between the two countries had virtually ceased. In time of war, passage on a military vessel was impossible and Robin's search to discover any other ship bound for any North American port had thus far failed completely.

Emily did not look up when Amanda returned to the room, and was equally ignored by her lovely cousin, who had all the audience she wished for in Galen.

When they had gone, Robin left his perch on the windowsill and came to sit across from Emily. "Do you know," he said conversationally, "I begin to think that little baggage is going to pull this one off. The betting at Watier's is now at three to two in Amanda's favor. I've got a pony on her myself, though I hold the bet in a friend's name. It would effect the odds if it was known how I placed my blunt."

Emily rounded on him so fervidly for this that he stared at her appalled. "Amanda is your sister," Emily said fiercely as the slender control she kept on her emotions gave way. "Betting on such a matter would be vulgar at any time, but in this case it is nothing short of disgustingly ill-bred."

Robin was far more astounded by her fury than offended by it. "No need to comb my hair about it. The way DeVere has been running tame about here for the past month, it seemed to me a sure thing. You know my pockets are always to let; I'd be a fool to pass up such easy money."

"You are a fool in any case," she retorted, and to her astonishment and dismay she began to cry.

Robin immediately rose and drew her out of her chair into his comforting embrace. In spite of the shortness of their acquaintance, a strong brotherly and sisterly regard had grown between them and Robin was the closest thing to a confidant that Emily possessed. He waited patiently for the strongest gusts of tears to subside. "Now what the devil is this all about?" he demanded gently. "I've noticed you haven't been in spirits much lately, but you're no poor honey."

Emily was a little ashamed of her outburst. "There are those who would not agree with you," she said with a watery laugh, thinking that it had certainly been Galen's first judgment of her.

"It's DeVere, isn't it?" Robin said astutely. "I thought for a time when we first came to town that you might cut out my vain little sister, but Amanda appears to have carried the day. Do you mind so much? Is that why you have been dispirited and wish to go back to Philadelphia?"

"I cannot stay here and watch them be married," Emily said, her voice catching again.

"DeVere is the fool," Robin said staunchly. "Dangling after Amanda and not knowing you are worth a dozen of her."

Bristling at Robin's well meant but lowering comparison of her worth to Amanda's beauty, Emily made a further admission. "He asked me to marry him."

"Good God!" Robin took a step back and held Emily at arm's length by the shoulders. "Then what the devil is toward, Emily?"

Now that her confession was begun, Emily could not resist the luxury of unburdening herself. Robin listened to her with great sympathy, but his response when she had finished showed a notable lack of this virtue. "Of all the bird-witted things to do. You would be well served if DeVere does make Amanda an offer, though I don't think *he* deserves such a fate."

Emily felt crushed by his response. Her tears had long since dried but she still held her handkerchief and she moved away from him to push it into her work basket. "I should not have told you," she said, her voice still catching only a little. "I hope you will respect my confidence and repeat what I have told you no one. I beg you will forget that I have ever spoken.''

''Stuff and nonsense,'' he replied rudely. ''If you had had the sense to tell me this weeks ago, I would have given you the advice I am about to give you now and saved you weeks of needless unhappiness. If you love him, don't let Amanda have him.''

''He doesn't love me,'' Emily said almost angrily as she turned to him again.

''Then why the devil did he ask you to marry him? He don't need your fortune.''

''I told you: it was because he felt he had compromised me and impugned his honor as well as mine.''

Robin shook his head slowly. ''It won't wash. The first time that might have been his reason, but not the second. When you refused to have him, you absolved him of all responsibility to honor, and there hasn't been the least breath of scandal about either of you in any case. If he asked you to marry him a month ago, he did so because he wanted to marry you and why should he if it isn't because he is in love with you?''

Emily wished desperately to be assured by her cousin's logic. ''He-he wants me, I think, but he has never made any mention of love,'' she said quietly.

Robin sighed. ''Speaking words of love doesn't come easily to all men, Emily.'' His grin was a little self-mocking. ''We aren't all poets, you know. If he's offering you marriage instead of a slip on the shoulder, that's something you know.''

Emily was not familiar with the cant phrase her cousin used, but deduced that he meant that Galen had not tried to seduce her without any intention of marrying her. ''He cares too much for his own honor for that,'' she said acidly.

Robin gave a sharp crack of knowing laughter. ''Don't you believe it, my girl. Honor's all very well, but few of us are virtuous enough to heed it too closely if we want a thing badly enough. If you want DeVere and he wants you, why the devil are you so determined to disbelieve it?''

Emily had no sensible answer for this so she said impatiently, ''Oh, go away Robin, you make my head ache.'' She sat down again beside the work table and leaned her forehead against her hand.

Robin meant well and was wounded by her attack. ''If you like,'' he said coolly, and withdrew, leaving Emily unhappily aware that she had alienated her one ally.

Emily knew it was her inability to answer Robin's very sensible question that had made her lash out at him. She did not understand it herself; she only knew it was abhorrent to her to marry without love on both sides and against the beliefs with which she had been raised. She was not so easily persuaded that love and lust were the same or that Galen was too inarticulate to speak his feelings. She had found him only too adept at saying what he thought when it suited him.

She sat lost in her thoughts for far longer than she supposed and was only brought out of her melancholy reverie by the sounds of arrival in the hall. She began to put things in her workbasket with more haste than care but in a quicker time than she would have thought possible, Emily heard voices and Amanda's high laughter outside the door. Emily shoved the few remaining pieces of linen into the workbasket willy-nilly, prepared to leave the room as soon as they entered, but when the door opened, only Galen came into the room.

His expression mirrored her own of surprise tinged with a bit of dismay. ''You are still here, Emily,'' he said as if to himself.

''Yes,'' she replied without looking at him, and picked up her workbasket. ''But I was about to go up to my room. If you will excuse me, my lord.''

''Please stay, Emily.''

Emily looked up at him. He was smiling faintly in the way that he had. His eyes, though, were quite serious.

"You mustn't call me that," she reminded him. "Amanda will doubtless be with us in a moment."

His smile grew and finally touched his eyes. "Not for several moments, I should think. She has gone to change her dress for luncheon."

So he was not blind to Amanda's vanities. Emily forced herself to smile and say lightly, "'Then she will be all of half an hour at the least. It is rude, I know, to leave you to amuse yourself, but I'm afraid I shall have to. I—I need to change as well," she added for an excuse, though she had had no intention of doing so.

"You look quite lovely as you are," he said softly.

Emily let out her breath and looked away from him, shaking her head slightly. "Don't start paying me compliments, Galen, please. Save them for Amanda. She craves them more than I do."

"Then don't tell bouncers," he advised. "You don't need to change your dress; it is just a polite excuse to escape me."

"I have no wish to escape you," she said, raising her chin.

"Then why are you trying to find passage back to Philadelphia?" Emily caught her breath at his words, and he continued, feeling some satisfaction that he had evoked a reaction in her. "Laelard asked me if I could help him find a ship to take you there."

"It has nothing to do with you," she said quickly. Too quickly. "Robin had no right to say anything to you."

He crossed the room until he stood beside her. "Why not?" he asked reasonably. "I have been a sailor for much of my life. I would know far better than he how to go about it. Laelard will never manage it for you."

"You do him an injustice. Robin is very resourceful."

"I have no doubt of it. But anyone hoping to find passage to North America in these times is facing an unlikely success."

"But it is not impossible," she countered.

"No. Not impossible," he conceded. "If one knows the right people to seek out, has sufficient funds to grease an army of palms, and does not mind making a circuitous route that could take as long as six months for the crossing. Money is not an object with you, and you might be willing to endure a long crossing, but I doubt you can manage the first."

"I suppose you could?" she said witheringly.

"Yes. I suppose I could."

She put her workbasket back on the table. "Will you help me?" she asked impulsively, though she had sworn to herself that she would not seek his help for any reason.

"Why do you wish to go back to Philadelphia now?" he asked instead of answering her. "I thought you meant to stay until September at the least."

"I find I miss my home more than I supposed I would," she replied, feeling it was the best answer she could give him without betraying the truth.

He held her eyes with his and she felt the now familiar, forbidden sensations come over her. Would it ever be possible for her to be with him without wanting him? She didn't think so; there was nothing else for her to do but put as much distance between them as possible. Even now, in spite of all that had passed between them, she wanted him to take her in his arms and to feel his hard body pressed against hers.

Perhaps her thoughts were mirrored in her eyes for he took a step nearer to her and cupped her chin with his hand. "Is that the real reason?" he asked softly, his face tantalizingly close to hers. His other hand traveled slowly up her arm, tracing a delicious trail of warmth on her skin. She shook her head, not in reply to his question, but in denial of her own feelings. He bent his head to kiss her, knowing she would not resist him, but at that moment the door opened and they sprang quickly apart.

Amanda stood framed in the doorway, her expression startled. Surprisingly, it was Emily who found her wits first. She picked up her workbasket again and said, "Lord DeVere was helping me put my things away. Is my aunt returned? I should go to her if she is, for she desired me to assist her with the invitations for her ball on the twenty-fifth."

Amanda smiled her lovely smile, and Emily, knowing how quickly it could dissolve into a frown if Amanda was crossed in any way, felt relief that her cousin apparently did not realize what manner of scene she had nearly witnessed. "Mama is just come in," Amanda replied with unimpaired good humor. "But I doubt she means to be writing invitations, at least not until after luncheon. She is just gone to her room to take off her hat and pelisse."

Emily murmured something about speaking with her aunt anyway, and at last made her escape. She sent the excuse of a headache to avoid going down luncheon. In spite of his attentions toward Amanda, Emily knew Galen still desired her. That was plain, but it was no comfort. What manner of man was Galen DeVere that he could flirt shamelessly with Amanda one moment and make love to her cousin the next?

13

Emily's room was at the front of the house and she heard Galen leave. Shortly afterward there was a scratching at her door and Amanda came in bearing a tray with cheese and fruit and a glass of rattafia. "Mama desired me to bring this to you, Emily. She says that it doesn't help the headache to starve it."

Emily got up from the chair near the window where she had been sitting for the last hour, an unopened book in her lap. "Please thank your mama for me, Amanda. I am not hungry just now, but if you will leave the tray, I may wish to eat later." Her tone was dismissive. She had no wish to be private with her cousin, enduring her usual self-centered chatter, particularly as today it was likely to be all of her drive with Galen and their conversation during luncheon.

But Amanda was not to be easily routed. She had not actually seen how close Galen and Emily had been to an embrace, but she had realized enough from their demeanor to draw conclusions that were far from her liking. Lady Laelard had already hinted to her daughter that Emily was not to be completely discounted as a rival. If nothing else, Galen's sudden departure from Sussex had proven to Amanda that his attraction to her was not as strong as she had supposed.

She was, however, much better at dissembling her feelings than was Emily. She put the tray on a piecrust table near the window and then, without being invited to do so, climbed onto Emily's bed and drew her legs under her in an attitude of comfortable repose. There was nothing at all in her expression or tone when she spoke to suggest that she had any more purpose than to enjoy an exchange of confidences with her cousin.

Since they had come to town and Amanda was reunited with her friends, she had seldom made any further effort to seek out her cousin's company in the way that she had at Whistley. Feeling that there was little common ground on which they could meet, Emily also did nothing to further their friendship, though she had the even stronger motive of not wishing to be made a confident of all the private moments that passed between Galen and Amanda.

Emily bit back an exclamation of annoyance. "Amanda," she said mildly but firmly, "I don't wish to be rude to you, but I am not feeling at all well today and I was just about to lie down on my bed when you came in."

Amanda shrugged. "Lie down if you wish, I shan't mind."

"I meant that I wished to sleep," Emily said less gently.

"Oh, but you cannot," Amanda exclaimed. "I have something I must tell you. Though I know I should not tell anyone yet, I feel as if shall burst if I do not."

Amanda was clearly very excited and her eyes seemed to shine with her delight, though it might have been no more than a trick of the sunlight that slanted across the bed where she sat.

Emily had a sudden sense of foreboding, but she knew she would listen to Amanda's news—whatever it might be. She sat obediently next to her cousin on the bed.

"You must wish me happy, Emily. I am to be married."

Emily was very glad to be sitting, even the bed beneath her seemed to sway a little. "Married? To whom?" she heard herself ask, though her mouth felt so suddenly dry that she wondered how she had managed to speak.

Amanda laughed. "To DeVere, of course. But you must tell no one, Emily. Promise me at once."

Emily felt as if her heart had frozen within her. "No, of course I won't say anything," she said mechanically, but then wondered why there should be any need for secrecy. "But why?"

"Because not even Mama or Papa know of it yet," Amanda said, lowering her voice confidentially, though it was purely for effect since they were quite alone and unlikely to be interrupted. "DeVere wished to ride *ventre à terre* to Whistley to speak at once to Papa, of course, but I persuaded him it was absurd to do so when my father will be with us here so soon."

This surprised Emily, for she would have supposed that Amanda would wish to flaunt to the world the excellent match she had made as soon as she could. It was even harder to understand why Amanda would wish her good fortune kept from Lady Laelard. Mother and daughter were clearly bent on the same goal of securing the best possible match for Amanda, but perhaps Galen himself had asked her to say nothing until he had formally applied for her hand. Emily had no difficulty imagining his insisting on observing the proprieties.

What she did not question was the veracity of what Amanda told her. She had herself been expecting and dreading to hear of their betrothal any time this past month, and according to Robin, it was what the whole of the polite world expected as well. Only the blessing of Lord Laelard was now required, and of that there could be no doubt.

"When did he ask you?" she asked, not from idle curiosity but because she wondered if Galen were base enough to make love to her again when he had already secured a promise from Amanda to be his wife.

Amanda looked surprised by the question. "Why today, of course."

"But when today?" Emily persisted, determined to know.

For the first time Amanda did not have a ready answer. There was a perceptible hesitation before she answer. There was a perceptible hesitation before she replied and her expression became guarded. "Actually, it was this morning just after you left us and before Mama came downstairs to join us. Does it matter?"

Emily forced herself to smile, though it was a wan effort. "I should think it would to you. I would never forget the moment the man I loved had asked me to marry him." And she knew that she never would, however unacceptable she had found his proposal.

"Of course I shall not," Amanda said a bit testily. "But you must not expect me to think of every detail when I am so excited."

"I am very happy for you, Amanda," Emily said, the conventional phrase sounding awkward to her ears because she knew it was so insincere.

"I hope you do not dislike it that I am to be betrothed to Lord DeVere, Emily," Amanda said, taking Emily's hands in hers.

"Why should I dislike it?" Emily asked warily.

"You say that you are happy for me, but you look as though you are not," Amanda said with a pretty pout.

Emily withdrew her hands and stood up. "It is my stupid headache, no doubt. I only wish you may be happy with Lord DeVere, Amanda. I—I came to know him fairly well during the crossing. He can be a difficult man at times."

Amanda gave a silvery laugh. "He is never so with me."

Emily's head was pounding in earnest. She would have said or done almost anything to have brought their interview to an end. "No, I suppose he is not," she said. "No doubt you will deal famously together."

Emily walked over to the window, unable to completely hide her agitation. With her back to her cousin, Emily did not see the catlike smile of satisfaction that spread over Amanda's perfect features. All that Emily was aware of was that Amanda at last rose to take her leave. "I suppose I should rest as well for Lady Sefton's rout. Mama says there will be informal dancing for the young people and I never know a moment's rest from the forming of the first set.''

She walked over to Emily and hugged her, not seeming to notice that Emily did not return the embrace. ''Mama has hopes that she can persuade Papa to join us in time for our ball next week, so perhaps we shall have an interesting announcement for our guests. Remember, dear Emily, until then this is our secret.''

Emily nodded, not trusting herself to speak, and felt the sting of tears in her eyes and throat form the moment the door had closed behind Amanda.

Emily did not eat the food on the tray Amanda had brought her, nor did she go down for dinner that evening, and she cried off from attending the Sefton rout party as well. Seeing Galen and Amanda together until the shock of Amanda's disclosure had worn off was more than she could manage in her present state. But the next day found her equally unwilling to go into company and her aunt insisted on calling Dr. Knighton, though Emily assured her it was no more than the migraine.

Dr. Knight, however, seemed to think that Emily might be sickening for the influenza, and though Emily knew it was no such thing, she did not demur for it had the effect of keeping Amanda, who was fearful of infection, away from her, as well as giving her an excuse to remain at home for the next few days without fuss.

But Emily could not be a recluse indefinitely as she had been in Philadelphia. Then she had had the very valid excuse of mourning the loss of her beloved parents, but no one knew that she had been foolish enough to fall in love with Galen DeVere and now mourned the loss of a love which had not even been hers.

A small fear that her continual rejection of him had forced him into Amanda's arms nagged at her and caused her a number of wretched hours, but ultimately she knew that it really didn't matter whether or not that was so. If she could not marry him, what difference did it make whom he married?

He had to have known that he meant to ask Amanda to marry him the morning that she had last spoken with him. Yet he had attempted to make love to her. It disappointed her that having failed to make her his wife, he would attempt to make her his mistress, but she seized on this proof of Robin's assurances that even a man of honor could possess a baser nature, and told herself that she had been very right to refuse to marry him without love. How soon would it have been after their wedding before he would have approached some other woman to mount her as his mistress? Perhaps it might even have been Amanda.

Eventually she had to face Galen again and she did so with a pounding heart and permitted him no opportunities for engaging her in private conversation.

As Galen had predicted, Robin still had no luck arranging passage to America for her, but Emily decided that even if it meant that she had to remain in England for the duration of the war, she would not ask Galen for help again. He was certainly not the only seaman among this island race and she had no doubt that in time she would find someone to help her. Help when it finally did come, was from quite an unexpected quarter.

Emily became more encouraging to Jeremy Cooke, particularly when Galen was near enough to observe them together. She knew he disliked Mr. Cooke, and even if it was not his heart she wounded as he had wounded hers, it gave her a perverse pleasure to let him see on whom her choice had fallen.

Emily was not blind to the danger of this. Cooke's manner toward her became increasingly ardent, forcing her to be quite resourceful in her efforts to avoid an unwanted declaration from him, or worse, another attempt to make love to her. She was successful until

Tuesday of the week of her aunt's ball, which was to be on Friday.

Emily was home alone when Mr. Cooke called and was quite startled when he came unannounced into the saloon where she sat writing a letter to her Aunt Lucy and Uncle Walter, which she was not sure would reach America any sooner than she herself would.

She stood up quickly and nearly tipped the ink standish over. She reached out to right it, but splashed ink onto her letter, quite ruining it.

Looking at the loss of a quarter-hour's work, she said frigidly, "You have startled me, Mr. Cooke. How is it that you are unannounced?"

Jeremy Cooke smiled, unperturbed by this less than warm welcome. "A gold coachwheel did the trick," he admitted. "I have been hoping for a word alone with you, Miss Hampton . . . Emily, for the past sennight. When your aunt's man told me that only you were at home and alone, I could not resist the opportunity to see you privately."

Emily silently cursed her aunt's nipfarthing ways, which caused her to pay her servants as little as they would take. It was no wonder that they could be bribed. "If you know I am alone, *Mr.* Cooke," Emily said with deliberate formality, "then you are aware that it is extremely improper for me to receive you."

He came up to her quickly as if he feared she meant to flee the room. His smile was entreating. "It would not be improper if you will smile upon me, Emily, and make me the happiest of men."

Emily nearly groaned aloud with dismay. "Please, Mr. Cooke do not say . . ."

He possessed himself of one of her hands and spoke over her words. "I must speak, Emily. I can contain my feelings no longer. You cannot be ignorant of the esteem in which I have held you since we first met on board the *Devon*. My ardency then was precipitate and offended you, I know, and I have been at some pains to keep my emotions in control this time, but I fear I cannot."

To Emily's horror, he actually slid to the floor beside her, coming to rest on his knees. She tried to pull her hand away, but he held it fast. "Mr. Cooke, do get up," she said, not bothering to hide her annoyance that he would continue with his proposal when he must see that she did not wish him to do so.

"I know that I daren't hope that you return my affection in the same degree," he said, ignoring both her words and her discouraging tone, "but I give you my word I would spend every waking moment of the remainder of our lives together attempting to make you happy. I would teach you to love me, Emily."

"That isn't possible, Mr. Cooke. Please get up," she repeated coolly, and this time he obeyed. "You do me honor by your sentiments," she continued quite insincerely, "but I regret that I cannot accept your offer or even encourage you to believe that I might later be persuaded to change my mind." She firmly withdrew her hand from his clasp.

He looked astonished. "But of late I have hoped . . . There is someone else?"

The word *yes* was fairly shouted inside her head but she said, "No. There is no one else. I think of you as a friend, Mr. Cooke, and nothing more. Pray do not continue to press me for you will only distress me."

"I see," he said after a full minute of silence broken only by the unnaturally loud ticking of the mantle clock.

His expression seemed a bit dazed and for the first time Emily wondered if he *had* come to care for her. She had always assumed him to be a fortune hunter and had received his declaration in that light. "I am sorry if I have wounded you, Mr. Cooke," she said more kindly. "But it is best if you understand how I feel. It would be very unjust in me to allow you to hope." Again he regarded her in silence and Emily began to feel uncomfortable. "If you will excuse me," she said at last. She held out her hand to him, but he was looking at her intently and did not even seem to see it.

His behavior unnerved her. The writing desk was behind her and he in front of her, blocking her way. She felt a sudden wave of panic and wanted to run from the room, but she would not let herself be intimidated. She made herself say calmly, "I think you had better leave, Mr. Cooke."

He did not move. His voice was quite matter-of-fact when he spoke. "Would you be gracious enough to entertain my suit if you knew you were not likely to receive any other offers?"

His voice had an odd, undiscernible quality that Emily found unnerving. "If you do not leave at once I shall call for the servants," she said, praying inwardly that he would not force a scene.

"If I leave without your promise to marry me, Emily, there will never be anyone else who will have you," he said with quiet menace. "Even your aunt may turn you out."

Emily wanted to ignore his threat, but could not. "What do you mean?"

"I mean the fabricated account you have given to the world of the wreck of the *Devon*. You could not have supposed that *I* would forget that you and DeVere were separated from the rest of us and had not yet found your way to Funchal by the time that the rest of us resumed our interrupted journey."

"No. How could you forget?" she said frigidly. "It was *your* fault that we were separated."

He shrugged. "An accident—I meant well. But my part is unimportant. You were several days—and nights—alone with DeVere before you reached Funchal, and you lied about it, allowing it to be assumed that we all arrived there together after we were shipwrecked. I know the truth and so does Mrs. Wilard, who I think might be persuaded to agree with my account if I contact her."

Emily's mother had always warned her against telling

lies. "Chickens always come home to roost," had been a favorite saying of Lady Regina's. Emily could almost hear clucking. "Say what you like," Emily said with angry bravado, adding what she hoped to be true, "I shan't be here to mind."

He laughed. "You certainly shall be if you are relying solely on Laelard for assistance. Yes, I know," he said in response to her patent surprise. "Laelard has been approaching nearly everyone who has ever been aboard a ship trying to find a way to make passage to America. It is surely an obvious conclusion that it is on your behalf that he does so. I might have been of assistance to him, but I have no wish to lose you, Emily. Unless," he added leadingly, "after we are married, you would wish to make our home in Philadelphia. I might easily be persuaded to that."

"Don't be absurd," Emily said angrily as she at last moved away from the desk and pushed past him. "I would never marry you just to return to America."

"The alternative is to stay here and face ruin."

It was also to remain and watch Galen and Amanda begin their life together. She turned to him again. "Do you really know of a ship that could take me there?"

"I know of one going to Lisbon and thence to Brazil. It may take a little time, but once we have crossed the ocean, it should be no big thing to make our way north, even overland if necessary."

She took a step nearer him again. "If you have any feeling for me at all, Mr. Cooke, please tell me how I may contact the captain of this ship. I cannot marry you, but I will make it worth your while for the information."

He gave vent to a short laugh. "I should be insulted, but I won't take offense. You can't realize what you are saying. Be you ever so intrepid, Emily, do you imagine yourself, after being alone and quite without protection on a common merchantman—very different from DeVere's elegant, well-ordered vessel—for upward of half a year, finding yourself set down in Brazil without friends and even less idea than you have now or how to finally reach Philadelphia? And it could be far worse —you might even find yourself without the means of making your way north. Even if your virtue survives such a journey, I doubt that your purse will. Only hope you don't find your throat cut for it.''

In spite of the fact that she was certain he was exaggerating just to frighten her, Emily shivered. She was determined to return to Philadelphia, but she was not blind to the dangers of a young, unattended woman making a long journey. She was prepared for insults, but it had not occurred to her that she might also suffer attacks on her person. She wished he had never put the thought in her head, but there it was, cheek by jowl with his other unpalatable suggestion, that she might find herself set down in a strange land still many hundreds of miles from her destination and forced to call on her own resourcefulness to make her way home. In spite of the strides she had made at independence, she could not but quake a little at the idea that Cooke might be right.

To her own astonishment, Emily found herself entertaining his proposal after all. It was not as if she had not liked Jeremy Cooke—she merely did not love him. But she perceived that there was a great difference between marrying a man she loved but who did not love her and marrying one that she simply did not love. Weighed against the alternative of heartache and ruin, the prospect did not seem insupportable.

"If I did agree to marry you," she said slowly, "you would be willing to return to Philadelphia with me?"

"*After* we are married, yes."

Emily sat down in a chair near the hearth. She chewed pensively on a finger as she weighed her options. Cooke sat himself on a chair near to hers and waited.

"Why should you wish for an unwilling bride?" she said at last. "I suppose it's my fortune?"

He shook his head. "Not entirely. I really have come to care for you, Emily, even though you do not hold me in a similar regard. But you shall have the tree without any bark on it. My pockets are wholly to let. I had prospects when I arrived, but they proved unfounded and I now have a number of obligations, some of them debts of honor, which I cannot possibly meet.''

Emily rose and took an agitated turn about the room. Again Cooke waited patiently. Emily desperately wanted to make the right decision, but nothing at all seemed right to her. Galen was to marry Amanda, who cared only for his fortune and title, and she was contemplating marrying a man who she also knew cared more for her purse than her person whatever he might say to make his offer more acceptable to her. So much for all her high ideals and belief that love would always run a true course and conquer every difficulty.

"If I do agree to marry you, Mr. Cooke," she said, returning to her chair, her tone becoming brisk and businesslike, "it must be upon my terms."

"And those are?"

"First, all arrangements for our return to Philadelphia must be made before any ceremony. In fact, I will only marry you on the day we are to sail. Secondly, I don't suppose you would agree to a marriage in name only, but I won't be ravaged. You must give me time to accustom myself to my change in estate."

His smile was lascivious. "It will be a difficult thing, but I give you my word on it."

For what that is worth, Emily thought, but had the prudence not to say it. For the present it would be as well if Cooke believed her resigned to her choice. But she agreed only out of present expediency; a part of her was not reconciled to it and she still hoped that she might yet find another more palatable solution to her difficulties.

He agreed to her every particular and the business part of their discussion completed, he would have returned to his attempt to convince her that he cared for more than her fortune, but Emily would not match his hypocrisy with her own by pretending to believe him.

She cut him short, saying, "There is one further thing. I wish nothing to be known of this even by my family until matters are well in hand."

His expression set and Emily thought he was finally going to balk, but he said, "That shouldn't take more than a sennight."

Emily nodded. "We shall inform my aunts and uncle of our plans only after they are too set to be changed. We may be married by special license from Portsmouth."

"One might suppose you were ashamed of me," he said, bristling.

"Not of you, Mr. Cooke. Of myself for being so cowardly. I think you should leave now. We have already given the servants enough to gossip about by being closeted together for so long."

It was clear from his expression that he did not like this dismissal, but he stood and held out his hand to Emily, which she ignored, looking up at him. "I have agreed to your extortion, but I won't dissemble."

"Count my blessings, should I?" He laughed. "Well, perhaps I shall teach you to regard me better once we are man and wife."

There was an ambiguity in his tone which Emily didn't like. Before she realized what he was about, he bent and swiftly kissed her on the lips. Emily recoiled involuntarily and she saw icy anger take form in his eyes.

But he smiled as he spoke. "Perhaps I shall manage to make our arrangements even sooner. Impatience to be with my bride will be my spur." He sketched her a bow and at last left Emily alone again.

14

On the morning of Lady Laelard's ball, which was ostensibly in her honor, Emily awoke with a headache. She knew it was a symptom of her wish that she could keep to her room again, but this time she would not allow herself to cry craven.

Emily could not look forward to the evening with any thoughts of pleasure. Lord Laelard, finally badgered out of his study at Whistley by his wife's persistent correspondence demanding his presence for her ball, had arrived the previous afternoon. As far as Emily was aware, Galen had not yet called to speak with him, but Galen would doubtless be present tonight and would have ample opportunity then. There might even be the interesting announcement that Amanda had predicted.

As if that were not sufficient to make her blue-deviled, it was also a certainty that Mr. Cooke would be among the guests. They had met only twice since he had extorted a promise of marriage from her, but each time her conviction had grown that she could not accept the solution he offered to her whatever the alternative. She even thought she might choose this night to tell him so, preferring to take all her misery in a single dose.

Both her Aunt Dorothea and Amanda subscribed to the belief that for a woman to appear at her best for an important evening's entertainment an afternoon of quiet and rest was essential. Emily certainly had neither rest nor quiet in her heart but she was determined to look her best for the confidence she hoped it would give her to get through this difficult night.

Physically, at least, she had completely succeeded in remaking her mousy image. The pale icy green silk gown overlaid with a half-dress of fine lace which she wore for the ball brought out the delicate rose tint in her complexion. Soft ringlets in which pearls that matched her necklace had been cunningly set on special pins, framed her face, and her eyes sparkled in the flickering candlelight. Hating herself for her weakness, she still could not help wanting Galen to see her looking so lovely.

Galen was one of those present at the select dinner before the ball, but they were seated at opposite ends of the table. Galen was placed at her uncle's right hand, though he was not the highest ranking guest by any means. Emily took this as proof that he was expected to offer for Amanda that night.

Mr. Cooke was not among those invited to dinner, nor was he among the early arrivals for the ball, and Emily had cause to be grateful for this. A number of young men made a point of asking her to dance before the ball was even begun and she found her dance card rapidly flling. At least Mr. Cooke would not be given the opportunity to monopolize her attention for the evening.

In spite of her predictions to the contrary, Emily enjoyed herself very much as the evening progressed. It was exhilarating to dance every set and to be made much of by attractive partners whose compliments added to the color in her cheeks. Mr. Cooke did finally arrive, but Emily was able to exchange no more than a word or two with him before joining the set that was forming and she saw him disappear into the cardroom shortly afterward.

He did not soon reappear and Emily recalled that he had told her that some of his debts were debts of honor, which likely meant gaming debts. On board the *Devon* he had also occupied much of his time playing cards, which made her think that he might well be an inveterate gamester, hoping to recoup his losses with her money.

This caused her features to set, and hardened also her resolve to tell him before the night was out that he might spread his poison about her and be damned; somehow she would make her own way back to America.

Though she tried to keep Galen and Amanda out of her thoughts, she was unhappily aware that she was constantly on the watch for Galen to disappear with Lord Laelard for the purpose of asking for the viscount's only daughter's hand in marriage. Her attention was necessarily imperfect, though, and as the time for supper approached, she acknowledged that that interview might already have taken place. Yet Amanda did not behave with the smug self-congratulation that Emily would have expected from her if it was a settled thing at last.

Galen had politely asked Emily to stand up with him when they had gone into the ballroom after dinner. She could not refuse him without being deliberately rude, so she had granted him the privilege of leading her into the last set before supper. Thankfully, it was a country dance which would keep them separated for much of the time and permit only limited and quite public conversation.

She had continued to afford him no opportunity to approach her since the morning she had been the unwilling recipient of Amanda's confidences, and though once or twice the look he had bent on her had been quizzical, he appeared to accept the distance she set between them. But that night Emily found him far less compliant.

When he bowed before her to lead her onto the floor for their set, she barely placed her fingers on his arm as if she disliked touching him, but he placed his hand over hers, smiling down on her in a way that all but melted her heart. She looked quickly away from him, but he made no effort to lead her onto the floor and she was forced to look up at him again, an obvious question in her eyes.

"Would you mind very much if we did not join the set

for this dance?'' he asked. "I traveled to Sussex yesterday and returned only a few hours ago and I fear my stamina is beginning to flag.''

Emily had no notion that he had been out of London. If the timing had been different, she would have suspected that he had gone to see her uncle about Amanda, but Lord Laelard was in town. "Of course I excuse you,'' she said with a bright smile and feigned indifference. "I have not had a moment all night to spend with my Aunt Caroline and would be grateful for the opportunity to sit with her for a time.''

"You misunderstand me, Miss Hampton,'' he said with a glinting smile. "I merely wish not to dance. You have promised yourself to me this half hour and *I* do not mean to excuse *you*.''

There was little that Emily wished less than to find herself forced to endure a half-hour's conversation with him. "If you are so tired, I suppose we could sit with the chaperones for a while,'' she said in a tone so flat it was nearly rude.

He shook his head. "These chairs are designed for maximum discomfort. To keep everyone dancing, I suppose. I see your aunt has set aside a number of anterooms for private conversation. We shall be more comfortable in one of these.''

"I don't wish for private conversation,'' she said baldly.

"But I do.'' He propelled her out of the room and it would have required physical force for her to resist him.

In the first room they passed two men were engaged in playing piquet; in the second were two couples holding a spirited conversation. The third was empty and he led her into this. He started to close the door but caught the alarmed look in her eyes and opened it again, giving her a faintly sardonic smile as he did so. Emily scarcely knew why she had permitted him to bring her here. She sat bolt-upright in the nearest chair, half dreading that he meant to warn her of his pending betrothal to Amanda. "I hope your journey was pleasant, my lord," she said stiffly, hoping he would take the hint from her formality that she wished to hear no confidences from him.

He sat on a small sofa opposite her. "Yesterday's journey was pleasant enough but today's was appalling. It began to rain about twenty miles from town and since I was in my curricle, even with the hood up, I received a soaking."

"You might have been wise to remain home tonight, my lord, rather than to go out and risk taking a chill."

His lips turned up in a faint, ironic smile. "My dear Emily, I risk being chilled whenever we meet. I seem to have the knack of offending you, though I wish I did not."

"I have no quarrel with you, my lord," she said quietly, meeting his eyes. "But it is true that we seem to be always at odds. Perhaps it would be best if we agree to disagree and meet as seldom as we may."

"I don't know why that has to be so."

There was a caressing note in his voice that made Emily acutely uncomfortable. She got up and walked over to the hearth, where a low fire burned to ward off the chill of the late March night. She shrugged with an indifference she was far from feeling. "What does it matter? I'll be leaving England soon in any case."

"Do you still believe that Laelard will be able to help find you safe passage?" he asked, mildly incredulous.

"No. I have found someone else to help me."

"Who?"

"Mr. Jeremy Cooke." She thought she heard the intake of his breath, but the fire chose to sizzle at that moment and she could not be certain.

"And have his efforts met with success?" he asked, and there was no doubt that his voice had hardened.

An impulse came over Emily and she did not resist it. "It is possible that Mr. Cooke and I may be married soon. We will return to America together."

"Married!" In a moment he was on his feet and standing beside her. "I don't believe it," he said. "You aren't a fool to be taken in by a captain sharp."

Emily turned and looked up at him defiantly, and instantly all her anger and hurt caused by his imminent betrothal to Amanda rose to the surface. How dare he condemn her choice in the face of his own? "And you, my lord? You are not susceptible to a lovely face and practiced coquettery? If I choose to marry Mr. Cooke, who are *you* to condemn him?"

Galen, looking searchingly into her eyes, saw something of her unhappiness there. She turned away as if fearing exposure.

Though he had observed her and Cooke together on obvious terms of intimacy, his instinct told him that Emily was not in love with his rival; what it did not seem to be able to tell was whether or not she was in love with himself. He was a badly shaken young man who for the first time in his life found that the self-assurance which some mistook as arrogance had deserted him. He found her behavior toward him so contradictory that it fed all of his self-doubt and cynicism.

It did occur to him, though, that perhaps Emily's unhappiness stemmed from the same cause as his own. Yet the fear still pricked at him that all his hope might be mere vanity. Emily might have meant every hard word she had said to him. But when he had held her in his arms, her response to him had told him something very different.

She stood beside him with her back partially turned toward him. He touched her arm and the simple touch was erotic to him. He knew she had felt it too as a slight shiver passed through her. She turned to him and hugged her arms to herself as if cold—or warding him off.

"You are right," he said quietly. "It isn't for me to criticize your choice, and I would say nothing at all if I believed you were in love with Cooke."

"My feelings for Mr. Cooke are not your concern."

"Are you in love with him?"

Emily longed to say yes, but with his cool, observant

blue eyes on hers, she knew she could not dissemble. "No. Are you in love with Amanda?" she added challengingly.

He did not reply, but shook his head slowly, which she regarded as ambiguous. He bent his head and lightly touched his lips to hers. "We have to acknowledge what is still unfinished between us, Emily," he said very softly. "I won't let you put me off this time."

Emily gave a shaky laugh. Her pulse was pounding; his nearness was having its usual effect on her. "When have I ever succeeded in doing that?"

"Every time I have asked you to marry me. I was used to think I possessed some address, but I see that I am really a very clumsy fellow. You found my proposal offensive."

"The manner of it, yes."

"I was drunk that night in Porto Santo and did the thing badly, I know.

"Oh, what does it matter?" Emily said impatiently, not wanting to recall her unhappiness when she had first discovered that he did not love her as she had come to love him. "It is the past and it doesn't change anything between us."

He touched her face caressingly. "I think it changed everything. But I didn't realize then that I was falling in love with you."

"Don't," she said pleadingly. "Don't say what you think I wish to hear. I am not such a gullible fool to allow you to make love to Amanda one day and me the next."

"The devil take Amanda," he said dismissively. "Why can't you believe that I could love you? Because of the rubbish that I said to you on one night when I was exhausted and half-disguised and smarting from your rejection of my advances? You are not indifferent to me, Emily, and it is not vanity that claims it is so."

"No, I am not indifferent to you," she said with anguish. "But I wish to be. I wouldn't marry you for honor or convenience so I suppose you hope to use the attraction I can't help feeling toward you to make me your mistress. I suppose I should be flattered; it says much for the improvements I have made in myself. I know well what your first opinion of me was; you were only kind to me when it was convenient. You were glad enough to wash your hands of me when we reached Portsmouth.''

"What the devil would you have had me do?" he demanded, but without heat. "You had just told me that you were determined not to marry me even at the price of your reputation and the least I could do was to see to it that your name was protected, which it would not have been if there was seen to be any intimacy between us."

But Emily found she had no stomach for a further quarrel. She lowered her head and said, "What does it matter anymore? I am to marry Mr. Cooke now."

"No." He gathered her into a hard embrace.

Every fiber of Emily's being screamed surrender. Their kisses became increasingly feverish as her response matched his in yearning and intensity. Emily knew in a moment she would be beyond the ability to resist him and she gathered her tattered self-control and pulled herself away from him.

"Emily . . ."

"No," she said forcefully. "I won't be seduced, whatever I may feel. Go to Amanda, my lord. You are more to her taste than mine."

Emily's words were meant to sting and she saw in his eyes that he flinched at the lash of her words.

"That is really what you wish?" he said, his eyes hardening to chips of ice.

"Y-yes." She faltered, but got the word out with enough strength to be credible.

"Very well, Emily," he said in a voice that chilled her. "Take Cooke, if it is he that you prefer. I've no taste for self-abnegation and I'm not as controlled as you think. If I leave you now, this is the end of it."

The cold that was spreading inside her made her feel

numb. She did not consciously will the words she spoke. "It is the end of it."

His ice-blue eyes held hers for what seemed to her an endless moment and then he simply turned and left her. Emily instantly dropped her head into her hands, but she did not cry. She felt too stunned by the finality of what had occurred. It was what she wished for, but, dear God, she had never guessed it would hurt so much.

She stood that way for a minute or so before she heard a sound and looked up. Jeremy Cooke stood propped in the door frame. He smiled in an insolent way. "My compliments, my dear. You acted very properly." He stood upright and advanced into the room. "I am blessed with an easy nature, but I am not complacent. I shouldn't like it at all if you allowed DeVere to make love to you."

He reached up to touch her face as Galen had done, but she slapped his hand away. Looking into his sharp, arrogant features, Emily's apprehension at telling him that she would not be coerced into marrying him fled. He behaved as if he already owned her and she knew she was going to enjoy wiping that superior smile from his face and damn the consequences. "My behavior is of no concern to you, Mr. Cooke. I have decided not to avail myself of your assistance. I shall find passage to Philadelphia from another source."

His eyes hardened and she saw the anger there, but he still smiled. "But can you find passage from another source soon enough? England will not be a very comfortable place for you in a very short time."

"But at least I shall not have married beneath me, which would be a worse fate, I think."

The smile disappeared, but only for a minute or so before returning in a more mendacious form. "As you wish, Miss Hampton," he said with a formal bow. "My regret at your decision is nothing compared to what yours is soon to be." But as he was leaving the room he paused at the door and turned to her again. "I shouldn't count on the Laelards to support you, or Lady Caroline.

Mud sticks, you know, and then they won't much like it when they hear that you have been making up to DeVere when they have quite other plans for him.''

Emily heard increased noise and laughter in the hall and knew that her aunt's guests were going in to supper. She was promised to Mr. Banfield, a young gentleman she had met only that evening. It would be unpardonably rude for her just to disappear, and if she went to her aunt and pretended to feel unwell, she would doubtless have to answer a number of questions about which she doubted her ability to dissemble at the moment.

She could not remember ever feeling more wretched in her life, but she called upon the reserves of her courage and went downstairs with the others, finding the anxious Mr. Banfield and allowing him to lead her into supper. Somehow Emily kept up her part in the conversation at their table and she even managed to eat some of the delicacies from the plate her escort had procured for her. She felt like a puppet, as if some unknown hand directed her movements and speech. By the end of supper she even felt able to congratulate herself a little that no one had guessed at her inner turmoil. But it was not to be that this wretched night would end with no further complications.

She had not seen Galen, but then she deliberately schooled herself not to search the room for his tall figure. Mr. Cooke came into the supper room a bit later and after wandering about for a bit speaking with friends he found a place for himself at the table where Amanda sat, surrounded by her usual court.

Emily returned to the refilling ballroom unescorted and stopped near the door to look about for a sight of Lady Caroline, with whom she meant to sit for the remainder of the evening. Thus occupied, she did not notice Amanda approaching her until her cousin stood directly in front of her. Emily took a step back at the fury to be read in the other's eyes. ''You wicked viper,'' Amanda said, her voice trembling with tears that were near to the surface. She did not bother to keep her voice down and several people nearby broke off their conversations to turn toward the two young women.

To Emily, it began to seem as if she had stepped into the middle of a nightmare from which she must surely wake soon. "Amanda," she said, deliberately keeping her voice at almost a whisper, "I don't know what I have done to upset you, but please, let it wait until we are alone if you have something to say to me."

"You know well enough what you have done," Amanda said, her voice forced and shrill. "My little American cousin so sweet and unspoiled, and all the while you have been laughing up your sleeve at me. You and that man," she said, pointing dramatically.

Emily turned mechanically in the direction of Amanda's outstretched arm and saw Galen standing a few feet behind her. "Amanda, please," she said in an urgent whisper. "Everyone is staring."

"I wish they may," Amanda said, the tears at last beginning to course down her damask cheeks. She was even lovely when she cried. "You have duped us all. Mama took you in and gave you a home and you have betrayed us. You know how I felt about Lord DeVere, but while he pretended to be interested in me it was just as a cover so that he could meet you without causing suspicion. Mr. Cooke has told me all; you have deceived us both. You are DeVere's mistress." This last was spoken in ringing accents, and all who were anywhere near to them were now unashamedly straining their ears to catch every word.

Emily felt ready to sink and perhaps even swayed a little, for she felt Galen's steadying hand beneath her elbow. "That is enough," Galen said in a voice that was menacingly quiet. "If you haven't any breeding, Miss Laelard, at least try for conduct. You disgrace yourself more than you have attempted to defame Miss Hampton."

While Galen spoke, Emily looked about her and saw a sea of avid faces, one of which belonged to her Aunt

Dorothea as she pushed her way past the throng of interested observers.

"How dare you speak so to my daughter," Lady Laelard said as she caught the now sobbing girl to her breast. Rounding on Emily she said brutally, "I should have guessed how it would be. Your mother was exactly the same sort, man-mad and not happy until she disgraced herself and her family by shamelessly running off with your father. I rue the day I ever had the misguided thought of recognizing her daughter."

The floor heaved beneath Emily and for a terrifying moment she thought she would faint in front of everyone. But a fury to equal her aunt's came to her aid and dispelled her weakness. "I will not permit you to say such things of my mother. She was honorably married to my father and they were happy and devoted to each other until the day he died."

"Your connection with this man is far from honorable."

"I won't have my private affairs discussed in this manner," Galen said with such icy menace that several people drew away from the immediate circle about them. "Since Miss Hampton is soon to be my wife, there could be no dishonor in any of our dealings."

"No!" Even Lady Laelard flinched at the force of Emily's expletive. "That isn't true and I won't say that it is merely to save my reputation. I have done nothing of which I am ashamed and I will not have the remainder of my life determined by lies." She was very close to tears herself at that moment but she swallowed them, ruthlessly searing her throat.

"Emily, you don't know what you are saying," Galen said with quiet intensity.

"I do." Looking at all the interested faces about her, Emily addressed them, even as a few had the grace to avoid her eyes. "Think what you like of me, it doesn't matter to me in the least," she said defiantly.

Eluding Galen's grasp, she pushed her way through those who stood in the doorway and when she reached the hall she almost walked into the arms of her Aunt Caroline. "My dear child, what has been happening? Lady Haverton came to fetch me saying that there was a wretched scandal brewing and that you were in the middle of it."

"Could I come with you to your house, Aunt, please? Now?" It was all that Emily could manage without succumbing to the sobs that threatened to overwhelm her. Lady Caroline nodded briskly and led her niece, ironically, into the same anteroom that Emily had so recently quitted. She rang to have Emily's maid gather together what Emily would need for the night and the following morning.

With great forbearance, Lady Caroline asked no questions of her niece, not even when they arrived at Upper Mount Street, and she assisted Emily, who seemed almost dazed, into the room she had previously occupied. Emily still did not cry, but her face was horribly white and drawn, as if she had suffered a great shock or a bereavement.

A chilling rain had begun during the carriage drive to Upper Mount Street, but even once inside Emily still shivered as if with the cold and she did not object when Lady Caroline's dresser helped her out of her dress while her aunt bullied her into drinking a glass of hot tea laced with brandy to warm her inside.

Emily willingly shut out all that had happened at her aunt's ball and let weariness lull her to sleep, but as she blinked awake in the first light of morning it all returned to her in a wave that almost left her breathless with misery.

She dressed in the cotton morning dress brought from Laelard House and went downstairs to the breakfast room, refusing the dresser's suggestion of a tray in her room because she did not want to be alone with her thoughts. But she was alone in any case, for her aunt's butler, Hillock, informed her that Lady Caroline had already left the house despite the early hour.

Emily could not prevent herself from reviewing the

events of the previous night, however little she wished to do so, and the more she did so the more hopeless her circumstances seemed. It did not even seem possible to her that she would be able to return to her home in Philadelphia, at least until the war was ended. Robin had not been able to help her, she had rejected Mr. Cooke's help as too costly, and it was all too likely that she would never see or speak with Galen again. Even if he had not meant what he had said to her in the anteroom, after her rejection of him in front of half the world he would never want to set eyes on her again, of that she was certain. Now that she was an outcast from society, she would find no one else to assist her either. She only hoped that her very fashionable Aunt Caroline would not abandon her as well, as too great a social liability.

Emily was heartily sick of her own unhappy thoughts when Lady Caroline finally returned. She came accompanied by a large trunk, two portmanteaus, and several bandboxes. It was all of Emily's things brought from Laelard House. Emily was glad of it, for she knew she could never go back there, but it brought home the frightening reality of her untenable position in the world now that even most of her family had cast her off.

But that proved to be not quite the case. Lady Caroline informed her that they were to leave on the following day for Whistley. "Dorothea feels it is the best thing for you to leave town for now," her aunt said. "She realizes it is best for us all if we do all we can to quiet the talk that last night's unfortunate scene caused, and she and Amanda will remain and continue to face the world. It is often the only way, however difficult. If we all turned tail it would likely only make matters worse. But you, of course, must retire from society, at least for a time. It will be some days before we can be certain of the severity of your disgrace, and it would only set people's backs up if you insisted on being defiant."

"I would not wish to," Emily said reassuringly. She

had the ironic thought that she had embarked on this visit to her family to come out of her retirement only to find herself forced into it again. But neither did she want to go to Whistley, even if the Laelards were not in residence. Lady Caroline insisted, however, and feeling that she had cause to be grateful that her aunt cared enough about her to share her exile just as the Season was getting underway, when she knew Lady Caroline disliked the country, Emily kept her objections to herself.

After those matters were settled and an early start on the morrow was decided upon, Lady Caroline took Emily to her sitting room and told her the version she had had from a still tearful and sullen Amanda of the events of the previous night. This proved to be remarkably accurate except that Amanda cast herself as the heroine of the piece and Emily as a shrill jade. But Emily, well acquainted with her cousin's character, surprisingly felt no rancor toward Amanda, whose injured vanity had precipitated the entire imbroglio.

In a quiet, calm manner, at odds with the very emotional story she had to tell, Emily related to her aunt all that had occurred, including those things of which Amanda could know nothing. Lady Caroline, when Emily told her that Galen had indeed made advances toward her which she had rejected, insisted on hearing the whole of their history, and Emily, tired of pretending, told it to her without restraint.

Lady Caroline was so silent when she finished that Emily feared she had greatly shocked her aunt. "I have been the greatest fool in the kingdom," her aunt said in accents of remorse. "It is all my fault that you are in this dreadful pickle."

"How could it be, Aunt Caro? You have been all that is good and kind to me since the day I arrived."

Lady Caroline bowed her head and put her hands over her ears. "Don't say so, Emily, or I shall never have the courage to confess to you.

Emily could not believe that her aunt could have anything to reproach herself for, but when Lady Caroline finally unburdened herself and told her of Galen's visit and letter, of which Emily had not the least idea, she sat quite as immobile as her aunt had done earlier.

"You answered his letter," she said in a dull tone, "and you never even told me of it. I thought he cared nothing for me, that it was only his pride and his sense of honor that mattered to him."

Lady Caroline was the one who was weeping, and she dabbed at her eyes with a lace-edged handkerchief. "I thought he was a fortune hunter, and even though I didn't know about the deserted island or anything else, I guessed that you were already half in love with him. He called the day after we came here and he was wearing clothes that my butler would not have donned had he had to go naked otherwise. How was I to guess that it was not your fortune he was after?"

Emily turned stricken eyes on the older woman. "But after we went to Whistley you knew the truth of it? Why didn't you tell me then?"

"I saw he was still interested in you and I hoped that it would all come about right in the end. I wanted to tell you, truly I did, Emily, but I could not. I was afraid you would hate me, which I can see you do." She began sobbing in earnest and Emily found herself incongruously cast in the role of comforter.

Emily was very upset, but she could not place the entire blame for her troubles on her aunt. Despite not knowing of Galen's visit or his letter, she could not exonerate herself. Lady Caroline had not been able to remember all that he had written, but what she did remember and relate was sufficient to convince Emily that it was she who was the fool. She could no longer blame Galen for fearing to bare his feelings to her if he had already done so in his letter of apology and received such a callous, second-hand reply. To a man of his pride, the insult must have been appalling.

But even if he had not spoken his love for her, she knew he had exposed his feelings in other ways to which she had been willfully blind. His desire for her which he was as unable to resist as she was hers for him, his persistence in the face of her repeated rejections, and even his continual calls at Laelard House, which she had assumed were to see Amanda because she had accepted Amanda's unsupported account that Galen wished to marry her, all of these things weighed against what she knew of his character might have told her that it could not be mere pride or physical attraction that accounted for his perseverance.

And she had sent him away. Deliberately. Intentionally. It was her pride not his that had destroyed her happiness. The public humiliation she had visited upon him, telling the world that she preferred ruin to being his wife, was unforgivable, but now she knew that she had lost something far greater than she had guessed at even in her misery of the previous night.

She assured Lady Caroline that she did not hate her, but she could not say the same about herself. There would be no peace or quiet in this retirement from the world, she was certain, only bitterness and regret. But in her attempt to buoy her aunt's spirits, she found her own lightened a bit as well, and by luncheon she at least felt the calm of resignation for what she would never be able to change.

Emily required her aunt's assurance that her Aunt Dorothea and Amanda did not mean to retire to Whistley as well, for she doubted she would have possessed the equanimity to reside in the same house with Amanda again, particularly as Lady Caroline had concurred with her suspicion that Amanda had lied about her incipient betrothal to Galen.

"He told me himself he was not at all serious in his intentions toward Amanda," Lady Caroline assured Emily when informed of this. "The minx probably was so sure of herself she thought she could bring him up to scratch before you discovered the truth of it." She snorted in an unladylike way. "I can just imagine her keeping such a thing from Dora, or Dora keeping *her* tongue about such a triumph, for that matter. Impossible." But though it gave Emily some sense of satisfaction to know that Galen had not preferred Amanda to her, it was cold comfort to her now.

15

On the following morning Robin Laelard called to wish them a safe journey, threading his way through the confusion of portmanteaus and trunks in the hall as they were being loaded into the baggage cart to find the ladies still in the breakfast room.

"M'mother decided to take Mandy off to Bath," he told them as she accepted a cup of coffee from his aunt. "Took her to Lady Ridge's rout last night and though there was whispering at first, it settled down after a bit. Until DeVere walked into the room, that is. Amanda made some silly comment about the disgrace of libertines being accepted in society that at least half the room heard. We all knew she meant DeVere, and of course the talk broke out like a rash again. The silly chit has more hair than wit and I can tell you m'mother was fit to box her ears. Mama decided on Bath because it would not put them quite out of the world."

"I really do blame Dora for all that has occurred," said Lady Caroline angrily. "I am sure I am very fond of Amanda, who can be a sweet girl when she chooses, but she has been allowed her head far too much and if it is not a mother's place to teach her daughter conduct, then I do not know whose it is. I think that Dora is more mortified by Amanda's behavior than she admits."

"Not a doubt of it," Robin agreed. "It's a damn shame that Emily and DeVere had to be splattered with Mandy's mud, but it did me some good to watch my sister make a spectacle of herself. Been expecting it for some time. If the girl had half as much sense as she does beauty, she wouldn't still be on the shelf. It'll be harder than ever to get her off our hands after last night.''

Emily, recalling that even in the midst of her tirade Amanda had somehow managed to lose none of her loveliness, doubted it, but it would probably mean a lowering of standards for both mother and daughter.

A footman appeared to inform them that the baggage cart was loaded and that the traveling carriage had been sent for and should arrive from the mews momentarily. Robin rose and wished them Godspeed. He embraced Emily and hugged her tightly. ''Don't let this cast you down, coz,'' he advised with his sunny smile. ''Most who know my sister know she's a spoiled baggage and won't take anything she says too much to heart. When all the fuss dies down, you'll be right as rain again.''

Emily returned his embrace and thanked him for his bracing words, but she didn't believe a word of them. It was not just Amanda's spite against her she worried about, but Jeremy Cooke's, for she had no doubt he would take full measure of his revenge upon her as well.

Their journey to Whistley was uneventful and made with little conversation passing between aunt and niece; each had a great many thoughts to occupy her. The only break in their peace occurred during the last stage of their journey when Lady Caroline ventured to suggest that now that Emily knew the truth about Galen's letter to her, it might be possible for them to mend their fences in spite of all that had occurred between them.

But Emily refused to hear of it. Galen himself had told her it was finished and she did not disbelieve him. The rupture between them was too great to be mended.

Now that the first confession had been made, Lady Caroline was quite prepared to present herself for self-immolation and offered to speak to Galen herself and admit the part she had played in fostering the misunderstanding between them, but Emily was immovable, and virtually forbade her aunt to speak to

Galen on her behalf. Lady Caroline was ever the optimist, though, and did not abandon the hope that all might yet end well.

Emily discovered that she did not feel at all uncomfortable being at Whistley. It was a lovely house and she enjoyed the quiet days occupied with her books and many small domestic chores which her aunt gladly left to her. She had not ridden since she had left Whistley in January, for neither of her aunts kept saddle horses in town and Amanda was too afraid of horses even to brave looking magnificent in a velvet habit riding in Hyde Park. Now Emily was permitted to ride to her heart's content, which she did every fine day, sometimes accompanied by her aunt and sometimes with only a groom for chaperone.

As April began they had a letter from Lady Laelard informing them that she and Amanda were comfortably settled in a very charming house in Bath and that Amanda was quite a success, with a court to rival the one she had enjoyed in London. Emily noted that Sir Edmund Timmons was mentioned as being among these and hoped that perhaps now that the dazzling prize which Galen's fortune had represented was out of reach for Amanda and her ambitious mother, his less brilliant suit might have some hope of prospering.

On a rainy morning several days later, Emily was both surprised and alarmed when she looked out of the drawing room window at the sound of a carriage being driven up the sweep and saw that it bore the familiar crest of the DeVeres. She stood transfixed by the window both hoping and dreading to see who would emerge, but it proved to be only Lord and Lady Haverton, stopping to call on their way to Landsend.

"Haverton has outrun our income again," Lady Haverton said baldly and as if her husband, who sat a little apart sipping sherry with unconcern, could not hear her. She sighed. "DeVere might have paid the most pressing of our embarrassments, but he would not. He told John from the beginning that he did not mean to be his banker and I, for one, do not blame him. John *will* play at Faro when he has not the least aptitude for the game. It is just the same as pitching the money in the river.''

"Does Lord DeVere join you?" Lady Caroline asked, earning Emily's gratitude for she did not like ask the question herself.

"No," Eugenia Haverton replied, unknowingly reassuring Emily that she need fear no accidental meetings. "He still has a number of things to occupy him in town, but he has said we might use Whistley to rusticate whenever we will. It is really too bad of John to make it necessary just now, when the Season is at its height." Lady Caroline then inquired after a mutual friend and the two ladies, who so loved town life but were forced to be out of the world just now through no fault of their own, launched into a lively discussion of what had occurred in town since Lady Caroline and Emily had left and speculated on the entertainments which they would now be forced to miss.

Emily wondered if Lord Haverton felt the same twinges of guilt that she did, but his expression was so placid it appeared bovine, and she dismissed the thought as absurd. When the Havertons at last rose to leave, Eugenia embraced Emily while Lady Caroline spoke with Lord Haverton. "It is not as bad as you might think, Miss Hampton. Caroline Lamb has been setting us all on our ears again and I doubt anyone even remembers that unfortunate little episode at your aunt's ball. If you were to return to town, I don't think you would find yourself snubbed at all."

"That is pleasing to know," Emily replied gratefully, "but I doubt I shall be returning to London. I had encouraging news in a letter from my cousin Robin, who is trying to help me find passage to return to my home in America. It is far from a certain thing, but I have some hope that I may be able to leave England before the summer is out."

"But I thought you meant to make your home here," Lady Haverton said, sounding surprised. "Your family and friends would miss you sadly."

Emily knew that this was far from true, but she responded appropriately and agreed with Eugenia's suggestion that perhaps they might meet one day and drive together into Hastings to shop.

But Emily had no such intention. It would never do to continue her acquaintance with Galen's sister; her only hope for serenity, she knew, was to put Galen and everything that called him to her mind out of her life completely. Accordingly, when Lady Caroline went to Landsend to return the call about a sennight later, Emily flatly refused to accompany her, and aunt and niece nearly quarreled over what Lady Caroline termed Emily's unreasonableness.

But harmony returned between them by the following day. It had been a rainy morning, but shortly after luncheon, the sun came out in full glory, resulting in a landscape that glittered like diamonds as rain dried on grass and leaf. It was an exquisite, crisp spring day and Lady Caroline suggested a ride to better enjoy it.

"It is rather wet to ride," Emily pointed out, "and very likely the ground is soft and muddy. I'm not sure we would have a very comfortable ride and it might even be hazardous if the horses have poor footing."

"We shall stay more to the roads today," her aunt rejoined. "I have quite set my heart on riding today, Emily," she said cajolingly, "and if you do not join me I shall have to take a groom instead and then I would not enjoy it half so much."

Emily, always conscious that her aunt had abandoned her own pursuits to bear her company in this quiet fashion, which was more to Emily's liking than her own, could scarcely resist this appeal and inside of a half hour they were walking their horses down the road toward Whistley Common.

But they had got only about halfway to the village when Lady Caroline pointed to a side road and suggested that they take that instead. "It looks fairly dry and not so well traveled, so we can let our horses out a bit."

Emily agreed readily, and setting their horses at an easy canter they took the other road. They traveled this for some distance until another village came into sight. "I don't think I have been here before," Emily said as they pulled up on the edge of what appeared to be the main street.

"No, I don't think you have. It is St. Catherine's and little more than a hamlet, really, without even a market-place." She pointed to another juncture that was adjacent to where they stood. "If we take that way I think it will bring us around again to the road into Whistley and then we may begin to make our way home."

Emily had not really paid much attention to their direction as they rode, but it seemed to her that the road her aunt suggested led away from Whistley rather than toward it. She suggested this, but Lady Caroline insisted that she knew the road and, of course, Emily had to bow to her aunt's superior knowledge of the country-side.

They rode at a comfortable trot, engaging in desultory conversation, enjoying the pleasures of a lovely day. Emily was quite at her ease and so thoroughly enjoying herself that the accident, when it happened, took her so completely off guard that she nearly lost her own seat.

The road narrowed nearly to a lane at one point and Lady Caroline had fallen just a little behind so Emily was not quite certain whether it was the sudden darting into the road of a rabbit or some other creature or some-thing else entirely that suddenly caused her aunt's mount to balk and rear. She heard the unexpected commotion behind her and turned in the saddle to see her aunt's horse with forelegs pawing the air. Her own mount began to sidle and there was nothing at all Emily could do but watch with horror as her aunt, with a small frightened scream, came tumbling out of the saddle.

Regaining control of her own mount, Emily quickly dismounted and went at once to Lady Caroline, who lay sprawled in the road. That lady was already sitting up when Emily reached her and was very inclined to be put out with herself for having lost her seat. "I cannot think how it happened," she said with vexation. "I should blush for such poor horsemanship. Give me your hand, dear, and then we will take our horses over to that convenient rock just ahead and remount." But as soon as Lady Caroline stood she gasped and immediately crumpled again.

"What is it, Aunt Caro?" Emily asked urgently. "Are you injured in some way?"

"It is my stupid ankle," Lady Caroline replied in exasperation. "This is really too much. Well, we shall have to get over to that rock somehow, for I certainly can't walk home in this condition."

Emily assisted her to rise again and they made their way slowly and painfully to the rock which they meant to use as an impromptu mounting block. It seemed to Emily that her aunt was in considerably more pain than would result from a mere sprain, and her anxiety rose when she returned to her aunt with the horses in hand and saw that Lady Caroline's expression was quite distressed. With Emily's assistance, Lady Caroline managed to reseat herself in the saddle with a minimum of difficulty and they started off again at a sedate walk.

Emily spoke lightly on various subjects, trying to divert Lady Caroline from thinking of her pain, but it seemed to her that the older woman looked increasingly peaked as they continued down the road. Turning to her aunt with a remark about an acquaintance, Emily saw her sway in the saddle and halted at once. "We cannot go on like this, Aunt Caro," she said firmly. "I don't think we are very near to Whistley and you look as if you can scarcely keep your seat another mile. Is there some house nearby which might have a carriage we can borrow to take you home?"

"I am not certain," Lady Caroline said vaguely. "It has been some time since I rode this way last. I do not like to give in to weakness, but it would be best, I think, if I did not have to ride all the way to Whistley. I am feeling strangely lightheaded and think I must have hit my head when I fell, without realizing it."

This is what Emily herself feared and her anxiety grew considerably. She had the sudden, unaccountable wish that Galen were with them. She knew for a certainty that she might lay this burden on his broad shoulders and he would deal with it competently. But the thought was both hopeless and absurd and was instantly banished. "There is a building over there on the left," she said. "It seems to be only a hay barn, but it must belong to someone."

Lady Caroline agreed. "If we take the lane just beyond it, perhaps we shall come to a house."

Emily was a little leery of leaving the road for the uncertainty of the lane, but there were no other signs of habitation along the road for as far as they could see and she supposed the lane was just as likely to lead them to someone who could help them.

As they traveled the lane, Emily, looking to her right, caught sight of a distant glitter and realized after a moment that it must be the sea. If that were the case, then they were considerably farther from Whistley than she had supposed. Obviously the road her aunt had assured her would lead them back to Whistley had led them away from it instead, as Emily had feared it would. This circumstance did not comfort Emily that her aunt's judgment concerning the lane they now traveled, was valid, but, after about a quarter hour's ride, a house, very large and clearly the residence of a gentleman, came into view.

At a distance it was an impressive sight, made of dark colored stone and rambling over a considerable portion of the property. There appeared to be several wings and many chimneys, but as they came closer to it, it was seen that much of the portion of the house that they approached, which was the rear, was in disrepair, though it looked as if some progress had been made at refurbishing both house and garden alike.

Emily would have taken her aunt directly to the kitchen, for it was the shortest distance, but Lady Caroline insisted they ride around to the front of the house as was proper and Emily, to avoid argument, acquiesced.

Either there were few servants inside or their approach was not noted by any one within the house, for no one came out to greet them and Emily was forced to dismount and leave her horse with her aunt while she sought admittance. A footman, wearing an apron and obviously engaged in household duties that were not strictly his province, opened the door after enough time had passed to cause Emily to wonder if the house were occupied. He was followed by a harried looking butler, who was immediately sympathetic to the ladies' plight and came out himself to help Lady Caroline dismount and come into the house.

He showed them into a small saloon which opened off the vaulted entrance hall. Emily had expected the interior of the house to match the neglected condition of the exterior, and was pleasantly surprised to find instead a cheerful apartment in which a low wood fire burned to ward off the damp left by the morning's rain.

As soon as the butler had seen Lady Caroline comfortably settled, he left them to fetch his master. Lady Caroline half-sat, half-reclined on a sofa near the fire but Emily was too restless to sit and stood near the hearth, absently slapping her crop against her thigh. In the fuss involved in getting her aunt inside the house, she had not thought to ask the name of the owner. "Whose house is this, Aunt Caro? I know it is not one we visited when I was at Whistley before."

But Lady Caroline was saved what would surely have been an awkward explanation, for almost immediately the door opened and Galen stepped into the room. He stopped on the threshold as if he had walked into an invisible wall. For a moment Emily read astonishment in his features and something else, less definable, but both were banished as the civil mask slipped into place. "Lady Caroline, Miss Hampton, I had no idea. Tomkins told me only that two ladies had called, one of whom had suffered some sort of accident. Pray tell me what has occurred and how I may be of assistance to you."

"It was the most stupid thing imaginable," Lady Caroline said, speaking rapidly as if to prevent Emily from speaking first. "My horse reared and I was riding with a slack rein and have paid for my folly."

Emily walked carefully to the nearest chair and sat down. "We didn't think it advisable to continue on horseback, my lord," she said stiffly, meeting Galen's eyes with some difficulty. "If you would be kind enough to provide a carriage so that my aunt could be taken home in comfort, we would be most grateful."

He was silent for such a long moment that Emily wondered if he meant to order them out of his house. After the way he had been used at her hands and those of her family, she could not censure him for wishing to do so. "Of course," he said finally. "I shall order the traveling carriage to be made ready at once. It is from my father's time and a bit dated, but it is well sprung and Lady Caroline should be reasonably comfortable."

Instead of pulling the bell to give his commands to his major domo, Galen excused himself to see to the arrangements personally. The minute he was gone Emily sprang up from her chair. "You have brought me here on purpose, Aunt Caroline," she said furiously. "How could you do this when you knew that above all things I wished not to see Lord DeVere again! Are you even injured? Oh, I shall never forgive you for this!"

"Of course I am injured. I did come off my horse, you know," Lady Caroline said defensively, but then added, "I brought you here for your own good because you were being so foolishly stubborn. Eugenia

Haverton told me that DeVere was expected by evening when I called yesterday.''

"And is she, too, a party to your perfidy?''

"Emily! It is no such thing! I doubt Lady Haverton even knows we are here.''

Emily slashed at the mantle with her crop to vent some of her anger, and Galen chose that moment to return to the room with his sister in tow. Emily felt warmth steal into her face and she abruptly turned her back on him.

"My dear Lady Caroline, whatever has happened?'' Eugenia said, going at once to sit beside the widow, while Galen took a chair opposite them after casting only a glance at Emily's rigid back.

Lady Caroline repeated the details of her accident, though she did so a bit falteringly, knowing that her niece did not now believe a word of it. As Emily suspected, the accident was contrived and all that Lady Caroline had suffered in sliding from her mount was a bit of dirt on her habit.

Lady Haverton gave no indication that she doubted Lady Caroline's account. She nodded sympathetically and when the story was done, begged her brother to pull the bell for the footman. "Our chaise is old enough to have been in service during the reign of the Conquerer and takes forever to outfit. You will be far more comfortable in my own sitting room next to the library.''

Lady Caroline nearly asked what the matter was with the room they were in when she gathered her wits about her and took Eugenia's lead. "I am sure you are right, Eugenia. You are most thoughtful,'' she said, gathering the heavy skirt of her velvet habit about her.

Emily turned and faced into the room for the first time since Galen had reentered it. "Wouldn't it be best if you did not move again until we are ready to leave, Aunt?'' she asked with a warning edge to her voice.

But Lady Caroline chose to ignore this and said instead, "You must keep Lord DeVere company,

Emily, while Lady Haverton and I enjoy a comfortable gossip over some sherry. It will restore me wonderfully, I am sure.''

"No doubt your ankle is feeling better already," Emily said, her voice heavy with a sarcasm which had no observable effect on her aunt, but which caused Galen to look searchingly from her to Lady Caroline and back to Emily again. There was the faintest up-turning of his lips. "Perhaps," he said, rising as the footman came into the room, "it would be best if we cut the boot off first. Peter, fetch the leather shears from the stables."

Lady Caroline looked startled. "That isn't at all necessary," she said hastily, thinking of the thirty pounds she had paid for the boots. She wasn't sure she was prepared to take her imposture to that extent. "As Emily said, I am feeling much better already."

Galen shook his head with concern. "It won't do, Lady Caroline, to be careless. If your ankle was so injured that you could scarcely stay in the saddle for the pain, it may well be broken and the boot should come off."

"I am sure it is not broken," the widow said firmly. "My dresser is most gentle and will manage to get it off when I return to Whistley without causing me further discomfort."

"But your ankle must be quite swollen, at the least. I am persuaded that you could not wish to continue in pain," Galen persisted. "If we get the boot off and wrap the leg in bandages soaked in cold water, your ride home will be considerably easier."

"For heaven's sake, Gale, leave it be," his sister said with exasperation. "Caroline knows what is best for her." She then instructed the waiting footman to give his arm to Lady Caroline to assist her out of the room.

"Is Lady Caroline's ankle hurt at all?" he asked gently when they were gone.

Emily let out her breath in a short sigh. "I doubt it,"

she said, mortified. "But I swear to you, my lord, I had no part in her pretense."

"I am certain you did not," he said with an enigmatic inflection. He crossed the room to stand before her. "I am glad you are here, though. I meant to call in another day or so. Emily, I beg your pardon for what occurred at your aunt's ball."

"But why?" Emily was startled by his unexpected apology. "You had nothing to do with it. You, too, were a victim of my cousin's spite."

"If I had not compromised you in the first place . . ."

Emily turned away from him. "Please, I have begged you not to speak of it." She made herself look at him again, refusing to flinch from what she knew she must say to him. "It is I who ask your pardon for saying what I did in front of everyone. I know you wish nothing more to do with me, but I have something that I feel I should tell you if you will hear it."

"Then let us sit for it," he suggested, and she tactily concurred. He led her to the sofa facing the fire and Emily eyed it askance, but sat beside him nevertheless.

Something of his old ironic smile returned as he noted her expression. Emily saw this and recalled that he had looked at her so the day he had first kissed her in her Uncle Walter's study. She felt a swell of unhappiness and began speaking quickly before her courage deserted her. "I wish you to know that I discovered only the day after my Aunt Dorothea's ball that you had called on me in Upper Mount Street when I first came to London," she said, her voice only wavering a little to show her nervousness. "I thought you felt that your charge to my Uncle Walter was complete when we reached Portsmouth and had washed your hands of me."

His brow knit. "I told you in my letter . . ."

"I never read your letter," she interposed, to get the words out before her courage failed her. "I only learned that same morning that you had ever written to me.''

His eyes searched hers as if he could pull an answer to his puzzlement from inside of her. "Dear God. I should have guessed. I have been a fool."

"No, it was my fault. I have always found it all too easy to believe the worst of you."

He laughed softly and without humor. "That is true enough, but it isn't entirely without cause. Would it have made any difference to us if you *had* received my letter?"

Emily looked into his clear blue eyes and felt suddenly shy of him again. "It must have done, I think," she said quietly.

He pushed back from off her face a curl that had come loose from its pins. "Does it make a difference to you now that you know I did write to you and tried to see you again?"

Emily had only told him the truth because she could not bear for him to think that she had dismissed his declaration of love so callously, not because she thought she could rekindle his feelings for her. Her heart began beating much faster. She did not quite dare to hope yet, but his tone was caressing and his touch gentle. She raised her eyes as she spoke and quickly lowered them again. "Yes."

He said nothing then and when Emily could bear the suspense of it no longer she said, "Does it matter to you that I had no hand in the letter you received in reply?"

His reply was not verbal. At the remembered taste of his mouth as his lips found hers, she could not prevent a small cry. He took her into his arms and the kiss deepened and lasted for as long as either had breath.

He rested his forehead against hers and said the words that she had so longed to hear. "I love you, Emily. But I have no wish to spend the rest of my days making you offers of marriage for you to cast back at me. For truly the last time, will you be my wife?"

Emily's eyes filled with tears of awe at the realization that she had been given another chance for happiness, and when she needed her voice to say the word that would make her happiness complete, she found she could not. She compensated by nodding enthusiastically and was once again pulled into his arms.

"Tell me that you love me, Emily," he said into her ear.

"I love you," she managed to say, though the words came out breathlessly. "I love you more than it is right to love anyone."

During the joyful embrace that followed this declaration the door into the room opened and Lady Caroline and Lady Haverton came back into the room, the latter no longer even making a pretense of her injury. "It is so satisfying to be given a chance to correct one's mistakes," Lady Caroline said happily to Lady Haverton, whom she had taken into her confidence. "It is even worth quite ruining my best riding habit by falling into the mud."

Galen and Emily, aware that they were no longer alone, parted reluctantly. "Is that why you would not let me perform surgery on your boots?" he asked.

"Wretched man. You guessed that there was nothing the matter with my ankle and suggested ruining my boots to punish me." His answering smile confirmed her suspicions.

"We are not here to disturb you, dearest," Eugenia assured her brother. "I just wish to tell you that I have rescinded your order to have the traveling carriage made ready and a message has been sent to Whistley. I also have informed the cook that we will require two additional covers set for dinner this evening. I daresay the two of you would rather be alone, but one must observe the proprieties," she added primly.

"Did Emily tell you everything?" Lady Caroline asked anxiously, perching on the edge of one of the chairs.

"Yes," Galen replied, but he smiled as he said it so that Lady Caroline felt considerably heartened.

"And you don't hate me for what I have done?"

"If Emily forgives you, how could I do otherwise?" Galen said handsomely. "In any case, you have completely redeemed yourself by what you have done today to bring us together."

"Though that too was deception," Emily pointed out. Emily got up and knelt before her aunt to put her arms around the older woman. "You must forgive yourself as completely as we forgive you, but please, Aunt Caro, from now on let it only be straight dealing between us."

Lady Caroline swore, her voice choking a bit, that she had learned her lesson well and was only grateful that she had had the opportunity to expiate her guilt.

"Dear me," Eugenia commented with distaste, "I think in another moment or so we shall all become quite maudlin. It is time for us to return to our gossip and sherry, Caroline."

"Yes, of course," Lady Caroline said, rising hastily. A sudden smile spread over her countenance. "It has just occurred to me that I shall have to write to Dora to tell her that we are to have a wedding in the family this Season after all. She will turn quite, quite green," she added delightedly, and followed Eugenia out of the room, carefully closing the door behind her.

Galen brought Emily closer to him again and she happily snuggled her head against his shoulder. "It will be no easy thing to convince me to let you return to Whistley tonight. I'll be in a quake until we meet again for fear that I dreamed this afternoon."

Emily laughed. "So shall I. After such an un-propitious beginning, it is a miracle that we are together at all."

"You mean after the cavalier manner in which *I* behaved," he said baldly. "Arrogant, overbearing, cold, and insensitive."

There was a note of sincere regret in his voice. She lifted her head to kiss him lightly but lingeringly. "And in my turn I was insipid, gauche, silly, and sharp-tongued."